Heart of the

THE LOST ROYALS SAGA
Book Three
by
Rachel Jonas

Heart *of the* Dragon

Description

Even the deadliest dragon warrior has a weakness ... his answers to the name Evangeline.

Liam suffered the loss of his mate once before, but with forbidden magic, Evie has returned to him. His reputation as "The Reaper" is one he earned ... one kill at a time. So, if there's any warning his enemies should heed, it's that he'll stop at nothing to keep history from repeating itself; will stop at nothing to protect her.

Evie senses the walls rapidly closing in as her role in the revolution becomes clear — a movement in which the supernatural order has begun to shift. All who stand for the cause have made sacrifices, including Evie who's faced several hard truths. The hardest lesson being one that brought loyalty into question — a single, careless act at the hands of someone she trusted.

Someone who nearly cost her everything.

Nick never wanted any of this. As he struggles to understand the nature of his dual identities, he's haunted by the pain and destruction he's caused as his dark side gains strength.

Escaping his cell and running was the only option, but that doesn't mean he'll escape the repercussions.

No one's out of the woods yet. The line between enemies and allies blurs for the Seaton Falls clan amidst rising tension, rumors of a traitor among them ... and the arrival of an uninvited guest.

Thank you for your purchase! I would love to get your feedback once you've finished the book! Please leave a review and let others know what you thought of

"Heart of the Dragon".

For all feedback or inquiries:

author.racheljonas@gmail.com

The Lost Royals Saga

The Genesis of Evangeline, Book 1 (Available Now)

Dark Side of the Moon, Book 2 (Available Now)

Heart of the Dragon, Book 3 (Available)

Season of the Wolf, Book 4 (Tentative release May 2018)

(Future Installment release dates to be announced)

Chapter One

Evie

"She's not ready." Hilda directed a hard glare toward Elise. "And at this rate, she never *will* be." Lines creased her otherwise smooth, dark skin when tension spread across her forehead.

Elise's posture stiffened at the sound of her oldest friend shooting down yet another attempt to speed up the process. A long breath puffed from her mouth as she stepped over me. I'd given up trying to speak for myself twenty-minutes ago. Tired of being outtalked and ignored, I sprawled out on the carpet where I now lay among the wrappers of the three candy bars I polished off while they went at it.

For all the excitement Elise expressed about Hilda—my father's sister and a powerful witch in her own right—joining us here at The Damascus Facility, it seemed all they did was bicker.

Mostly about me, about the role Elise hoped I'd fill in bringing her sons back.

I felt like a kid caught in the middle of a nasty divorce. Only, these two weren't separating, which meant I'd just have to deal with it.

"I don't understand what's taking so long. We *need* them here," Elise reasoned, raking through her long, brunette hair as she paced. "To protect Evangeline, to protect this facility … The greater our numbers, the better our chances."

It was no secret tensions were running high this past month, especially for Elise. It started with Nick's disappearance and the hell-storm of bureaucratic red tape that followed. There was not only one, but *two* families breathing down the Council's neck—the Stokes's on Nick's behalf, and Officer Chadwick on Roz's. She was his accomplice, the reason Nick was able to escape, and now they were in the wind.

The whole situation had turned into quite the mess, actually.

After the incident with Scarlet and her sisters, Nick's fate hung in the balance, according to Elise. Within hours, she'd been contacted by the Elders of Seaton Falls and several other members of the Council, and they all wanted answers. For starters, Baz demanded an explanation for what happened to his witches. When Elise shared that I was the one who'd taken their lives out of self-defense, he dismissed it.

Although, the *self-defense* argument wasn't entirely true.

I hadn't acted to defend myself. I killed them in a blind rage after what they'd done to Liam—crippled him with their magic, nearly ending him.

It came as no surprise that Baz didn't reprimand my behavior. In his eyes, I was the rightful heir to the lycan throne, and to some degree, above reproach. However, what was *less* easily swept under the rug was how the incident resulted in Nick going rogue.

A question that forced Elise to admit security wasn't as airtight here as she promised, thus delivering another crushing blow to her peers. It did nothing for her credibility. Already, as a dragon inducted into an organization of lycans, her standing with them was conditional. Her contribution to the cause made her an asset, but now … none of us were sure how long it'd be until her welcome had worn out.

Nick was on a streak ruining lives.

Starting with mine.

He was the reason my parents' temporary memory loss was now permanent. The witches he called on, the ones he had been willing to let kill Liam … they were the key to fixing all this.

And now they were dead.

I took a deep breath and shifted an arm behind my head, feeling soft carpet beneath it. I thought of them often, my parents. Living apart hadn't gotten any easier and I guessed it never would. The only comfort I had stemmed from knowing this horror was one-sided. They'd been given a gift, the luxury of thinking ours had only *ever* been a family of two. They no longer even knew I existed. I was the only one who lived with the shattered memories and the echo of our last goodbye.

Thanks to Nick, there was no going back.

Liam reminded me often that I still, technically, had a mother. Not that I'd forgotten, but … it wasn't the same. Yes, I'd grown to love Elise—her kind spirit, her fierce devotion to a cause bigger than any one being or supernatural race, but something still lacked; the bond between mother and daughter. In *this* lifetime, I only ever had that with Rebecka Callahan.

"She's not a witch, Elise. Plain and simple," Hilda said on the tail end of a frustrated sigh.

The words echoed in my head, hearing them clear as day, spoken in her now familiar accent. Unlike many of the supernatural beings I met, she wasn't a drifter. As she put it, her home had always been, and always would be, Bahir Dar, Ethiopia—the birthplace of my father and, technically, I'd been born there once, too.

Elise, a French native, hadn't been back to Ars-en-Ré in decades—the town where her side of our family originated.

Painful memories, I guessed, but she never spoke enough about it for me to know for sure. In short, everyone seemed to either stay or leave home for their own reasons. And I guessed Hilda, like everyone else, had hers.

We'd gotten to know each other well in the month since our first meeting. Since I now understood her tough exterior was merely camouflage, I didn't take offense to her frustration. It wasn't with me, personally. The issue lie with Elise tasking her with a job she wholeheartedly believed was a lost cause.

As Hilda explained it, I came from a long line of powerful witches. All the women on my father's side, including herself, were born with gifts. She believed there was a trace of witch within me. However, it was only residue—enough for me to be born female despite a curse placed on my mother long ago to only bare sterile sons. Enough to make me immune to magic *still*, but … likely not enough for me to assist with this spell.

She believed the gift missed me because I'm not human. As a rare hybrid born to one of two original lycans and the *only* original dragon, it was her understanding that these aspects of who I am made it impossible to be a witch, too.

So, here we were, back at square one.

"Why can't we just … bring in someone we know can actually get the job done?" I suggested, trying anything to get them to stop fussing.

Elise sighed heavily before answering. "We've been over this a thousand times, Evangeline. This spell, bringing your brothers back ... no one can know what we're doing. No one can know who you are," she explained before her eyes fell on me and she added, "It has to be you."

No pressure.

"The spell we did to bring Evangeline back was different," Hilda pointed out. "Taking her soul from the talisman and placing it back in your womb where it started was sort of a ... a reset," she explained. "But it's an entirely different task to bring back, not one, but six full-grown, fully developed, and functioning hybrid shifters."

Silence.

Defeat.

I wasn't sure which was loudest.

I sat up and pushed the candy wrappers aside, scooting closer to the table. There, in a beautifully-crafted, wooden box, sat six large rings, telling of the size of the men who once wore them. I traced the dark stone of one with my fingertip, trying to imagine them—my brothers. *Would we look alike? Would we get along? Would they remember me? Would they think it's strange that I'm so unlike the old Evangeline? Would they be the same as before?*

Not that I'd know the difference ...

I had a ton of time to come up with these questions. Mostly as my eyes glazed over whenever Hilda made me study her huge, ancient books on my own.

Listening to Elise breathe a sigh of frustration somewhere behind me, I glanced toward one ring in particular. It stood out to me since the first time I saw the collection. While all the rest were intact, this one was broken, a part of its stone missing. I asked Elise once if she thought the damage might make it impossible to bring back whomever it belonged to. The question, which I later realized was incredibly insensitive on my part, brought tears to her eyes as she tried to answer. But I realized something that day. To me, these were just rings. I had no attachment to my brothers because I didn't remember them. But to Elise, these rings were all she had left of her family.

Besides me, anyway.

Although, I often wondered if my lack of attachment hurt her as much as not having me around at all. Or, maybe it was worse.

"Put those down, child." Hilda's gruff voice caught me by surprise when the ring I held was all but smacked out of my hand before she closed the box, tucking it beneath her arm as she shuffled away. "They're not toys."

"And she's no child," Elise reminded her.

I stared at the back of Hilda's head, the colorful, decorative scarf of purple, turquoise and gold she wore around her graying hair.

Did she really think I didn't know they weren't toys? Did she think I'd forgotten that this entire month had been all about how important those rings were?

I fell back again, staring at the ceiling as the two went back to discussing my life and, in so many words, how inadequate I was.

I didn't want to be here anymore—in Elise's quarters while they argued. My heart, my thoughts, were several floors down where a very anxious dragon had me on his mind, too.

How did I know?

Because he'd just made his way inside my head, invading my thoughts as if he weren't already in them.

"*Still with Hilda?*" he asked.

"*Of course. You know we're practically joined at the hip now. World's worst BFF.*"

Morning, noon, and night, if I wasn't in class or asleep, I was with Hilda. She'd done her best to teach me to wield whatever magic might be inside me, but the bottom line was, there wasn't much to speak of. Once, I managed to make a lightbulb glow, but I'm still not sure that didn't have more to do with faulty wiring. In short, I was no closer to being who or what Elise wanted me to be than I was four weeks ago.

"*Tell them you have to leave,*" Liam suggested. "*You were supposed to be mine the last half of the day.*"

My cheeks warmed at the sound of his words floating around inside my head. It was strange and amazing all at the same time, freely owning my feelings for him and being able to freely accept his for me.

Before answering, I lifted my wrist into the air, cutting my line of site off from the ceiling fan that whirred above on its lowest setting. My eyes landed on the leather band I hadn't taken off in weeks. The one symbolic of a union that existed between us centuries ago, a piece we exchanged when we vowed our love was forever.

"Just ... go to the dining hall without me. I'll come find you whenever they take the leash off." It was impossible not to roll my eyes. I'd come to feel like somewhat of a prisoner. A useless one at that.

"I'm starving, but I'll wait."

To most, his response would've seemed like little more than a polite gesture, but I knew better. His nightly routine of escorting me down to dinner had more to do with the fact that Nick was still on the loose. Liam, like the Council, didn't have much faith in this place's security anymore. Not that he ever really did.

But I wasn't worried.

My confidence no longer had anything to do with my belief that Nick's friendship would stop him from taking my life. After he called on the witches, I, too, thought he might be capable of much more than I originally imagined. My lack of worry was based on nothing other than the fact that I wasn't afraid.

I don't know ... maybe it came from taking on Scarlet and her sisters. My dragon was stronger than she'd ever been that night, and even now, I felt her. No, I hadn't suddenly become a prize fighter overnight; I still struggled in combat training, but deep down I was confident that, if it came down to it, she wouldn't let me fail.

While Nick wasn't my favorite person in the world, I still hoped it never came down to that—a physical confrontation between us.

I once believed that my being a descendant and Nick being the Liberator didn't define us. Much like I didn't believe my past with Liam meant we were destined to be together.

Now, my thoughts were quite different.

As I laid on Elise's floor feeling electricity scatter across my skin at the mere *thought* of being near Liam ... I also believed Nick and I were doomed from the start. It was simply a matter of time before we accepted it.

"I'll be fine going down by myself later," I assured him, drowning out the heightened volume of Hilda and Elise's conversation. *"Besides, I think Beth's going late, too. I'll eat with her."*

He hated the idea. I knew it before he even responded. It had nothing to do with being possessive or wanting to consume all my time; he wasn't that guy. His concern was that I'd be cornered by Lucas and Chris, like they'd done a few weeks ago, asking questions I couldn't answer. They weren't hostile, just concerned about their friend.

"It's fine," I reiterated.

He hesitated to respond and I knew that meant he was wrestling with himself—wanting to protest, but remembering my request to be treated like an adult.

"Fine," he sighed. *"But this means you're mine tonight. No exceptions. No interruptions."*

I smiled. *"Done."*

To most, his request would've seemed suggestive, but I knew better. The night Liam stopped me from throwing myself at him amidst an emotional haze, I realized something—we had *forever.* That was the very thing he wanted me to accept when I realized we were mated. We didn't suddenly start behaving like some old, married couple. Instead, we enjoyed the slow burn of watching what we'd become evolve and change with each passing day. We'd get to the other stuff, eventually, but there was no rush. So, I was still me. Liam was still Liam. We were just us, but … together.

I severed our connection and cleared my throat, gaining both Elise's and Hilda's attention.

"What do I need to do to get this right?" I wanted out of there so bad.

Both sets of eyes were on me when I asked the question.

"Study harder? Push myself harder?" I suggested.

Guilt washed over Elise as soon as our eyes locked. Her fingers flitted through her hair again.

"No … Evangeline." Her tone was sympathetic, like she only just realized I was in the room and heard everything. "And none of this is your fault or a sign that you've done something wrong," she explained.

To that, Hilda nodded in agreement before adding her two cents. "She's right, which is why I've been hoping your mother would come to see things my way. You cannot demand a square peg to become a marble and expect it to be so. That's simply not the way things work."

So, now I was a square peg. Mmm… got it.

"You are what you are and it's time we *all* just learn to accept that." With those words, her gaze hardened and slipped toward Elise.

The room was thick with tension, and for a moment, I forgot these two regarded one another as friends, *family*. The moment only grew more uncomfortable when Elise responded.

"You're asking me to give up on my family?" The question was clear, pointed, and somehow void of emotion despite her expression saying the opposite. It said she was a woman desperate for her heart and her family to be made whole again.

Lowering my head, I couldn't help but to sympathize.

"Your family is mine, too," Hilda reminded Elise. "And nothing would please me more than doing what you've asked, bringing them back. But … what sense is there in getting our hopes up if we're hoping for the impossible?"

The question lingered in the air a moment, but then, Hilda took slow steps toward Elise, taking her hand once she was close enough.

"I won't be responsible for breaking your heart," were Hilda's final words on the subject.

For the first time in hours, I understood why they were so close. It wasn't because they always got along or agreed with everything the other said, did, or desired. It was because they loved one another. Even if that love meant the true words spoken between them weren't always easy to hear.

Elise glanced up and I didn't miss the remorse behind her eyes when she addressed me. "We'll stop," she said. "I hadn't taken time to think how this must all be affecting *you* and that wasn't fair. You're just as important to me as my boys are."

And I believed her.

She sat on the couch, blinking before her blank stare settled on the carpet. "I've got a lot on my plate," she admitted. "Listen to me … ranting at my friend, my daughter … like a crazy person." Her dark hair shifted when she shook her head. "I'm expecting a call from the Council by nightfall and … I suppose that has me more on edge than usual."

As I laid there, seeing her coming undone at the thought of giving up, I suddenly saw past myself, saw her pain.

Losing family was something I could relate to, and if there was anything someone could do to fix it, I'd like to think they would. So, because I had a chance of helping Elise put ours back together, I wouldn't steal that hope from her.

Even if I was agreeing to take part in an endeavor that might, in the end, prove fruitless.

"I'm not giving up."

Her eyes—suddenly full of life, unlike before—landed on me. "No, I can't let you do that. You've been at this for a month already and you've got your own life to live."

Shaking my head, I interrupted her thought. "This isn't too much," I assured her. Everyone handled me with kid gloves, so I knew that's what she was thinking. "And time is relative, right?" I added with a smile. "What's a few more months of trying when you've got forever?"

Warmth filled her expression again and, finally, she smiled back. "Evangeline, you have no idea how ... thank you," were the words she settled on when she got choked up.

I gave a casual shrug and felt content with the decision to continue our course. And, to sum it all up, there were four words that seemed to fit.

"That's what family's for."

Chapter Two

Evie

The portion of cold spaghetti I was served slid from the Styrofoam plate as I dumped it in the trash. I wasn't sure it tasted much better warm, but it couldn't have been any worse.

Beth checked the time as we passed through the threshold on our way toward the dining hall exit. She'd done that about three times in the last five minutes, so I had to ask.

"Okay, what the heck is up? Am I keeping you from something?" My tone was lighthearted, so she knew her incessant tracking of every second that passed hadn't really gotten under my skin.

She smiled, pushing golden waves behind her shoulder. "Errol and I are supposed to meet in the gym. He's never seen me in action on the field, so he's doubting my soccer skills. I'm headed there to school him," she added as her grin widened.

We passed Chris, Lucas, and Theo at their table. Each gave either a casual nod or wave, and as I waved back, it wasn't lost on me that they hadn't been themselves since Nick left. Several times, they'd asked if I knew why he took off with Roz, and if I knew of anything that may have made him run. Every time, I had to lie through my teeth.

The Elders, the Council, Elise ... they all made it clear we were not to discuss the incident leading up to Nick's disappearance.

Not even with three guys who were so worried about their friend it was practically eating them alive.

"Catch up with you later," Beth said, smiling as she headed in the opposite direction. She was on her way to dole out a butt-kicking Errol wouldn't soon forget.

"Don't embarrass the poor kid," I teased.

"No promises."

I stepped out into the hallway alone, hearing metal chair legs scraping tile, followed by footsteps.

"Evie, wait up," Chris called out. I turned to find that all three followed, not just him. "Anything new?"

I hadn't known Chris long, but knew he wasn't the sensitive type. The type to wear his heart on his sleeve. He was huge, formidable just like most of the *other* guys from Seaton Falls, and with that same naturally intimidating presence. It said a lot that I saw worry in his eyes.

All they knew was that Nick stepped off the bus after their return following Christmas break, then they never saw him again. Even telling them he'd run off with Roz when they cornered me with similar questions weeks ago was more than I'd been given permission to say. I couldn't stand it, though— seeing their concern growing by the day. Like now, as none of the three before me bothered to hide their true emotions, letting their vulnerabilities show through.

I sighed, darting my eyes around before speaking. "He got into some trouble," I shared, keeping the details to myself. "That's why you saw Dallas pull him aside."

It was nothing but dumb luck that they hadn't seen Liam that day. He'd gone topside with Dallas to retrieve Nick from the bus, but must have stayed out of the guys' line of sight. If they knew he played a part in this, it would've colored their whole perception of the situation and raised suspicions that didn't need to be raised.

I couldn't be sure what they knew about Liam and I, but I was sure Nick had shared *something*. After all, they were his closest friends. Even I, eventually, spilled to Beth after swearing her to secrecy. But now … she knew everything.

About Liam and I, our past.

About my lineage.

About Elise.

"What kind of trouble? What'd he do?" This time, it was Lucas who asked.

I shrugged, pretending to be all out of answers. "Not sure, but I overheard a couple monitors discussing it. Missed the details, though."

My eyes bounced from one to the next, hoping I was convincing enough.

"Nick doesn't get in trouble," Chris added. "I mean, not the kind that would warrant a punishment severe enough he'd have to run away from it."

"Doesn't sound right," Lucas agreed.

"But he's done it before," I interjected. "He took off right before we all ended up here, remember?"

I hoped that, by showing them there was actually a pattern, they wouldn't think it so strange. Nick *had* disappeared without a trace for days without so much as a phone call, a message in a bottle, *anything*. I, nor his family and friends, heard a word from him until he was good and ready to reach out. So, was it so farfetched that he'd do the same now?

They seemed to suddenly accept that this wasn't new behavior. "You're right," Chris sighed. "Just let us know if you find out where he is."

"Will do," I promised.

And I'd keep my word. They deserved to know Nick was okay. Even *I* wanted him to be okay, just … not anywhere I'd have to look at him.

Not yet.

Maybe not ever.

I turned, headed in the direction I was going before the guys stopped me. While I walked, I thought about everything. So much had gone wrong since I became a part of the clan. Couldn't help but wonder if anyone else felt that way and just hadn't had the balls to voice it.

Seemed I was a bit of a jinx.

Sure, this thing with Nick came up because he'd been making piss-poor decisions lately, but even *that* was simply one scenario in a long list of many that had gone wrong since my arrival.

The thought stayed on my mind the entire walk to Liam's room. Before I could knock, he answered. He felt me when I got close just like I felt him, so it wasn't a surprise. I did my best to smile and pretend nothing was wrong, but he had a way of reading me.

"What happened?"

I moved toward the couch as he locked us inside. "Do you think I'm a jinx?"

The question left my mouth as I dropped down onto the cushion. The soft fabric touched my thighs where my shorts cut off.

Liam smiled and a breath hitched in my throat at the sight of it. I hadn't seen him all day, thanks to Hilda and Elise. I hadn't really laid eyes on him when I first walked in either because I was preoccupied, but ... now I did.

A tight-fitting tee hugged his solid chest, doing little to conceal what lie beneath it—a hard body corded with muscle. My eyes lingered there a moment when he first filled the seat across from me, but then they drifted up to a hazel stare and a handsomely rugged face framed in dark, shoulder-length hair. I could feel the loose waves between my fingers like there was no space between us at all. It wasn't until he spoke to answer my question that I realized I'd zoned out observing him.

Again.

A smile touched his lips and they parted with a question. "Why would anyone think you're a jinx?"

I sighed before responding, and all that'd gone wrong echoed inside my head again. "Because of all the bad things in Seaton Falls, because my parents' memories were taken away ... because the spell for Elise isn't working."

My chest tightened as all the pressure hit me at once. It felt like so many people hoped I'd become someone I wasn't. Whether the hope was that I'd be the one to bring my brothers back, or one day reign as queen, I had no confidence I'd succeed at either. It didn't seem anyone was satisfied with me being me.

Plain old Evie Callahan.

"Is that what this is about?" he asked.

I sighed again, spilling the contents of my heart at the feet of the one person I knew I could be completely open with.

"Is it bad that I'm secretly disappointed this spell isn't working? But not just because I want Elise to have her sons back?"

Liam's brow twitched curiously and I went on to explain myself.

Shaking my head, I let him in a little deeper. "I don't want the title," I admitted. "I don't want to be anyone's queen."

I kept my gaze trained on the carpet while I thought of all it would eventually entail—heavy decisions, *more* high expectations, self-sacrifice. I wasn't cut out to lead anyone.

"If I'm able to bring them back ... then one of *them* can lead," I added, confessing my hidden intentions. "They're from the same bloodline and they're all older, so ... once they're back, one of them can have it."

I hated what admitting these things said about me. Most would jump at the chance to be royalty, to be revered by the masses. But not me. I wanted nothing more than to be normal. That's all I'd wanted this whole time—to live the life of a normal, teenage girl. Only, fate had other plans. I was anything but *either* of those things. Heck, if I was being honest, I wasn't even a teenager if we were counting the hundreds of years I lived before.

These were just very confusing, very stressful times.

My eyes followed Liam when he stood, casting a large shadow with his six-foot-plus inches. He crossed the room, his heavy, boot-clad feet echoing with each slow step. My body slumped toward his when he sat close and I leaned into him, settling my head into that space between his neck and shoulder like always. Strong arms covered in ink that told his life story closed me up tight against his chest. I hadn't breathed this easy all day.

"You're no jinx, Evangeline. And, if anyone thinks otherwise, tell them to come see me."

There was an air of jesting in his tone, but I *also* knew he'd have no problem teaching someone a lesson, even for a *lesser* offense. God forbid they hurt my feelings …

My arm warmed where he rubbed it, soothing away the stresses of the day with a simple touch.

"The crown is yours. The *title* is yours," he reiterated. "Regardless of your brothers being older or more fit for the role in your eyes."

I listened, a sense of calm coming over me as I breathed his air.

"Your father saw something special in you from the beginning." With mention of my father, I listened harder. "When you were young, he put it in writing, signed a decree stating that, one day, if he was no longer able to rule, you would take his place as leader of his kingdom. And your mother never objected because she knew you were special, too. It was always just fact that, when the time came … it would be you."

A heaviness filled my heart. Mostly because I knew Liam was telling the truth. Partly because it sealed my fate even more so than it already had been.

I let that sink in—that my life was laid out for me and I didn't have much say.

"What's going on?"

Liam's question should've been a simple one to answer, but it wasn't. There was a lot riding on my ability to meet everyone's expectations and, maybe, I wasn't so sure I wouldn't let them all down.

Or … maybe I was sure I *would.*

Instead of drawing this out and making myself feel worse, I pretended to be over all of it and faked a smile. "It's nothing."

He knew better than to accept that as truth, but didn't force me to talk about it. I liked that about him. Since I made it known that I wanted to be treated like an adult, and have my feelings taken into consideration more often, he'd been mindful of doing so.

"How was dinner with Beth?" he moved on.

"Other than the food itself? Good. She went to meet Errol after," I yawned, drawing my feet beneath me as I snuggled deeper into his side. He was so, so warm. Like a blanket.

A big, sexy blanket.

The ridiculous thought made me smile as my eyes drifted closed. A soft kiss went to the top of my head and I could have stayed there forever, with my hand resting at the center of his chest, feeling his heartbeat beneath my palm.

Love.

It was as much a part of this room as the air we breathed, as tangible as any piece of furniture, as real as Liam and I ourselves. I was guilty of trying to drown myself in it, letting the feeling *and* him consume me.

He made it clear on several occasions he couldn't do this again without me. Not after knowing what it was like to exist on his own, and I understood after nearly losing him a month ago.

A gentle touch to my chin tipped my head back, and then … lips.

Warm.

Soft.

Familiar.

No, I hadn't regained any of my old memories, but I *had* spent my fair share of time kissing him lately. Seemed we could hardly keep space between us when we were alone, although it had never gone further than this, had always remained innocent.

Well … *innocent* may be the wrong word.

Strong hands made their way to my waist, and with one tug, Liam brought me to his lap—solid thighs pressing into the softness of mine as I straddled him. His palms roamed up and down my back beneath the vintage *Transformers* t-shirt I borrowed from Beth. My chest melded to his.

There was so much raw energy between us. Now. Always. It only added to it that we kept it locked inside, never acting on it completely, inadvertently forcing it to build like pressure inside a teakettle.

Heat and desperation covered us both like a living, breathing thing, only retreating when a frantic knock hit the door.

The sound left us both sighing with frustration. Liam eased my body aside, placing me back in my original position on the cushion. I straightened my clothes, licking my hot, damp lips that still tasted like his.

"It'll just be one sec," he promised me, rising from the couch right after.

Watching his every move as he strode toward the door, I sarcastically counted that one second out loud. By the time I got to four, I sank deep into my seat, disappointed.

When I groaned audibly, he glanced back with a smile just before letting Elise in. She was just as frantic as her knock, wringing her hands as the redness in her cheeks spread.

"What is it? What's wrong?" I got the words out before Liam could.

Elise's eyes shifted to me as the answer spilled out. "They're shutting us down. The facility," she clarified. "The call I was waiting on from the Council? It came through and they're giving us two weeks to get things in order. Then, they'll send for all the kids."

Bewildered and at a loss for words, Elise dropped down into the armchair on the opposite side of the coffee table.

"I just ... I don't understand why they would do this. We never had a breach where anyone got in," she rambled. "Our only issue has ever been keeping Nick from getting *out*."

At the mention of his name, my blood ran cold.

"I mean, I understand they see it as a risk we can't afford to take, with so many valuable lives in our care, but ... we're owed another chance," Elise reasoned, peering up at Liam. "After all we've put into this. After all that's been sacrificed."

She fell silent again and I imagined what a bitter pill this must have been to swallow. These facilities were a huge part of what she envisioned when joining forces with the Council and lycans across the globe. Closing even *one* was a huge loss in her eyes. She dreamed of unity between both races, a bridge that would bring us all together to fight our common enemy—Sebastian De Vincenzo, the Sovereign.

For a man I'd never crossed paths with in *this* lifetime, he'd done so much damage. I could only imagine the havoc he'd wreak should we ever meet face-to-face. In fact, the thought of it made me shudder.

"So, what's their next move?" Liam asked, visibly concerned given Elise's news. "I've never exactly been this place's biggest fan, but I'm also not a fan of leaving the job half finished. They were supposed to learn something from this," he added. "Being here was supposed to make up for the clan dropping the ball all these years. And I don't know about you, but from where I stand, that mission's nowhere *near* complete."

He was totally right. Yes, we were more knowledgeable, getting stronger, but … there was still so much work to be done.

Distraught, Elise nodded. "My sentiments exactly. And now, they want to send them all home like the same threats that made this place necessary suddenly don't exist. And do you know what their weak, half-cocked solution is?" she fumed. "They want to continue their training at home in Seaton Falls. They're equating the preparation of these young shifters for war to some trivial, after-school activity." She stood to pace, raking her fingers through her hair before going on. "It's not good enough. It's nowhere near good enough."

"There has to be something we can say. The least the bastards can do is finish what they started. They're willing to let one rogue shifter change their whole plan?"

Elise sighed sharply before answering Liam's question. "Apparently, with the fuss parents in Seaton Falls have been making, this decision is meant to pacify all parties involved."

Clearly, that meant all parties other than Elise.

"My frustration has nothing to do with the millions I, and other investors, have sunk into this place. It's about the fact that ending our program speaks volumes about our mindset, our preparedness," she explained. "If these families can't even see the value in what we're trying to teach their children, if they don't feel the same sense of urgency, then … maybe it really is a lost cause."

Defeat marked Elise's expression. In her own right, she was a soldier, one who'd been on the frontline of a movement many centuries in the making, a soldier only a select few had any confidence in. Two of which were right here in this room.

Liam was all out of suggestions, and from the way Elise's shoulders slumped beneath the white silk of an expensive blouse, I guessed she was, too.

"I suppose there's nothing to do but notify the staff and prepare the facility for our departure."

Another frustrated sigh puffed from Elise's nostrils and a thought occurred to me…

Where the heck would I go?

I wouldn't dare ask the question out loud because I was no one's responsibility, but my heart did race. The thought of being displaced, or a burden someone would feel obligated to take on, was scarier than I could put into words.

'Home' had become such an abstract concept for me. My parents didn't remember me, so I, technically, didn't belong anywhere. My life was in the strangest limbo, dangling somewhere between being the top priority to some, and still managing to matter so little in the big scheme of things.

While I knew Liam hadn't wandered inside my head, it was as though he heard my thoughts.

"I'll need to make arrangements for Evangeline and I before we head back," he asserted, passing Elise a confident glance. It was as though he had no worries at all for where we'd go or whether we'd thrive. And I guessed he *wasn't* worried about that, because knowing him, he'd be content wherever we landed. If I chose to live out the rest of my life in an arid desert, he'd be okay with it, as long as we were together.

"Actually ..." Elise chimed in, "that might not be necessary."

Liam's gaze shifted toward her, and mine did the same. With a softer expression than the one she wore as we discussed the Council's decision, she rounded the table to join me on the couch.

"My mind's going a mile a minute and I can hardly fathom what's happening right now," she confessed, "but the one thing I'm sure of is that I want our family to stick together."

Inside my chest, when she said that word—*family*—my heart began to flutter in the strangest way.

"I don't want either of you to worry about anything," she said softly, taking my hand in hers when she went on. "I know Rebecka and Todd were the only parents you've known, but ... not having them doesn't mean you're alone, Evangeline. Yes, you've got Liam, but you have me, too."

Tears stung the corners of my eyes, but the tightness spreading across my chest only intensified when she said more.

"I'll be making housing arrangements for myself back in Seaton Falls. I need to sort things out with the Elders, the Council," she added with a sigh. "Whether they like it or not, they'll need help looking after the young shifters there," she reasoned. "Dallas will be with me, of course, but I'll be purposely seeking accommodations that will suit us *all*."

A smile touched her lips despite the stress I knew she was under.

"If you'd do me the honor, Evangeline … I'd love it if you'd stay with me." My eyes lifted toward hers and she added, "*Both* of you. Having you two with me again will be the only positive thing to come of all this." She managed a small laugh.

Her gaze rose to Liam then. Her love for my brothers and I extended to him as well. It didn't surprise me at all that she wanted him close, too.

Liam seemed just as moved by her offer as I did. "As long as Evangeline agrees," he said, "it's a yes for me."

Elise nodded. "Of course." Her eyes shifted to me again with a hopeful smile, one hardly dimmed at all by the bad news she just received. "Evangeline?"

I glanced toward Liam and breathed deep. The ball was in my court now. Spending so much time with Elise lately had brought us closer than I ever imagined we would be.

Considering how adverse I was to the idea of letting her in when we first met. However, I believed I understood her now, sympathized with her in ways I didn't think possible.

So, feeling no reluctance whatsoever, I nodded. When I did, her smile broadened.

"Then it's settled," she beamed.

And so it was.

I never would've imagine we'd be returning to Seaton Falls so soon, and certainly not under these circumstances, but the Council had made their decision. In two short weeks, we would return to the place where it all began.

Chapter Three

Nick

"Dad, please. Just ... another couple hundred bucks."

Worried seemed to be Roz's default expression these days. Especially now, and every *other* time she had to call and beg her father for money. Our survival out here kind of depended on it. I hadn't had the nerve to reach out to my *own* family yet and I was sure that, when I did, they'd have one thing to say:

Come home.

Only ... home wasn't an option right now, and honestly, it may *never* be.

Flipping through channels helped keep anxiety at bay while Roz pleaded with her father. Every commercial was either an advertisement for jewelry or sites for ordering flowers online. We were creeping up on Valentine's Day, which meant we'd been away from the facility for five weeks now.

Away from friends.

Away from family.

... Away from reality.

I'd done things I wasn't sure I could come back from; things I wasn't sure I'd be forgiven for. In short, I hurt a certain girl I never meant to. The nature of me and Evie's relationship had changed drastically. We were nowhere near romantically involved at this point, but I still felt something for her. Respect, concern, and now guilt for what I'd done.

For what I cost her.

Late that infamous night, before Roz snuck down to my cell, she'd gone to my room. Not realizing what had taken place several floors below with the witches, she got tired of waiting for an update and headed for my sector. She thought I'd returned without bothering to come to her room like I promised. When she got to my quarters, she overheard a conversation that led to a haphazard chain of events—her knocking one of our combat instructors out cold, freeing me from my cell, and, eventually, us breaking out of a facility built to be inescapable.

She had no choice.

During the conversation Roz overheard, certain phrases were used. Phrases that struck fear in us both.

Reckoning.

Exile.

It was also during this conversation that Roz learned the part I played in injuring Evie, about the witches and how my summoning them led to her being permanently separated from her family.

That part, whether I realized it at the time or not, was on me. My actions led to Evie having to intervene; led to her chances of breaking the spell the witches cast being ruined.

Her back was against a wall. I inadvertently made her choose—let Liam die, or forfeit a future with her family.

She chose.

The decision to seek out the witches for help was made during one of my dark moments. Agreeing to their terms happened during an even darker one. But my emerging nature was no excuse. No matter how ugly my actions, my choices, they were mine and I had to own that.

Whatever fate lie ahead for me, it would be fair.

I hadn't laid eyes on Evie since seeing her distraught and broken in Liam's arms—covered in blood, screaming as she mourned the loss of her parents. Fearing for Liam's life turned her into a savage, a one-woman killing machine as she slaughtered three powerful witches I'd just watched bring *Liam* to his knees.

But not Evie.

There was no fear as she took the three out one-by-one, canceling their plans to end Liam.

Canceling mine.

She hated me now. I knew that without even having to look into her eyes to confirm.

Why wouldn't she?

It wouldn't matter to her that I had no idea those witches were important to her in some way; no idea she needed them. It was all just one, big misunderstanding.

Or, at least that's what I kept telling myself.

But Evie wasn't the only one thoroughly disgusted by my actions. Over the last five weeks, Roz only spoke to me when she had to. It was clear that, running away with me only meant she didn't want to see me locked up forever or worse. It didn't mean she no longer thought I was infallible.

It seemed she finally believed my warning, that a monster dwelled within. But, now that she'd been convinced, I hated it; hated seeing the disappointment in her eyes whenever she looked at me.

I used Liam as a bargaining chip. I should be ashamed of how easy it was to say yes when Scarlet made her terms clear. All she wanted in return for helping me, was him. His life. And I handed him over willingly.

He'd been a thorn in my side since before I even realized he existed. Before he was on *my* radar, he was definitely on Evie's. He was the reason she could never really let go and give in to whatever we had, whatever we might have become. Even when she was with me, she wasn't really with me; her thoughts were always someplace else. Only, I didn't realize where at the time. Part of her was tied to him, or, in her words, *tethered* to him.

The problem ran deeper than my ego being bruised; deeper than me not *'getting the girl'*. Once, not so long ago, I loved her, but I was the only one that seemed to matter to. She tried denying her feelings for Liam—to me, to herself—but at the end of the day, whatever hold he had on her was stronger than any words or any actions I could've put into the universe.

He won her heart.

And I hated him for it.

A heavy sigh, followed by a loud crash when the phone slammed against its cradle, meant the conversation hadn't gone well. Roz sat back against the headboard of her bed opposite the nightstand between us. She stared at the ugly, paisley comforter that'd seen better days.

Consequently, those days were likely back in the seventies.

We'd hopped around from one seedy motel to the next, trying to sort things out. Trying to determine what our next move should be. Roz's father, Officer Chadwick, had been our lifeline, the only one we'd been in communication with since breaking free from the facility. With no clue what the Elders or the Council would do when they found me, going home was not an option.

Well, it wasn't for *me*, anyway.

Which was why I couldn't understand why Roz hadn't left. Every morning I awoke to see her sprawled out and snoring in her bed, I asked myself the same question: *Why hasn't she bailed yet?*

The best meal we'd had thus far was when a diner up the road had half-off meatloaf dinners. Otherwise, the vending machines had been our go-to. We were broke, scared, and unsure of what would come next.

Reaching for the remote beside my leg, I turned the TV off before speaking.

"What'd he say?" I asked, as if I didn't already know the answer. It'd been the same every week when she called and asked for help.

"He said for me to come home," she replied with a now familiar chill to her voice. Of *course* he wanted her home. And he was right to say it.

"Roz, maybe you should listen to him. You don't have to be out here roughing it like this. You're not the one who messed up," I added. "*I* am."

Even before the incident with the witches, I managed to get myself locked in a cell because I did the one thing I'd been trying to avoid lately. I hurt Evie. Granted, it'd all been an accident, but, given her title, that didn't matter a whole lot. Putting her in danger, injuring the rightful heir to the throne, came with consequences even if very few people knew her true identity. I was only aware because I put the pieces together on my own. Otherwise, she never would've trusted me with that kind of information.

Roz stood from her bed and began to pace slowly in front of the large window overlooking the parking lot below.

"We've already had this conversation," she sighed. "I'm not going back without you. Technically, I'm the one who got us into this."

"No, you're the one who rescued me," I corrected. "Truth be told, I have no *clue* what they would've done to me if I stayed."

"And we have no clue what they'd do with you if you went back," she countered. "Back to the facility, back to Seaton Falls."

She fell silent then, and so did I. She was right; if the Elders had caught wind of my behavior, I could only guess how they'd deal with me. When I first shifted, my brothers made it clear how making waves within the clan was frowned upon. I knew death was on the table for any lycan who went without shifting for too long and eventually shifted without the ability to turn back. Who's to say the same punishment didn't stand for a lycan who couldn't seem to control himself? A lycan who blacked out and woke up in strange places? A lycan destined to end the life of a girl they hoped to be their future queen?

Still, my life hanging in the balance didn't have to mean Roz's should, too.

"Call him back," I asserted, making her steps halt.

"He'll just say the same thing and I don't want to hear it," she said in a clipped tone.

I stood this time, taking the long, corded phone from the nightstand where she'd just slammed it down. When I stopped in front of her and held the receiver out, her eyes lifted to meet mine.

"Call and tell him to send you the money," I clarified.

Frustration spread through her expression as she stared. "He made it abundantly clear he's not sending anymore." She crossed her arms over her chest, covering the words on the navy-blue t-shirt she bought at a gas station last week.

"He'll send it because it's not for the motel," I assured her. "... It's for a bus ticket home. *Your* bus ticket."

She didn't break her gaze and neither did I. Not even when her eyes pooled with fresh tears. Her lower lip trembled, but she stopped it by sinking her teeth into the flesh, proving this time on our own hadn't broken her, hadn't made her any less defiant. A trait I hated and admired all at the same time.

"Nicholas Stokes, if you don't get that freakin' phone out of my face, I swear I'll shove it so far up your—"

Stepping closer, my presence quieted her. I looked her over. She'd gotten thinner since being on our own—something else for me to feel guilty about.

"Roz … you have to know I'm right."

Glaring at me as the whites of her eyes shaded pink with frustration, she breathed deep. So deep her shoulders rose and fell with each surge of air she drew in. I wouldn't back down on this. I wouldn't let her suffer because of me. She deserved better, and even if *she* didn't know it, *I* did.

"Call him. *Please*," I urged.

A dark gaze focused intently on mine, leaving me to wonder what she was thinking. After mulling it over, she shook her head, and now *I* was the one frustrated.

"No," she asserted. As pissed as she was at me, she wouldn't go.

"What do you mean '*no*'?"

She plopped down on the edge of her bed, an act of defiance. "I mean I'm not leaving you out here to fend for yourself. I mean I'm not gonna sit at home beating myself up for not sticking it out just 'cause it's not easy, wondering if you're still alive."

I stared at her as she stared out the window.

I hadn't quite figured her out completely, but what I did know about Rozalind Chadwick was that she was stubborn as a mule, the smartest person I'd ever known, and she was loyal almost to a fault. Like now, she could hardly stand to look at me, but it was still evident that she cared.

I took a seat beside her and stared out the window, too. With a heavy sigh I accepted that I'd never change her mind.

"Well, what next?"

She shrugged and it never ceased to amaze me that, even when she was visibly worried, she kept her head.

"We've got fifty bucks left. That's enough to grab a tent and a couple sleeping bags from the secondhand store. Maybe a few cans of beans from the market," she suggested.

Apparently, we were about to take 'roughing it' to a whole new level.

There had been a knot in my gut for the last several weeks. One that grew and grew with each passing day, every time I dared to think back on my mistake.

"I'm sorry." The words fell from my lips and landed at Roz's feet. There were many I owed an apology, but I'd start with her. She put everything on the line for me. Not because she agreed with my choices or thought I deserved saving.

But because she was a good friend.

Her eyes strained red as she continued to fight back tears. However, instead of saying she forgave me or even that she *didn't* … she simply nodded, keeping her eyes trained on the paved lot outside.

The knot swelled again as I wondered if I'd lost her forever; if I crossed a line with her I couldn't recover from.

"Whatever you're thinking," I said quietly, "please … just say it out loud." She might not have known this, but I was begging, desperate for her to speak her mind so there might be a chance for us to move on. If she kept it bottled up, we'd never make any progress.

It didn't matter that we sat hip to hip, breathing the same air. She felt so far away.

"Roz ... please." Now it was *clear* I begged.

A quiet breath entered through her mouth and exited through slightly flared nostrils before she spoke.

"I'm angry," she fumed, breathing deep as a lone tear spilled over her lashes. "At you. At myself."

My hands ached when the inclination to hold hers came over me, but I held back, refusing to interrupt while she vented.

"I'm pissed that you're so blind." Frustration marked her expression as she went on. "All this time, you've been so worried about becoming a monster, that you'd become the thing that would eventually hurt Evie, but somehow you managed to miss the fact that hers isn't the only life that counts, the only one that matters."

I lowered my head, letting that sink in, imagining how weak I must seem to her.

"And, okay, you hate Liam. Big friggin deal. There's still *zero* excuse for what you did." She paused and I held my breath when a fresh wave of disappointment swept over her. "I had no idea you had it in you to do something like that. But I guess that's my fault because you tried to warn me. I just ..." Her voice trailed off and I felt sick.

Kind of like a guy who'd just let his friend down.

"You're forgetting he's wanted me dead since the first time he laid eyes on me," I reasoned.

As soon as the words left my mouth, I knew I shouldn't have made excuses, but I was desperate to justify what I'd done. Not for me. For Roz. So she wouldn't always look at me like she did now.

"And yet … you're still here. He's never *actually* tried to take you out, Nick." The tone she took made me feel small. "But this isn't about Liam." Her gaze dropped to her lap. "This is about me knowing you're better than this."

I let that settle in, really gave her analysis some thought. And the conclusion I reached was that I definitely wasn't as good as she thought I was. If I had been, we wouldn't be hiding out, jumping from motel to motel, begging her father for money. But I couldn't take back the things I'd done. The only thing in my power was to try living up to the standard Roz once thought I met.

I guess what it came down to was … I wanted to be better.

For her.

Chapter Four

Liam

Word spread quickly. Within a few days of news coming down from the Council to the Elders about the facilities closing indefinitely, all staff and students had been brought up to speed.

The concern was that, with such high concentrations of young shifters packed into these places, and with security now being an issue, they were sitting ducks. If someone, the

Sovereign, were to find out where even *one* facility was located, the outcome would be tragic.

Whereas I'd once been sure leaving was in everyone's best interest, I wasn't so sure now. The uncertainty was starting to get to me.

I wasn't the only one. I'd seen a wide range of emotions pass through my lecture hall. Some were relieved to return to their hometowns, their families. Then, there were those who were content to be here, saw the value in learning how to defend themselves, and understanding the history of their species.

Most of the staff saw the mass exodus as a huge mistake. Did I think this place was Fort Knox? Absolutely not, but scattering all the shifters back across the map wasn't ideal either. There'd be no way to rally everyone together quickly when and if trouble came, but the decision had been made.

The young shifters weren't much more prepared for what was to come than they were when they first arrived nearly six months ago. Sure, most could shift and use basic defense moves, but we'd only begun to scratch the surface. Despite my mixed feelings throughout our time here, despite wanting Evangeline to be better protected, it was hard to deny what was best for the majority.

They needed this place.

I paced the carpet between my desk and the front row of seats. Right there, in the middle of the room, were two empty chairs, symbolizing the fall of this facility. Nick and his accomplice, Roz, were the sparks that ignited this firestorm, and now they were long gone, leaving the rest of us to deal with the fallout.

At the thought, I glanced toward the one who'd taken the hardest hit — Evangeline.

The closer our return to Seaton Falls came, the more she seemed to drown in her own sadness. I understood. Being so close to her parents and yet, unable to be with them. I couldn't imagine.

Elise had been sympathetic, too, going out of her way to include Evangeline in the moving process — getting her opinion on furniture and paint choices before making final decisions with the designer. She wanted her to know this home would belong to *all* of us, but there was no lifting Evangeline's mood. She'd never been one to care about material things. All she wanted was her parents.

The one thing I couldn't give her.

She wasn't the only one with mixed feelings. They all seemed to have them. The class was so quiet you could have heard a pin drop. I wouldn't lecture today because there was no point. This place would be in our rearview mirror in a few short days, so I had other plans for how today's class would be structured. These kids had been silenced enough, forced to pretend they weren't at the epicenter of this entire fiasco, but they were. It was *their* lives being shifted back and forth. So, I offered them the only thing I could.

Honesty.

A hand shot up the moment I opened the floor for questions. I pointed to a girl in the back row.

"None of our other teachers will tell us anything," she began. "But what happens now? Are we just supposed to go home and pretend nothing's changed? None of our towns were strictly lycans and dragons, so where do our teachers and friends think we've been?"

I stopped in front of my desk and rested against it.

"Many towns used their witches to cast mass spells to cover their tracks. Others, like Seaton Falls where a few of you are from, have shifters planted in high positions within the school board, local government, law enforcement. Within that network, they cover one another's tracks whenever anyone gets suspicious. It works."

Another hand went up and, before calling on them, I glanced over at Evangeline. She'd been distracted the last few days, seeming to have checked out mentally, emotionally. I looked away and pointed.

"Yes?"

The kid cleared his throat before asking, "Is it true all this is happening because a couple kids went missing."

In my peripheral, I saw Evangeline's eyes lift from the paper she'd been scribbling on since she first took her seat. It would have been so easy to lie, but I'd grown tired of all the secrecy, and if I had to guess, the kids were tired of it, too.

"That's a big part of it."

Low chatter picked up all around the room as speculation had just been confirmed. There might be a hell-storm of backlash for telling the truth, but I didn't care. There was no sense in hiding it.

"Were they taken?" came from the left side of the room.

"Was it the Sovereign?" came from the right.

I shook my head, easing their minds. "No, they weren't taken. They left on their own and video footage proves it. As far as we know, all of the facilities are still operating in secret."

As far as we know …

"And what about when this war finally comes?"

"I'm still not sure I even believe there will *be* a war."

"Maybe this was all the Council's way of pushing their own agenda."

Questions and comments flew at me faster than I could address them. Despite what the Elders thought, these kids weren't stupid. They weren't satisfied being moved from place to place without explanation and this latest decision was the final straw.

"Settle down." At the sound of my voice, the volume in the room lowered to a hushed whisper and then it was quiet. "I know we're all a little confused about what's happening, but we have to face the facts. We'll all be leaving here in a couple days whether we like the idea or not. From this point forward, my only advice to you is that you continue to put what you learned here into practice. Starting with the concept responsible for the first brick of this facility ever being laid."

I looked around to make sure I had everyone's attention before explaining. "Stand up for yourself. Ask the hard questions even when they try to shut you up. Fight back when you're treated unjustly. And never let *anyone* make you powerless; you're only as weak as you allow yourself to be."

No one said a word.

"If you take nothing else from this experience, the one thing you should've all learned is that your differences don't have to divide you. Each species has their strengths, their weaknesses. Bring your best to the table and band together when it counts … against your *real* enemy."

When we first arrived, there was immeasurable tension in this room. Being in mixed company had most of these kids on edge without fully understanding why. They knew they sensed each other's differences and some had even been *taught* not to trust anyone of another species. However, as I stood before them today, that segregation had vanished. They'd come to trust one another, which was a huge part of what this course was about.

My only hope was that it'd been enough.

After dismissal, Evangeline stayed behind, standing beside me in the empty lecture hall. We leaned against my desk, both staring out at the now vacant seats, maybe sharing the same unsettlingly pessimistic energy.

She hadn't said a single word yet, just … lingered. Maybe she just needed to be close, needed to breathe. Uncrossing my arms, I reached for her hand and she laced her fingers with mine. Right after, she released a breath she'd been holding, and let her head fall to my shoulder.

"I'm scared for them," she said, speaking about her peers just above a whisper. "For their future," she added. "Maybe a little scared for ours."

A surge of air swelled my chest when she shared her thoughts. In the moment, I wished I had the ability to look into the future, wished I could assure her there was nothing to fear.

But I couldn't.

The only thing I had was the truth — *mine*.

Squeezing her fingers gently, she rubbed her cheek against the fabric of my shirt. There was never a time I didn't feel like my reason for breathing was to protect her, but, right now, that feeling was like a life source coursing through my veins.

"I'll never let anything happen to you."

Some might say this was a foolish vow to make, assuring someone with definite certainty something will *never* happen, but, to me, this wasn't an empty promise. It was a fact. As long as there was breath in my body, I'd make sure Evangeline was safe. If I had to lay down my own life to make sure of it, I'd do so without question.

A short laugh puffed between her lips and the sound of it was a relief.

"I know I'm safe with you," she replied. "But not everyone has their own personal warrior. What if ..." she paused, thinking of the other shifters I was sure. "What if things get bad for them? Are their clans equipped to fight?"

Again, I wished I had all the answers, but the only one I could give was steeped in more speculation, more uncertainty.

"We just have to trust the Council knows what they're doing." It was an answer, but more than that, it was a gamble.

One I'd never take with *her* life.

My shoulder went cold when she lifted her head. "Shoot, I have to get to Hilda."

This was her routine—rushing to eat an apple or granola bar to take the place of an actual lunch so she could study with her aunt.

"I'll see you at the end of the day," she said in a rush, pressing her lips to mine before attempting to run for the door.

It truly *was* only an attempt, because I caught her wrist before she could get away. She gasped as I yanked her to my chest, holding her by the waist now. She did her best not to smile, but it didn't work.

"You're gonna make me late," she protested weakly. "And we both know how Hilda gets when I'm late."

She was right, I did, but a few stolen seconds would be worth the glare and lengthy lecture. I just wanted a little more of her time.

The world seemed to slow as she gave in, surrendering her lips. Her weight rested against me, pressing her body flush against mine, no real distinction between where one ended and the other began.

Smiling, she pulled away. "Okay, I have to go. For real this time."

I heard the words leave her mouth, but then she swallowed them down again when she came in for a second kiss.

This time, she braced her hands against my chest. "You're a terrible influence and I won't let you corrupt me," she teased, managing to put significant distance between us.

I tilted my head, enjoying the view as she walked away, glancing over her shoulder several times with longing in her eyes. She wanted to come back to me as badly as I wanted her to. She had the soft flesh of her bottom lip clamped between her teeth as she pushed the door open, and then I was alone.

My eyes went to the band I wore, the one that matched hers, and I could only smile. She'd always had a way of making me ache for her, and even after centuries apart, that hadn't changed.

***

Evie

"You're late."

There was always a bit of a scowl on Hilda's face, but it deepened whenever I skated in after our agreed upon time. I swallowed the bite I'd taken of my apple before apologizing.

"I'm sorry, I had a ... a thing after class and ..."

A dark, slender hand lifted into the air, silencing me as silver bracelets clanged on her wrist.

"Tell Liam, from now on, his ... *groping* ... can wait until day's end. Not on my time. Not when we have serious business to tend to," she glowered, flipping through pages of a book that looked about as old as she was.

I lowered my gaze and took a seat at Elise's dining room table — our makeshift workspace.

"Understood."

She peered over the frame of her glasses and then focused on the page for a moment before shoving it across the table to my chest.

"Start there," was her grumbled command.

Little effort went into these sessions anymore, mostly because Hilda had given up hope that we'd ever make progress. It went like this nearly every day — she'd shove a book at me, then she'd wander around Elise's quarters doing whatever suited her until time was up. Almost daily, I thought about throwing my hands up of the entire thing —

giving up on her, giving up on *me*. The only thing that stopped me was remembering that hollow look Elise held when we last discussed it being pointless.

If I could avoid having her lose hope by coming here for an hour a day, then I'd do it.

Even if it did prove to be fruitless.

A shadow loomed above me and I peered up. Hilda stared as a vile of red liquid dangled from a chain just above her blouse's neckline — lycan blood. She always kept one close by and I could only guess the supply she must have brought with her considering how long she'd already been here, how long she'd have to stay if her date of departure matched the date I finally got this spell right. Once, in class, Liam shared that lycan blood was what kept a witch a life beyond their *'natural end'*. The same held true for Hilda. No matter how powerful she was, she was still at the mercy of the lycans she was allied with in Ethiopia.

"You're not focusing," she snapped, her gruff voice stabbing my senses.

"I was, um …"

"Daydreaming," she interjected.

I lowered my head, knowing there was no sense in arguing with her. We'd been at this a while, several weeks, and during that time I'd gotten used to her short fuse and inability to sugarcoat, well … *anything*. So, when she took the seat across from me, I could only guess what would come out of her mouth. She'd surprised me on many occasions, so I braced myself now.

"You're thinking about Liam?" she asked, managing to sound slightly less irritated than before.

I shook my head. "No," I lied. That wasn't true because I was sort of *always* thinking about him, but that wasn't what had me preoccupied.

"Then what is it?"

My lip ached as I gnawed it, trying to put into words how I felt. Hilda was hard, tough. That made it difficult to share my thoughts with her when they were steeped in emotion. I always wondered if, to her, I sounded like some sniveling brat who'd replaced the niece she once knew, and from what I heard, revered. You'd never guess it by how she spoke to me now. How she *looked* at me now.

At the thought, I observed those dark eyes glaring.

"It's nothing," I quickly replied, deciding to keep my thoughts to myself. The last thing I needed was her thinking I was weaker than she already did.

When I lowered my gaze to the book again, I gasped as it was snatched right from beneath my nose. No, she hadn't reached to take it; she used magic, bringing it right to the edge of the table as she stared at me intently. *So* intently I wondered if she read my thoughts, but then remembered she couldn't even if she tried. Being immune to magic was about the *only* thing I'd gotten right.

"You were always difficult. Even before."

I was pretty sure she almost smiled.

Almost.

"Your head needs to be clear," she sighed. "So … clear it. Tell me what's wrong so we can move on."

See? Never sugarcoats a freakin' thing.

I leaned away from the table and just spit it out.

"I'm not ready to go back." Before she could tell me to suck it up because I had no choice, I spoke again. "I know it's already been decided, and I know there's nothing I can do to change it, but that doesn't stop me from dreading being in Seaton Falls again."

Those dark eyes of hers were unfeeling, like she'd never had an emotion course through her veins a single day of her life. But I knew that wasn't true. Once or twice, her heart had shown through, although I believed the reveal was in error. Still, even through her toughness, I knew she cared at least a little. If only because we were family.

"You're right; it *has* been decided," she began. "However … I can understand why this might be difficult."

She glanced toward the wooden box Elise kept on the credenza and I think we both thought of what that box held — the souls of my brothers, more family I had and lost. More family I couldn't remember.

I had a thought and, in my absentmindedness, blurted it while I zoned out. "Can magic restore a person's memories?"

I glanced toward Hilda again when she snickered. "On most, yes, but you've got a clever way of being immune to magic, so ..."

I breathed deep. "I know. I was just wondering if it was possible."

She studied my face, but said nothing for several seconds. She did that a lot. Stared wordlessly, analyzing me.

"Have you ever asked yourself if maybe it's a blessing your mind is a clean slate?"

The question caught me by surprise and my brow twitched. "Why would I? If I could remember who I was, if I could remember Liam, or Elise ... it'd make things so much simpler."

"You've named the good things," Hilda replied. "Of course, *those* would be helpful, but what about the rest?"

She made me think long and hard about that one. I recalled the story Liam shared of the day I died. Would I want to remember being ripped apart by the beast that came for me?

My gaze met Hilda's again. "I mean, I know there were bad things, too, but ... wasn't I happy? Wouldn't I want to remember my brothers? My father? All the memories I shared with Liam?"

Hilda's brow lifted a bit as she shrugged. "I suppose," was her lackadaisical response. "But ... has it not been exciting to ... *claim* your true soulmate twice?"

She did this bouncy thing with her eyebrows that made me laugh, hinting at a physical connection Liam and I had yet to reestablish. She could assume what she wanted, but the question *did* make me think on all the stolen moments he and I managed to carve out in our day, how it felt to be held by him, protected by him.

Kissed by him.

The love between us felt new to me, but I had a feeling it would *always* feel just as exciting, just as necessary, as it did right now.

"Besides," Hilda chimed in again, causing thoughts of Liam to scatter at the sound of her voice. "You've been given something only a handful of others were granted — a second chance."

My head tilted. "Only a handful?" I couldn't imagine why more hadn't taken advantage of something so useful, so *convenient*. My guess was something else Elise had shared. For me to return, because she only had the help of one witch, she could only restart my life from the beginning. I'm me, but without any knowledge of my past life. But to do what Hilda and I have set out to do, bringing back my brothers ... a spell like that required at least two.

Hilda relaxed in her seat a bit when she let out a breath. "The kind of magic your mother and I used to bring you back, the kind you and I have been studying for weeks to do the same for your brothers," she began, "it's forbidden."

My heart sank as I listened.

She saw my surprise and veered off topic for a moment. "Didn't your mother share this with you? Share what she risked bringing you back?"

I shook my head. "No. She wasn't exactly open about it because the Council—"

With the wave of a hand, Hilda scoffed and interrupted. "Of course. The Council," she mumbled, rolling her eyes. "Well, *she* may have sworn her allegiance to them, but I certainly have not." Crossing her legs beneath the table, she situated her long, heavy skirt of expensive, purple fabric over her knee before going on.

"Resurrection spells were forbidden centuries ago. In fact, there are witches planted all over the globe charged with one task only: detecting the use of *'restorative magic'*. Anyone found guilty will suffer a fate worse than death."

I frowned. "What's worse than death?"

Hilda's eyes met mine and I took note of the grave expression she wore. "Being captured by the Sovereign, forced to do his bidding until he feels you've atoned for your transgression … and *then* he ends your life. A gruesome, painful death too despicable to speak of."

Every time someone mentioned this man it gave me chills, made my skin crawl.

"That's why she, your mother, waited so long to bring you back. Not because she feared losing her *own* life, but because she knew I was the only one who'd ever even *think* about helping her, and she thought it too great a favor to ask."

I stared when she smiled. "And ... it was, but ... I suppose we all do stupid things for family," she added.

I smiled back, noting this as one of those rare moments she didn't remind me so much of a statue.

Newton's third law—for every action there is a reaction. This was the analogy Elise used when explaining why she didn't rush to bring me back. She knew saving *my* life could potentially end Hilda's.

And yet both were brave enough to go through with it anyway.

"So ... if you and I get caught ...?"

Hilda laughed out loud this time—a booming sound I think I'd only heard once before. "Your mother would never think of putting your life in danger. Before we began the spell to reincarnate you, I received a blessing from one of the Oracles—a chief member of the High Council," she explained. "I was owed a favor and I figured this was as good a reason as any."

Reaching for a thick gold chain around her neck, one that rested beneath the vile of lycan blood she kept on hand, she revealed a large, gold pendant. The symbol reminded me of a flower, but definitely wasn't one.

"This," she went on, "it hides me from the Sovereign's witches, the ones all over the world hunting for those who dare to resurrect the soul of a deceased supernatural being. With it," she added, "you and I are completely safe, free from that devil's ever-watchful eyes." A look of disgust filled her expression at the mention of him.

I had another question, one Elise refused to answer because of her vow to the Council. However, Hilda made it abundantly clear she, herself, was not bound by any oath. So, I just asked it. The worse she could do was tell me to mind my business and shove the spell book back in my face.

"What made Elise bring me back when she did? I know there's more to it than just her hope that I'll one day serve as queen, but ... I'm still confused."

A hard look came my way, one I couldn't read. "She really didn't tell you much, did she?"

Feeling like a naïve little kid, I shook my head. "No."

There was a long pause. Long enough I thought Hilda had decided not to explain.

"The oracles again," she sighed. "Only this time, they reached out to *me*, after two of the three shared the same vision. They saw a great war, one where much blood will be shed, but, luckily, it was afar off — decades," she added. "Enough time to prepare as much as we're able."

"So, it *is* just about me serving as queen." My stomach turned at the thought of it, taking such a weighty position, one that never appealed to me.

"It is," she answered. "...Because they *saw* you."

My brow tensed again. What did she mean '*they saw me*'?

I knew there was a prophecy about the war, knew I'd been brought back to be queen should the clans succeed in bringing down the Sovereign, but … I had no idea that I, specifically, was part of this prophecy.

"It was that vision of you reigning that made the Oracle agree to this blessing," she explained, touching the large, gold pendant again. "It was the reason I agreed to help Elise. All prophecies are provisional."

"Provisional?"

She nodded. "Yes. They are never etched in stone. The actions, or *inactions,* of others can directly affect them. For instance, the vision of you reigning pointed toward you being queen as long as you're alive, present when the opportunity presents itself. However, if you were not, if you *are* not … then the position would go to someone else," she explained. "Your mother and I simply decided to do our part in ensuring things were in alignment when the time comes."

"As long as I manage not to get myself killed, that is." When I smiled so did Hilda.

"I suppose *that* part is up to you."

"Duly noted."

The large book was shoved at me again. "And now, you study."

Running my hand over the brown, leather cover worn on the edges, my fingertips grazed a gold emblem at its center, one that matched Hilda's pendant.

Lifting my eyes to her, realizing how much thought and effort had gone into bringing me back, how much had gone into seeing to it that I sat here today, I nodded.

"And now, I study."

Chapter Five

Evie

The two weeks the Council gave us to prepare came and went quickly. It was time. Today was the day we'd all be moving back to Seaton Falls.

Beth stuffed the last item from her drawer into the navy-blue suitcase resting on top of her bed. Forcing it shut, she tugged the zipper closed before perching both hands on her hips.

"I think that's everything," she sighed, taking a look around the room we shared for nearly six months.

She, too, had mixed feelings about leaving. While, yes, she missed her family, she'd also gotten close to Errol — an easy on the eyes lycan she met when we first arrived. As luck would have it, he lived in Maine—quite a long way from Michigan.

As I watched Beth now, I found her expression hard to read. Not that this was unusual for her, I guess I just expected a stronger display of emotion, considering.

"You okay?" I asked, hoping to get a feel for what was going through her head.

She lifted her eyes to meet mine, smiling a bit. The weary kind.

"I'm cool," she sighed.

I set aside the small box of books I'd brought with me and went to her. Standing closer, she wasn't able to hide her feelings like before. That twinge of sadness I expected to see was definitely present. Even if not as strong as I would have imagined. But she was a tough girl. One of the toughest I'd ever known.

My hand went to her shoulder. "We'll take a road trip to Maine as soon as the weather breaks," I promised.

Another smile, but her response surprised me. "Appreciate it, but it's probably best to just ... let go."

My brow tensed when I frowned. These two had been inseparable for months, and now she seemed so indifferent.

Seemed being the operative word.

"You don't want to keep in touch with him?"

She shrugged. "I guess I always knew it couldn't last forever. You know ... like more of a *'for now'* thing than a *'forever'* thing. Our clans are so far apart and neither of us have plans to leave them. Just doesn't seem to be written in the stars," she reasoned.

She was so levelheaded. Always. Most girls would've been a crying mess, covered in tears and snot, but not my best friend. Nope. Beth was a rock.

"So ... ready for another round at Seaton Prep?"

At her words, images of plaid skirts and crested blazers were all I could think of. *Those* uniforms were a step up from the ones we were given here, but that didn't mean I was particularly fond of wearing either one.

"Let's just say I'm glad we only have a few months left until graduation," I said with a smile, one that faded quickly.

Graduation ... another milestone my parents would miss.

She must've seen something in my expression because, the next moment, hers became solemn. "How are *you* doing with everything?"

My answer came quickly because there was only one response to give. "I'm dealing."

To be honest, I'd become kind of numb to it all, choosing not to feel *anything* just to block out the negativity. I expected Beth, and everyone else, to be watchful over me today. She knew all my secrets. Everything, including the symbolic loss of my parents. Yes, they were still living, but all ties we had with one another were dead. She knew about my past, who I really was — the eventual queen of the lycans should things go according to plan.

Not *my* plan, but ... *a* plan. Someone's.

It was also no longer a secret between us that Elise was my birth mother and that it'd initially been a struggle forgiving her for sending me away. Although that had changed — my struggle to forgive — I still felt orphaned most of the time. Like I kind of manifested out of thin air, like I came from nowhere.

"Looking forward to shacking with Liam?" Beth asked with a cheeky grin, bouncing her eyebrows suggestively. I was actually surprised she even made a joke about him. After finding out his history, that she'd read about him in books while growing up, he was somewhat of an idol to her. Someone she held the utmost respect for.

"It's not like that," I said, feeling heat spread through my cheeks. I've got my own room and he has his."

My response had Beth eyeing me as I crossed the room to secure my last bag.

"Separate bedrooms or not, dude, you're still kinda … married, or mated, or whatever you want to call it." She paused and shook her head. "I mean, I know you're technically much older than eighteen, but that's gotta be kinda heavy."

I could see how she would think that, but she didn't know what I knew. Didn't feel what I felt. Liam completed me. No, not in some *desperate-girl-who-can't-function-without-a-guy* sort of way. He was my missing piece. My other half. And besides, he hadn't pressured me to act like his wife in any traditional sense of the word. If anything, he'd taken somewhat of an old-school approach to our relationship. Courting—that's the word that came to mind whenever I tried to define it. He'd never been anything but a gentleman, and the one time I tried to move things along quicker, he was the one who pumped the brakes, slowing me down before I did something I might regret the next morning.

Although … I doubted I would.

Without realizing it, Beth had been watching the whole time I ran through my analysis of what Liam and I had grown into. I guessed I was smiling, because now she was, too.

"You two are the real deal, huh?" she asked as I became content with her being able to see right through me.

I caught a glimpse of the band on my wrist as I reached for my hoodie, slipping it on while answering. "As real as it gets."

I meant that from the bottom of my heart. There was no doubt in my mind that what Liam and I shared was unlike anything anyone else had ever experienced. Our souls were inseparable. How I ever thought I'd fight it was beyond me.

We were inevitable.

"I hope I find that one day," Beth confessed, surprising me with such sentimental words.

"It'll happen."

A casual shrug was her only response. Not words to indicate whether she agreed or disagreed with me.

I perked up seeing her grab something that didn't belong to her—a laptop bag with Roz's name stitched on it amidst hand-sewn patches of planets and stars. Per her father's request, she was bringing a few of her cousin's belongings despite them not exactly being close.

Actually, they kind of hated each other.

"Has your family heard from her? Roz, I mean?"

Beth looked up when I asked and, of course, her face told it all. She said several times these past two weeks that the facility disbanding was on Roz, her fault as much as it was Nick's. Now, she resented the idea of being her gofer.

Another indifferent shrug came before a blunt response. "Don't know. Don't care. I just grabbed her things like I was asked to do. As soon as we're back in Seaton Falls, I'm dumping this trash right on her dad's porch and being done with it."

There was always so much animosity between the two. Not that I was *Team Roz* or anything, but she seemed okay. When she wasn't giving me the stink eye for talking to Nick, that is.

"What's *with* you two?" I'd been wanting to ask for months now.

Beth sat Roz's things by the door before answering. "I just don't like the girl," she said plainly. "She's a know-it-all. She's a brat. She's needy. She's—"

"Everything you're not?" I cut in with a smile.

Chuffing a short laugh, Beth nodded. "You could say that."

It seemed like they still would've found a way to coexist without every interaction between them being a cold one, but I couldn't judge. I had issues of my own.

We gathered the things we could carry, leaving the rest for the staff members who'd be by to bring it topside once the facility cleared out. Beth and I stood at the door, glancing back at the room we shared. I think we both perceived the uncertainty the future held.

***

Liam

The busses were filling fast.

That was the plan—get these kids out of here as quickly as possible. Having them out in the open, all at once, was the most critical part of this entire operation. I stood off in the distance, resting against my truck, watching the tree line for disturbances.

A set of heavy footsteps accompanied by the lighter variety approached from my right. I didn't turn, shifting my eyes toward the entrance of the decoy house where Evangeline would be exiting any second.

"We've got ourselves a problem." The announcement came from Dallas, the words rolling out slowly in his Southern drawl.

My shoulders heaved with a deep breath. "What else is new?"

Seemed all we had these days were problems. Here we were, leaving the facility, and they were *still* coming at us.

"I've heard from the Council just this morning," Elise chimed in. "Apparently, Nicholas' mother, Mrs. Stokes, has been inquiring about ... *'the girl'*."

I glanced at Elise just long enough to confirm she meant Evangeline, turning toward the house again when I asked, "What about her?"

"It seems Mrs. Stokes never approved of the short-lived relationship between the two and has suggested they consider what role *she* may have played in her son's disappearance."

"He didn't disappear," I said flatly. "The jackass ran away."

Because that's what cowards do ...

"Either way, she's making waves, calling attention to the problem, calling attention to Evangeline. Neither of which we need at the moment." Elise paused and the air around us thickened, causing me to give my full attention when she went on.

"She spoke to Evangeline's parents."

My brow tensed and, instinctively, both fists clenched. "What do you *mean* she spoke to them? They don't even remember her."

Elise breathed deep. "Her intention was to find out if Evangeline had mentioned anything that might allude to where Nick's gone, or any inkling there was more going on than their family has been told. Of course, the Callahan's knew nothing, looked at her like she was insane for insisting they even *had* a daughter." She paused again and I knew this was going to go from bad to worse when she turned away, choosing to watch the busses instead of looking in my eyes.

"In short, Mrs. Stokes is demanding answers," Elise sighed, "threatening to seek help *outside* the Elders, outside the Council if need be, but she assured them she *would* get answers."

I could take care of all this. Easily. However, as soon as I opened my mouth to suggest it, Elise spoke.

"And, no, you can't kill her."

"It'd fix the Council's problem. It'd fix ours, ensure the woman can't do anything stupid," I countered.

"Makes perfect sense to me," Dallas mumbled in agreement.

Elise eyed us wearily. "Need I remind you both of the importance of maintaining a low profile?"

"That'll be hard to do if Momma Stokes's antics compromise us," Dallas added, taking the words right out of my mouth.

Shock filled Elise's expression when Dallas continued to butt against her. "Just sayin'," he added, lifting his hands in surrender.

Her gaze slipped back toward me. "Just be patient while I find out more."

"No promises," I said honestly.

She ignored my response and relayed the rest of the Council's message. "In the meantime, they won't allow Evangeline to return to Seaton Prep. Not just because of this latest issue. It would have required more magic to reintegrate her into the system, seeing as how she's been wiped from half the staff's memory. They've arranged for a tutor to come to the house twice a week and that will ensure she's able to finish her coursework for the year. So, Liam, if you wouldn't mind—"

When I took a deep breath and shoved off the side of my truck, Elise knew I understood. She wanted *me* to be the one to break the news.

I felt Evangeline before spotting her and Beth as they lugged heavy bags down the porch steps. I went to her, leaving Elise with a few parting words as I walked away.

"I'll take care of it," I sighed. "I always do."

The twisting in my chest spun even faster when Evangeline and I locked eyes, tripled when she smiled. We were close now, the three of us within a few feet of one another.

I nodded toward Beth. "Afternoon."

She nodded back, but didn't speak. She was always so formal around me and I guessed it was because she knew me only as her instructor.

"Evie, I'll text you in a bit," she said in parting, offering another of her tense smiles. Before she could step away, I stopped her.

"You're welcome to ride with us if you want," I offered, aiming a thumb over my shoulder toward my truck. It'd be a little cramped, but there was room. Mostly, I just wanted her to know that, despite all she read about me, she could relax.

Her lips were tight when they turned upward. "Thanks," she began, blinking profusely. "But I already had the guys hold a seat for me."

And by *'guys'* I assumed she referred to Chris and Lucas.

I smiled back. "Suit yourself. Just text Evangel ... Evie," I corrected, "if you change your mind."

"Will do." With that, she headed for the bus.

The weight of a black duffle bag shifted from Evangeline's shoulder to mine when I relieved her of it. Our steps toward my truck were slow as we exchanged words for the first time today.

"You'll have to forgive Beth," she said with a smile. "In her mind, you're basically a celebrity."

The idea of anyone regarding me in that way was laughable.

"She's like your super fan or something."

I shook my head. "Kind of strange she'd find anything honorable about my darker years."

All the killing. The bloodlust.

"Beth's a different breed," Evangeline said with a laugh. "She's a bit rougher around the edges than the rest of us. She likes the blood and guts of it all."

I tossed the duffle into the bed of my truck and caught her gaze before heading around to open the passenger side door. There was a look in them that wouldn't let me go.

I smiled a bit. "What?"

Evangeline's head tilted to the side as she studied me. "You really don't think there was *anything* honorable about your past? About the wars you fought?"

During that time, my heart was as black as night—cold, empty. While the side I fought on may have been the side of righteousness, my reasons for getting involved were anything *but* righteous. I wanted to kill, wanted to bring pain and darkness to others because it was eating me alive. I *liked* taking lives.

Not wanting to taint her innocence with such a response, I simply shook my head. "It's not that simple."

Maybe she sensed it in my tone that I didn't want to talk about it, because she didn't press. Instead, she climbed into her seat and only thanked me.

By the time I got in and started the engine, the busses had done the same as a few stragglers rushed from the facility. The compartments with the remaining pieces of luggage the staff brought up were closed tightly. In front of us, the brake lights of a black sedan glowed red as Elise and Dallas prepared to lead the way back to Seaton Falls—a journey I don't think anyone dreaded quite like Evangeline.

I reached for her hand, squeezing when I took it. There was nothing I could say to make this easier, so I didn't bother trying.

My gaze shifted toward the decoy house we'd dwelled beneath for so many months, thought of all that had changed while we were here. In this place, she reunited with her mother, found her way back to me, found herself.

She took a deep breath as I put the truck in drive, pulling off right behind Dallas as he drove Elise's car carefully through the rough terrain. The busses were leaving as well. I watched from the rearview mirror, still keeping an eye out for anything out of place.

After weeks of preparation, we were on our way.

The first few hours were mostly quiet, especially after I broke the news of her being tutored for the rest of the year. She said she didn't mind not going back to Seaton Prep, but I imagined this, along with everything else, just added to the mounting changes she was going through.

Had it not been for the radio, it would have been completely silent. Evangeline changed positions every ten minutes or so—from leaning on the window to leaning on my shoulder. Restless.

"Looking forward to having your own room again?" I asked just to make conversation.

She forced a weak smile and shrugged. "Sharing with Beth wasn't bad. She's good company."

"Well, rest assured, whatever house Elise picked out, your bedroom is likely to be the size of a modest apartment. She's always had grandiose taste," I said with a laugh.

"Have you seen pictures?"

I shook my head. "No, but I know your mother."

Evangeline smiled. "Maybe I'll wander inside your head if I ever get lonely."

"Or ... you could always just wander down the hall and visit," I suggested.

Glancing over, I noted the red twinge to her cheeks before she spoke again.

"My mom would've loved you," she said amidst the bubbly sound of easy laughter.

"And your father?" I asked.

The question earned me a huge grin. "Are you kidding? You would've been his worst nightmare."

I didn't take offense. Actually, I found the answer amusing. "Why's that?"

A warm glance passed over me, landing on my arms just beneath the hem of a white t-shirt, then my chest, and eventually my face before answering.

"Because ... you look like the authority on talking your way into girls' beds," she grinned.

I turned away, keeping my eyes on the road ahead, but feeling the smoothness of her leg beneath my palm.

"Not *'girls'*, plural," I corrected. "Just one. Doesn't that count for something?"

My knuckles warmed when she shifted in her seat, unconsciously squeezing my hand between her thighs.

"It may not have made a difference to my *dad*," she replied vaguely, leaving me to reach my own conclusion — that being the one and only mattered to *her*.

My heart, nor my body, had ever wanted another.

Her head made its way back to my shoulder, and this time she was more content, running both hands up my bicep as she settled in.

"I'm okay with going back," she said out the blue.

I listened, but didn't speak. This was a far cry from where her head was a few days ago. Maybe she'd put things into perspective between then and now ... or maybe she just wanted to seem brave, fearing the rest of us would think less of her if she didn't.

"I talked with Hilda the other day and I think it helped me focus," she added.

Talks with Hilda had a way of doing that, helping you focus on the issue at hand because she wasn't one to deal with the extra fluff.

"What changed?"

She shrugged, gathering her thoughts and, meanwhile, I tried to keep mine clear. Easier said than done as the tips of her fingers traced a tattoo. Her touch had always, and *would* always, be a distraction.

"Hearing her break everything down just made me grateful — grateful to be alive, grateful my parents didn't meet a worse fate, grateful I have Elise." I felt the heat of her stare when she went on. "Grateful I have you."

She pressed a kiss to my arm. At the feel of warm, sticky lip gloss against my skin, coating her fleshy lips, I toyed with the idea of pulling off the road. Maybe no one would notice if we disappeared from our convoy for an hour or two. I went over the entire scenario as the heated tension between us thickened. It was always there — heavy like sultry air before a downpour. The waiting ... it was enough to bring me to my knees, begging.

But then she rested her head against my shoulder, and just like that, I was reminded of her innocence. Reminded of our unspoken vow to take things slow and steady.

"As long as I have you, I'll be okay," she breathed.

Those words settled on my heart. I waited half my life to hear her say she felt that way again.

Her hand slipped down to mine. She caressed my palm a moment before letting her fingers travel to my ring — one that matched her brothers'. I only recently believed I had reason to bother wearing it again. Before, I didn't much care whether I lived or died.

"Promise you'll never take this off." It was a solemn request, one filled with the knowledge of how final death would be if I did. Long lashes that shrouded the most beautiful set of eyes I'd ever seen fluttered toward me.

"Promise me," she breathed a second time.

I nodded, assuring her. "You have my word."

With that she settled again, getting comfortable at my side, watching the back of Elise's car as Dallas barreled down the freeway—fast, reckless, like an immortal with a million lives to live.

We had several driving hours under our belts and when Dallas pulled off at the next rest stop, I guessed either he, Elise, or Hilda needed to stretch their legs.

Evangeline stayed seated when the engine went quiet. Moving my fingers from the handle, I leaned back in my seat, waiting to see if she intended to step out or not. When she continued to gaze out her open window, I guessed she didn't.

Her tongue peeked out from between lush lips when she wet them, breathing deep right after. Something seemed to be troubling her, but I never expected the words, "I'm sorry," to tumble from her mouth.

I frowned, wondering why on Earth she was apologizing. "For?"

Her lids shielded me from the brown centers of her eyes when she blinked—long, hard, contemplative.

"For fighting you all this time about Nick. For not believing he was who and what you said he was," she explained. "I'm sure that caused you undue stress."

It was completely unnecessary for her to even bring it up, but I appreciated it nonetheless.

"Apology accepted," I said quickly, no need to even give it a second thought.

"You never asked." She turned after making the vague statement. "When we left Seaton Falls, I was hellbent on making things work with him. Then, when we got to the facility … I barely said one word to you about him," she added. "And you never asked why—never asked where things stood between he and I."

She didn't seem upset, just puzzled.

When I shrugged, I put my thoughts to words. "Because he never mattered."

That was the simplest way I could put it. In the big scheme of things, with the centuries Evangeline and I shared, Nick was merely a blip on the radar. There wasn't a doubt in my mind she'd eventually realize it, too. And I had nothing but time to wait until she did.

One corner of her mouth tugged up into a smile. "You were that confident I wouldn't let things go too far with him?"

I replied as honestly as I could. "No, but I did know you'd eventually feel what I feel, and you'd be just as powerless against it as I am."

Truth was, she'd always been stubborn as a mule. No one could make Evangeline do anything she didn't want to. No one could stop her from pursuing something she believed in. And, for a while, her relationship with Nick was one of those things she believed in. There was nothing I, or anyone else, could tell her to change her mind. It would take her seeing it for herself.

And, while I wasn't sure what the tipping point was exactly, I was sure he'd shown her whatever she needed to see.

So, here she was, beside me, latched to my arm. Right where she belonged.

Elise approached the open passenger-side window with a cheeky grin and bag in hand. Passing it to Evangeline without a word, she headed back to her car. The plastic rustled when Evangeline dug inside, and the moment she smiled, I guessed what she'd been given.

"Seems she didn't forget my weakness either," she grinned, dangling one of several candy bars between her fingers.

The bag was tucked between her feet where she could easily reach it when she wanted, and then her eyes went to Elise. Warmth filled her expression and the look gave me hope where none existed before.

Evangeline may not have fully accepted it yet, but I wasn't the only one she needed. Her mother was waiting for her to come around, holding back all the love she had to give for when her only daughter was ready to receive it. Evangeline couldn't have understood how important she was to all of us and it had nothing to do with anyone wanting her to be queen. For all we cared, she could run from the throne all her life and it wouldn't change how we felt about her. When she was gone, we all fell apart, went to dark places, at times hoping for death to quench the loss.

Now that we had her back, we'd *all* been given a second chance. Not just her.

Her heart was incredible. She had the capacity to love and forgive like no one I'd ever seen before. These were only a few reasons I was confident that, when the day finally did come that she must choose to accept her role as queen, she'd be the fairest the lycans could ever hope for. Under her rule, it'd be the dawn of a new day.

To them, she'd be the compassionate sovereign they always wanted, always deserved.

To me, she'd be what she's always been.

Everything.

It was only a matter of time before she, too, saw herself for who she really was.

Chapter Six

Evie

No expense had been spared. It was obvious the second we walked in.

My socks slipped and slid over the marble tile when I removed my gym shoes and set them aside. It was nice to finally be out of them after traveling so many hours. The seamless, black and white stone stretched from the foyer, well beyond the kitchen, and into the nook. It was a straight shot across hundreds of square feet, allowing visitors to see clear through from one end of the massive house to the other. To my right, stairs with a massive landing decked out with floor to ceiling bookcases. Elise had her decorator fill them to the brim. To my left, a coat-closet the size of my old bedroom. Echoes of our steps ricocheted off cathedral ceilings adorned with ebony-toned, wood beams, forming diamonds against their white backdrop. In the center, a wrought-iron chandelier the size of a small car.

So many windows. They were everywhere, showcasing the beauty that lie just beyond them—the woods of Seaton Falls, made more beautiful by the freshly fallen snow, the incoming winter storm. A gentle squeeze to my shoulders brought my eyes toward Elise when she approached with a smile.

"I know we've only just walked in, but … do you like it so far?"

When she asked, I glanced around at the breathtaking views beyond each window—leafless trees with branches dressed in sleeves of white snow. That was all there was to see for miles from what I could tell. Out here, it was just us and nature.

"It's … amazing," I breathed, trying to take it all in.

My answer made her smile grow wider. "I'm glad. I wanted nothing but the best for you."

She'd done all this for me?

Her arm slipped from around my shoulder and she moved forward. "Let me show you the rest," she beamed.

A quick glance toward Liam proved he was far less impressed than I was, which may have meant he'd seen better.

Lived in better.

Maybe my father's kingdom in Bahir Dar, our home, made this house look pitiful in comparison. I'd never know.

"A large kitchen was a must," Elise explained. "I intend to prepare homecooked meals for everyone. I know the food at Damascus left much to be desired."

No one disagreed with her. Hilda had mostly converted to a diet of fruit and muffins because she said those were the only edible items in the entire dining hall. If you ask me, including the muffins was pushing it.

Pristine, white cabinets with brushed-metal knobs reached the vaulted ceilings. Countertops of white and black quartz gleamed in the daylight, the sun bringing out small flecks of glitter. The appliances were all state-of-the-art, and glancing around, it was easy to tell who had inspired the facility's décor. At every turn, clean lines and bright white surfaces met my vision. Potted plants had been placed strategically around the room—near windows, beside detailed floor-to-ceiling pillars, beside doorways. While, no, this house wasn't nearly as cold and sterile as the facility, the similarities were just enough to catch my attention.

"There's more to explore here on the first floor, but I'm sure you're anxious to see your bedroom." That broad smile was back as her voice echoed in the large space. She paused, seeming to read my expression, causing the corners of her mouth to turn down again.

"Of course, if you're not completely satisfied once you take a look, I'll have the decorator come back and redo it to your liking."

I didn't say it out loud, but I'd never consider having someone come back and do double the work. Not even if I hated whatever design ideas Elise had for my space. Love it or hate it, I'd live with it.

"You always liked turquoise," she rambled as we climbed the stairs. "Does that still hold true?"

I nodded. Turquoise was my favorite color, actually. I noted that this was another small piece of me that hadn't changed — another missing piece I could now fill in.

Liam's and Dallas' heavy, boot clad feet thudded against the wooden steps behind Elise and I as we approached the landing. My fingers trailed a row of books on the shelf as we passed, on our way to more steps that curved us toward the upstairs hallway. A word came to mind. One I wouldn't typically use to describe a house, but it was so fitting here.

Grand.

This house was enormous and elaborate, fit for a queen.

At that word, my eyes flitted toward Elise, to the long, black coat trimmed in fur and the sleek pumps she'd worn during the long trip we'd just taken. Only a queen could be so poised, so glamorous all the time. This home suited her.

But I, on the other hand, felt out of place.

In this house.

In this town.

Doing my best to ignore the sense of being … unfit … the feeling spread through my gut as I stepped into the doorway of a bedroom.

"This is it," she announced with a hopeful grin set on her face.

I stared, blinked, stared some more. The sheer size of it had me speechless. White carpet met our feet once we ascended the stairs. It carried on through my bedroom and all the others from what I could see. Left, a huge walk-in closet. Right, a bathroom big enough to live in if I wanted. Even from here, silver fixtures gleamed in the sunlight through a large picture window above the tub. Outside it, the same breathtaking view I'd have beside my bed when I awoke every morning.

A black and white striped comforter covered a king size bed adorned with pillows. So many pillows. Black, white, turquoise. A dark desk with a clear chair tucked underneath it, a laptop the same shade of pale turquoise found sprinkled throughout the entire room. It wasn't so much that it was overwhelming the otherwise muted tones she selected, but enough that it broke up the stark contrast of black and white. Beside a lamp at the desk's corner, sat a glass jar filled with colorful candy. I smiled at that, the small touches of *me* she hid here.

Above my head, I peered up into the shimmering crystals of a chandelier I was afraid to know the price of. Straight ahead, French doors with white sheers at either side drew my attention. I stepped closer until my hands touched the cool knobs. Pulling them open, I moved out onto a balcony that overlooked the woods. Just beyond the trees, the sound of rushing water. The falls were close by and hadn't been frozen by frigid temps.

"Well?" Elise asked, that hopeful look returning to her eyes.

I glanced left as a strong gust of chilled wind lifted her dark hair into wispy swirls of brown, looking not a day older than twenty, although I knew that to be false. There was such emotion, such warmth emanating from her, it transferred to me.

"It's perfect."

The trouble she'd gone through to make sure I'd be comfortable here, despite all the drama and scrutiny surrounding the facility we just left … it was an incredibly sweet thing to do.

She seemed shocked when I attacked her with a hug, feeling her arms tighten around me, too.

"Thank you for taking time to—"

"It was no bother," she interjected, her accent coming through stronger as she wrestled with emotion. "Anything for you."

Connecting with her hadn't been easy. Mostly because I'd set a barrier between us. I *had* a mother already, and all this time, I'd been vigilant to remind myself that Elise was not her. There was no substitute for Rebecka Callahan.

But … the more time I spent with Elise, the better I got to know and understand her, see her strength, her fierce love … my heart expanded to let her inside it, too. So, while there was only one Rebecka, there was also only one Elise — the woman who'd brought me into this world twice and proved her love and loyalty at every turn.

We finished touring the upstairs, including Liam's room directly across the hall from mine. His had a rugged set up that suited him — dark grays and navy blues against dark wood. Elise knew us both like the back of her hand. Liam and I, her children.

A room had been decorated for Hilda as well, despite her stay being only temporary. She was fond of purple, finding a way to work it into every ensemble she wore, even if only a bracelet or two. So, it was no surprise that Elise had been thoughtful enough to have subtle hints of plum and lavender tastefully arranged throughout — throw pillows, a vase on the dresser filled with fresh lilies, a candle on the nightstand.

She knew us all, had taken bits and pieces to make these foreign dwellings feel like home.

This *was* home now.

Dallas grabbed his, Elise's, and Hilda's things from the trunk of Elise's car. They all retreated to unpack and start settling in, but not Liam and I. We lingered in the hallway alone, taking it all in—the house, the adjustments to our lives, everything.

"She did a great job with the place." My eyes danced from one elegant furnishing to the next—crown moldings that trimmed the ceiling and each light fixture, the banister and its ornaments carved from a single piece of wood, the view down into the foyer from where we stood.

A grin touched Liam's lips and the sight of them had me licking my own.

"It's nice," he crooned, "but still not the most beautiful thing she's ever created."

His gaze lingered on me as the subtle compliment brought heat to my cheeks. Large hands swallowed my waist and I moved into his arms, correcting a thought I had a moment ago. No, this house was *not* home.

This was ... locked in his embrace, close.

"I've got an idea," he breathed, soft, fleshy lips grazing the rim of my ear.

Inhaling the mild, earthy scent of him, I managed a question. "What's your idea?"

He shrugged and, for a moment, seemed too distracted by whatever rogue thoughts rushed through his head as we gravitated closer.

"We've been on the road all day. What do you say we head outside for some fresh air?" When he smiled, I was intrigued. "I think I know a way we can all blow off a little steam."

My head tilted as I tried to make sense of the cryptic statement, but before I could ask, Liam traipsed toward Elise and Dallas' room, pounding a heavy fist against the door.

The sound brought Hilda out into the hallway as well, standing beside her door with both fists perched on her hips. She stared at the back of Liam's head, clearly fighting the urge to chastise him for keeping up so much noise. He caught her watching and countered her scowl with a smile.

"Get your coat, Hilda. You're joining us, and I won't take no for an answer."

"Joining you where?" she huffed.

He didn't let her iciness back him down. "We're heading outside for a lesson."

The word 'lesson' only confused me further. I didn't feel much like training today, but wouldn't shoot down his idea with how excited he seemed.

Hilda glowered at him a moment longer, and then, like me and every other woman I'd seen in Liam's presence, his charm got the best of her. She smiled the easiest smile I'd seen her give since arriving. Snorting a laugh when he broke her, she waved him off.

"It's cold out there, and unlike you, I'm not a walking furnace," she pointed out, heading back into her room where I guessed she intended to stay.

But Liam had other plans. He rushed to her doorway and gently took her shoulders. "That's what coats are for," he reasoned.

To my surprise, Hilda didn't argue. The most resistance he got was an eye roll to accompany the half-smile she gave.

Elise finally surfaced with clothes draped from both arms. The urgency of Liam's knock had startled her while she unpacked if her tense expression was any indication.

"What is it? What's the matter?" she asked, bearing that heavy, concerned mom tone.

The look faded when she took in Liam's light expression.

"Grab Dallas," he insisted. "Meet us outside. Thought now would be a good time to show Evie around."

My eyes flitted toward him. Show me around? I'd gotten to know my way around the woods and the rest of Seaton Falls pretty well. Why would he think I needed a tour guide?

My hand warmed in is and I didn't have time to think or speak as I was rushed down the stairs, and then spun toward the kitchen. Liam scooped my shoes from the front door on the way. Apparently, we were headed out through the back.

"Wait … my coat," I protested, thinking the hoodie I wore wouldn't be enough.

"Don't need it," he called back over his shoulder. "I'll show you how to keep warm once we get outside."

My brow twitched at more vague words.

We paused at the sliding door that made up a large part of one of the nook walls. I only had time to slip my shoes on before Liam swept me outside behind him, into the blistering cold and blowing snow.

February in the Midwest can be brutal and that was the perfect way to describe the weather today. Coming from Chicago, I hadn't forgotten, and Michigan was no exception to that rule. Frosty air stung the tip of my nose and my eyes watered accordingly. It was practically a blizzard out here, reducing visibility to half a mile at best. Even for those of us with supernatural vision.

Being half dragon, I was sure I ran hotter than the average person, but still. I could feel my knees quaking as I hugged myself when an angry gust of wind swept between Liam and I.

Speaking of, he was seemingly unaffected by all of it. While I felt snowflakes gathering on my lashes and in my hair, it landed on him and instantly trailed down his skin like he was standing in a rainstorm and not a blizzard.

"How're you doing that?" I asked through chattering teeth.

It was clear he'd tapped into some secret ability I didn't realize I was capable of.

"Hold out your hand," he called over the sound of howling winds.

Dreading the idea of pulling my arms away from my body, I did as he asked. My wrist was gently twisted until my palm faced the sky.

"Now watch," he said, nodding toward his arm.

I stared, thinking he was insane for being out here in only a t-shirt, jeans, and boots—nothing covering his flesh other than the snow turned to water.

But then, there was something else—streaks of light just beneath the surface of tanned, inked skin. His veins were alight with glowing movement, like lava flowed through them at a sluggish pace. I squinted, watching as warmth spread from his body to mine.

My eyes lifted toward his. "How'd you do that?"

He quirked a smile. "It's easy. Focus on shifting," he instructed, "but right before your flames ignite, you'll feel a surge of heat. Contain it. Hold it inside and let it move through you."

A deep breath puffed from my nostrils, the warmth of it crystalizing in the bitter cold. I sucked at new things. It generally took me weeks to master an unfamiliar technique, so I was almost positive my effort would result in fireballs shooting out my ears or something stupid like that.

As if he heard my thoughts, Liam laughed a bit before encouraging me to give it a try.

"You can do it," he insisted.

With another breath, I closed my eyes and did everything he said to. First, I awakened my dragon, and then, just as she was about to burst from within, I harnessed the energy she supplied and concentrated to spread it through my limbs, my quivering lips.

"First try," Liam said. Even with my eyes closed, I knew he was smiling. I could hear it in his voice.

My lids fluttered open and my vision was settled on my wrists just beneath the cuffs of my sleeve. I took in the sight of the same glowing veins and slow-crawling lava moving inside mine as I'd seen in Liam's. Pushing my sleeve further up my arm, I noted that the glow ended somewhere between my elbow and shoulder, but it kept me warm all over.

Pleased with my progress, I smiled up at him. Suddenly warm, I only kept my hoodie on to stay somewhat dry.

Behind us, the sliding door opened and Hilda stepped out bundled in a coat, scarf, hat, and gloves, clutching a mug of coffee. She conjured it, I guessed, seeing as how there hadn't been time to brew any. Elise and Dallas emerged next, wearing nothing more than athletic gear. His black shorts and tank matching Elise's. She wound her hair into a tight bun before bouncing her brow at Liam.

"I knew exactly what you had in mind," she smiled. "And it's been far too long since I spread my wings."

At first, I thought it was just an expression, but as Dallas made a show of stretching and readying himself with a watchful eye trained on the sky, I knew I'd been wrong.

Elise, literally, meant it'd been too long since stretching her wings. I whirled to Liam and I could only guess how the excitement showed through on my face.

"Wait … you're teaching me how to fly?" I asked, bouncing on the balls of my feet as I stuttered.

Liam gave a nod.

Excited didn't even describe how I felt about this. Since finding out flying was even something I could do, I'd been looking forward to this day. Once or twice, I pressed him to teach me, but understood there were more important things to perfect first.

But now … Liam thought I was ready.

My gaze lowered when he gripped the hem of his shirt and raised it a few inches, revealing skin the shade of sand, covering a tight, ridged stomach. I swallowed a breath and forced my eyes toward Dallas when he spoke.

"May as well ditch the sweatshirt, kid," he said with a laugh. "It's gonna get soaked once we get moving."

He was right. I was already drenched and had only stood in one place. I could imagine how it'd be once we were hundreds of feet in the air. So, reluctantly, I took it off, draping it over the ledge of the porch. I never would've thought I'd be warm standing outside in freezing temps, wearing only a tank and yoga pants, but I was.

"Since this is your first time up, you'll be with me," Liam explained. "Eventually, once you're comfortable, I'll show you how to get airborne on your own."

I couldn't contain the huge grin his words brought to my face.

"See you up there," Elise winked.

The very next second, my head shot back to follow her into the sky—a blur of smoke and flames. She took off like a rocket emerging from the cloud of displaced snow where she once stood. It wasn't at all what I expected. I thought it'd be more like watching a bird take flight, but … it wasn't. There was so much force, so much power in the motion.

I stared at two streaks of fire in the sky, Elise and Dallas. He chased after her and the sight of it made me so much more anxious to get up there on my own.

"Hold on tight," Liam instructed, lifting my arms to his neck where I gripped him, knowing I'd need to if his takeoff was anything like Elise's.

I stepped closer, chest to chest, face to face, body to body, feeling the smooth heat of his shoulders as I clung to them. My eyes followed his when he lowered just a few inches and I noted the devilish grin he wore just before the backs of my thighs warmed. His palms pressed into them as he hiked me up off the ground, locking my legs around his waist. The movement made a breath hitch in my throat, but my gaze never left his.

My heart thundered in my chest. Or maybe it was his. We were so close it became impossible to tell one from the other. That was us—a tangle of warm flesh, scorching emotion, and thundering hearts.

"Don't let go. Getting off the ground can be kinda rough," he warned, grazing my ear with a breath. "Then again ... I can't recall *rough* ever being a problem for you."

The words registered, but I barely had a chance to take note of their double meaning when the ground disappeared from beneath my feet. Snow-topped trees became greenish-gray smudges, roads reduced to winding streaks of dark thread. My stomach sank at the feel of being flung into the air, weightless.

"Breathe," he said against my ear, making me aware that I hadn't exhaled since leaving the ground.

My arms cinched his neck, forcing my cheek against his. The only thing that kept me from plummeting to the ground was his unwavering embrace—solid arms locked around my back, squeezing me to his bare chest.

Following the surge of power that went into getting us off the ground, it was easy to feel the instant we slowed, losing momentum as gravity took hold of us again. That churning in my stomach was back tenfold. Liam must have felt my body tense against his because he spoke to calm me, more whispered words, so soft they made no sense amidst this otherworldly experience.

"I've got you," he promised, forcing me to suspend reality a moment as we drifted back toward Earth, sinking like stones in water.

When he first came back into my life, before I accepted that we were timeless, he often asked me to trust him. And I did. With my life, my future, my heart. So, despite feeling it'd be perfectly okay to panic right now, I didn't. Because he had my trust now even without having to ask.

One word fell from his lips, one that sparked confusion. "Ready?"

Unable to speak, I only nodded, waiting with great anticipation. What more could he possibly show me? What more was there than flying?

And then, I got it, understood fully why he posed the question.

Brilliant orange and white light seeped through my closed lids, and when I opened them ... beautiful.

Large wings that spanned nearly twenty-feet commanded the wind, moved it to-and-fro with authority. This space between heaven and Earth, it belonged to us. Heat cut through the cold, warming my face with every burst of movement. The elegance had me in awe, trying to imagine myself possessing something so stunning.

We reached the peak of Liam's intended flying height. As we leveled off, the ground was no longer beneath my feet, but beneath my back. So I'd feel secure as he hovered above me, those solid arms were like bricks now, rigid as they locked me in. I'd never felt so alive, never more free than miles above the ground. It was a rush, like adrenaline times a thousand. My breathing was wild and erratic. Not from fear.

From excitement.

My face rested in the crook of his neck, inhaling his scent — still potent to my heightened senses even as air whipped around us at a greater speed than I'd ever traveled. One might think the experience would be disorienting, but it was the opposite.

I was more aware of my dragon, more aware of Liam.

Especially ... Liam.

He didn't flinch when my mouth brushed the tender flesh beneath his ear, feeling his pulse surge against my lips on contact. They trailed the length of his broad jaw, desperately seeking more, suddenly needing to be closer. The motion was slow and unhurried, unrushed despite being in flight. When I found his lips, he released a tightly wound breath that breezed over me, telling of how much he was holding back, contradicting the incredible willpower he seemed to possess in every moment except this one.

We were weightless, drifting in this space like nothing else mattered. Because it didn't. Our physical limbo mirrored that which we existed in emotionally every day — two hearts sure of the love they share, desperate to reconnect after so many years had been stolen away.

A tug to my bottom lip followed the sensation of teeth lightly grazing it. A jolt coursed through my limbs — a deepening hunger for him when I hadn't realized such a thing was even possible.

He spoke and I swallowed the words greedily. "Are you ready?"

My head swirled and intentions were relative at the moment. Hence the reason I moaned a misguided, "Mmm hmm," against his lips.

It was the sound of his deep laugh vibrating in his throat that alerted me we were talking about two totally different things.

"I'm asking if you're ready to fly solo," he clarified.

I should have been embarrassed he'd so thoroughly turned my head into a marvelous mess ... but I wasn't. There was no shame in feeling the way I felt for him. After all, we were mated and he was, technically, mine anyway.

Slightly more sober, I forced myself to abandon the kiss. Still, I couldn't speak and only nodded against his cheek.

"Ok, good. When you're ready ... I'm gonna let go."

That made my heart race even more than it already was. "You mean ... we're doing this way up here? We're not starting on the ground?"

He shook his head. "It'd be too hard to synch up with you quickly enough if something were to go wrong. For now, just don't let go and focus on bringing out your wings. I have to move my arms out of the way."

I didn't even know where to begin, but nodded anyway. He waited a moment before releasing me, but then cool air replaced his warm embrace. It was time for me to give this a try. I wriggled my back muscles, thinking I'd feel something instinctual that would help. But there was nothing—no feeling, no wings.

"It's not working," I sighed.

"It might be easier if you shift," he suggested, but I didn't want that.

He was ... well ... *him*. No flames to speak of aside from his wings. I wanted to know how to control my shift the way he could, choosing to allow certain parts of my body to burn while others didn't.

"Okay," he agreed, "but it'll be harder that way."

That was fine with me.

"Call up your dragon," he instructed. The term made me imagine myself summoning her from a dark corner, seeing the faint light of her flames as they came into view, growing brighter with each step.

"Now, let her show you," he went on. "Everything doesn't have to be logical. In fact, the less things make sense, the better."

I smiled at that, unable to help acknowledging how that statement also applied to the two of us.

"She'll guide you if you let her."

I closed my eyes again, surrendering to that side of myself, allowing the dragon within total control. I made a request and would wait for her to do the rest.

And, as always, she was happy to oblige.

A powerful thrust nearly ripped my arms from Liam's Neck, but he seemed to expect it, grabbing my hands before I drifted away. He brought me in and slowed his speed until we weren't moving at all, only hovering as his massive wings kept us both afloat.

My nerves were shot. Trusting him was one thing. Trusting myself was another. I got distracted by Elise and Dallas a good distance away, shaming my remedial dragon skills as they soared elegantly, swirling around one another in brilliant bursts of light.

"Focus," Liam said firmly, bringing my eyes back toward him. His hands settled on my waist and I was painfully aware of the difference in how my wings moved compared to his. Mine weren't in sync. They fluttered irregularly like a graceless baby bird. My chest heaved as I struggled not to panic.

"Breathe," he said again gently.

"I *am* breathing," I snapped, which brought a laugh out of him. "Breathing I can do. It's this flying thing that's scaring the crap out of me."

He bit down on his bottom lip to keep from chuckling again. "Remember what I taught you," he asserted. "Your dragon is more you than *you're* you."

I nodded, trying to convince myself.

'She's me and I'm her,' I chanted inside my head hoping *false* confidence would be enough until the real thing kicked in.

But that left me as soon as I felt Liam's grip loosening. I pawed him like a cat headed into the bathtub, flailing my arms and legs to get a better hold on him. He suppressed another laugh, but I didn't care. It was a long way down from here and I wouldn't depend on these clumsy wings to save me.

"Relax, Evangeline."

"That's easy for you to say," I scoffed. "You've been doing this for hundreds of years."

He grabbed my hands once again so I'd focus when he countered with, "So have *you*."

Things shifted into perspective. He was right. Completely and totally right. Although, it'd been a while for me, I still had centuries of flying experience even if I didn't remember it. My body had done this before. Maybe it was like what they say about riding a bike, how you never really forget. It might be like muscle memory. Maybe I just needed to try it and ...

"Okay," I blurted, knowing I'd lose the nerve quickly if I didn't. "So ... I should just ... let go?"

Staring with certainty, Liam nodded. "Yes, and you'll be fine."

He'd never lied to me before, never steered me wrong. I had to trust he wouldn't start now.

Deep breath.

Deep breath.

Slowly, I drew my hand away from his, feeling my balance tilt the moment I was no longer relying on *his* strength, but my own. I gasped, but with a nod, he assured me I wouldn't die today.

"You've got this," he insisted.

The tips of my fingers teetered on the ends of his … until it was just me. I was up here, hovering above the world … all on my own.

An elated laugh burst from my lungs and Liam smiled. I wanted to celebrate, wanted to scream, but I was too afraid I'd lose concentration if I did. Clamping my bottom lip between my teeth, I slowly reached for his hand again. All I needed was to prove to myself that I could do it. That was enough for today.

Retracting the wings was much simpler than spreading them. There was no longer a counter-wind pulling me from Liam as he held me close. I wrapped my legs around his waist again and our descent was slower than the takeoff. On the way down, I got to soak in the beauty from here, drifting among the falling snow.

We came close to a white pine and I reached to graze the needles, my heat melting snow from the tips on contact. It amazed me how much perspective changed the world, brightened it, made it seem wide open.

Liam's boots hit the ground with a thud, sending snow shooting up into a plume of white that surrounded us, settling and melting on our hair and shoulders when it fell again. The massive wings tucked away gracefully, disappearing beneath the flesh like they'd never been there at all. With wide eyes, amazed, I ran my hands down his skin when I finally let go of his neck.

I was mildly aware of Elise, Dallas, and Hilda heading back inside, leaving the two of us alone in the worsening blizzard. But ... you couldn't have told me today wasn't perfect. Couldn't have convinced me the sun wasn't out, shining against the bluest of skies, because for me, it was. Always. Whenever we were close.

Our lips met when the gravity that exists between us got to be too much. He'd shown me so much today, including another side of my abilities.

I barely remembered the time before him, back when each day was a little lonelier than the last. That feeling was so foreign to me now. The loneliness had been replaced by moments like these that made up for all the lost time.

In so many wonderful ways ... he'd given me my life back.

Chapter Seven

Evie

Sleeping in a new bed, in a new house, took some getting used to. Twice I stopped myself from wandering into Liam's head to talk, for comfort, but didn't because I could hear him snoring across the hall. He was exhausted from the long drive, from the flying lesson. I couldn't bring myself to wake him.

So, most of the night, I lie there staring at the ceiling, thinking.

Training sessions would be starting soon. Three evenings a week, those of us who returned to Seaton Falls from Damascus Facility, would meet to keep up our combat regimen. We were lucky enough to have Dallas and Liam to work with us—two highly skilled dragons. As for the other kids in other states? We could only hope they had similar resources.

Apparently, my tutor would be making his or her first visit in the coming days as well. Can't say I was looking forward to it, but I understood. According to how Liam explained it on the way home, the decision was made after some blanketed threats Nick's mother made to the Elders. Threats that she'd take matters into her own hands if they didn't produce answers. Threats that she'd gladly go over their heads if they didn't act quickly.

She was pointing a very suspicious finger toward me, suggesting I had something to do with his disappearance.

I could only guess what she meant by stating that she'd go *over Council members' heads,* could only guess what her intentions might be, whose help she might consider enlisting.

That particular thought kept me up the latest.

This morning, Hilda was bright-eyed and bushy-tailed while I slumped over the table from my seat. Elise had her designer set up a work space just for Hilda and I. A large attic spanned from one end of the house to the other and had been decorated with the same furnishings as the main portion of the house. No shortcuts simply because it'd mostly be the two of us spending time up here. Elise had gone all out in *this* space just like all the others.

A tall, white bookcase already housed many of Hilda's books—the ones she requested Liam and Dallas bring up last night. A shorter one beside it was where she kept the various herbs and other strange ingredients I mostly couldn't pronounce. I sat at the long table directly in the middle of the room, holding down a seat at the head. Right in front of me, a box—the entire reason I was stuck up here. While Hilda rummaged through a large bag in the corner, I lifted the lid and peered inside. Six gold rings. It was hard to believe there were souls inside them. Hard to believe mine had once been held inside a similar stone.

"How'd Elise get them all?" I asked with a yawn, still feeling the effects of a poor night's sleep.

Hilda glanced over her shoulder, and then turned back to the bag she'd been searching through. I'd wondered about that before. The only way my brothers' souls would be inside was if they died. How on Earth had she managed to collect them all?

"It was simple really," Hilda began to explain. "After you were taken and Liam recovered your necklace by some small miracle, Elise realized how close she came to losing you for good despite her efforts. She saw the flaw in her plan." A heavy sigh left Hilda's mouth and she stopped searching for a moment.

"She came back to me, asked if I'd alter the spell I'd already placed on the stones. This time, she wanted to ensure they'd be back in her possession if something were to happen to them," she explained. "I cast a spell on that box you're always poking around inside."

At her stern words, I pulled my fingers away.

"It was designed to summon the rings of her sons should they be cut down. Unfortunately, almost immediately after Liam returned your necklace to your mother, he took off. She never had a chance to amend the spell cast on his, which was why, once tales of him in battle stopped reaching her, she assumed he was dead."

I fell silent at those words. The mere thought of him not existing made me shiver.

"One by one, as more supernatural battles raged on, the rings began to appear in the box. The Lunar War alone claimed three." Hilda paused to replace items she removed from inside the bag before adding, "She even had one made for your father."

My interest was piqued, and I was suddenly less tired than before. "So, he's—"

"I didn't mean to mislead you," she cut in. "Your father is most certainly no longer with us. When Elise presented him with his, he had it destroyed right away. It was his belief that, should he die, it was his appointed time."

He was an honorable man. Every time someone spoke of him, this fact was only confirmed. While I might not understand fully why he wouldn't take the kind gesture Elise offered him, I respected the decision. However, there was one decision he made I still hadn't wrapped my mind around … naming me heir to his throne.

"Were you present when he chose me?" I asked. "When he decided it was me he'd make his successor?"

Hilda gave a shallow nod as she approached the table with whatever she'd been looking for — a thin book she placed on the table.

"I was," she confirmed. "And I agreed with the decision."

Her response surprised me. Here I was thinking she perceived me to be at *least* as inadequate as I did.

I took a deep breath as I thought of it all — the role I was expected to one day fill.

"Why do I always feel so ill-equipped for whatever purpose my life is supposed to serve?" I asked the question rhetorically, so imagine my surprise when Hilda had an answer. A blunt one at that.

"Because you *are* ill-equipped."

My eyes darted to hers. Somehow, her candor always caught me off guard, although I ought to expect it by now.

She caught the look I gave and held my gaze when she asked a question. "How can you expect to feel whole when you don't embrace your full self?"

My brow tensed, and I was too tired to untangle riddles. "What do you mean?"

Hilda sighed and answered my question with another. "How many times have you called forth your wolf?"

My stomach sank, and I stammered a bit. "It … uh …"

She stared at me so deeply I felt it, realizing she'd never believe me even if I tried to lie.

"Never," I admitted.

A knowing glare passed my way, followed by a cynical, "Mmm-*hmm.*"

"But it's not my fault. I'm surrounded by dragons and no one's ever taught me how to shift into—"

She held a hand up. "I can't help you." The words were cold and unfeeling. "I can only help you *see* the problem. You're immune to magic, which means I cannot *fix* the problem. This is something you'll have to come to terms with on your own."

I sat. I thought. I hoped she'd eventually interject some sort of insight, but that wasn't her way. She preferred I grasp things on my own; said experience was a far better teacher than she could ever be.

Our study session went mostly like all the others, except I left feeling worse than usual. It was the realization that, despite all the progress I felt I'd made, I wasn't even halfway done.

Hilda was right. There was more to me than just Evie, more than just my dragon. There was the wolf I inherited from my father's bloodline—an aspect of myself I had yet to meet.

And, according to Hilda, it was time to change that.

***

Nick

The sun was setting, which meant Roz had been gone way longer than expected. She insisted on making the walk into town alone to call her father this time, and now that I was sitting here with no idea if something happened to her, I regretted agreeing to it.

We'd been roughing it in the woods for a solid week now. Surviving off canned goods and water from a nearby stream. The large tent and used sleeping bags we snagged for next to nothing from the thrift store were our only luxuries here in the wilderness. For lack of a better term, we'd gone feral.

Nothing lets you know you've hit rock bottom like washing your underwear in the same place you bathe. For the life of me, I couldn't figure out why Roz hadn't abandoned me yet. I was sure her offense would easily be forgiven by the Elders. All she'd done was break me out of my cell. I, on the other hand, had done far worse.

A twig snapping in the distance had me on my feet, drawing my hands back from the fire that warmed them. To the human ear, the sound wouldn't have even registered, but I heard it in stereo—all around me. Everywhere.

I focused my eyes as far as I could, until I spotted what— or should I say *who*—caused the sound.

Roz trudged back toward our camp with the same solemn expression she had every day. She was miserable just like I was. Her clothes were dingy, but not filthy. She made frequent trips to the stream to keep them as clean as possible. Her hair wasn't its usual vibrant brown anymore either. The hints of bronze that used to glimmer in it had faded. It didn't surprise me, though. We hadn't eaten anything of substance for quite a while. And toiletries were a luxury we simply couldn't afford.

Easing back down onto the log where I sat before she startled me, I eyed the few cans of food we had left. Tonight's choices were ravioli or beans again.

It didn't take me long to decide on the ravioli.

She approached just as I took out the can opener, eyeing me as I dumped it into our only pot. Things between us were still tense following the discussion that took place just before leaving the motel, but at least we were on speaking terms. There wasn't much I could do to restore the way she felt about me, but I wouldn't give up trying.

She once believed there was more good in me than bad. While I didn't necessarily believe it myself ... she made me want to try.

"Did you get a hold of him?" I asked, referring to her father.

That'd been the point of her journey. I wasn't sure if she meant to beg for cash again, but I halfway hoped she wouldn't even come back. I wouldn't have been mad if she didn't.

She yawned, stretching her hands toward the flames. "I did. Just to check in," she added, dashing my hopes that he may have finally talked some sense into her. However, it was comforting to know I wasn't the only one she refused to listen to.

"He's doing okay? Things are good back home?"

She nodded, but this time I could tell there was more, something that troubled her. "Everyone went back."

I paused after placing the pot on a contraption we rigged to hold it above the fire. "What do you mean they're back?"

"He just said the Elders ordered everyone home and they've been there a few days now."

My head spun — thinking of the reasons they would have made such a drastic move after making a big deal about bringing us to Louisiana in the first place. The answer hit me right in the gut.

It was because of me.

I stared at the flames and those words Roz overheard that night near my quarters before we ran away — *reckoning, exile.*

"Everyone's returning to school Monday," she added. "And training's gonna continue a few evenings a week."

"...Wow." I couldn't think of anything else to say. I'd caused so much trouble; had changed so many lives.

Richie warned about making waves, warned about the consequences, but I'd done just that. If I had to guess, my name was on the lips of Elders and Council members around the world. It was bad enough that, as the Liberator, they were likely already watching my every move. Now, I'd done nothing but proved them right. Proved I couldn't be trusted.

I was drawn out of my thoughts when Roz placed a hand on her forehead. Her eyes squeezed shut right after and concern spread through me like wildfire.

"You feeling okay?"

It took her a moment to answer and, when she did, she shook her head. "Not really. Headache," she explained. "It started on my way back. Now I'm kind of nauseous, too."

My heartrate picked up as I glanced around at the few belongings we managed to scrounge up out here. It was no wonder she was coming down with something.

"If you want to lie down, I'll bring your food to you when it warms up."

She didn't put up a fight. Nodding, she headed for the tent. "Thanks."

My eyes followed her when she unzipped the flap and then eased down onto the red sleeping bag.

I was failing her. On top of everyone else I disappointed, I failed Roz.

My best friend.

Dinner finished cooking and I ate alone, not bothering to wake her. Instead, I covered her portion with a cloth and set it aside for whenever she got up. Aside from our fire, it had gone completely dark. I reached for my backpack and internally thanked Roz for getting it to me before Dallas hauled me off to my cell. It held all my grandfather's journals, where I packed them before heading back to the facility after break.

I took one of the later installments, one I wasn't as familiar with as the four I'd gone over at least ten times. These still held secrets within them, secrets I most likely missed the first time I skimmed. Then, I'd been in a rush to find out more about getting cured. Tonight, I had nothing but time.

Thumbing through pages, I was taken on an adventure, reading of how he traveled from Italy across the Tyrrhenian and Mediterranean Seas on a whim, following a hunch that something he sought awaited him. It was described as an unquenchable thirst he could neither identify nor explain. He just knew the journey was necessary.

He spoke of the day he spent aboard a large merchant vessel that took him from Italy to Tunisia. Then, crossing the desert of Egypt by camel with his mute guide, Samir. Apparently, the irony was entertainment enough, considering there was no conversation to pass the time.

I read quickly, anxious to see what was so urgent that he traveled all this way. What was it that *'beckoned for him like a lighthouse to a drifting ship'*?

His exact words.

I imagined myself walking in his shoes, passing through the Nile Valley of Sudan, the Libyan desert. The terrain was brutal, but still, he pushed on.

Until he arrived in Ethiopia. Bahir Dar, to be specific.

My eyes lifted from the page as the faint smile that'd been on my face the entire time I read disappeared altogether.

Bahir Dar ... it was familiar to me for a reason. We discussed it in class—the fallen kingdom of the *other* original lycan, Noah. My heart raced as sickness spread in my gut. I was naïve to hold out hope that what my grandfather had come all this way for wasn't ... *that.*

To claim the life of a lycan princess.

My mouth felt dry and I reached for the canteen I filled earlier at the stream. It was cool going down my throat, contrasting the heat that crept up my chest and neck.

'... *beckoned for him like a lighthouse to a drifting ship'.* That's how he described the sensation. *'An unquenchable thirst he could neither identify or explain.'*

No matter how much I tried to convince myself otherwise ... there was no doubt in my mind he was on his way to Evie.

To kill her.

I had to read on, had to understand what triggered him. Maybe if I could figure it out, I could fight it. Maybe even *stop* it. I just ... I had to know.

I skimmed the pages quickly, passing over the brief adventures he had in route. It was unimportant that he spent a night with the Tigraway tribe; unimportant how beautiful he found Lake Tana. All I cared about was what drew him there despite the treacherous journey.

And then ... I found my answer.

It was there, at Lake Tana, that his thoughts became linear. It was there that he felt it, felt her.

Heard ... her.

Bathing in a pool at the foot of a waterfall he called *Tis Abay;* that's where he first spotted her. He'd been wandering one afternoon when that feeling overtook him again, drawing him out of his camp. He described her, said she was as beautiful as the day is long, but something about her spread hatred within him. He referred to it as *'the sickness'*. He realized all the darkness that existed within him was because of her.

And he knew the key to ending it was to stop her heart.

'The sound nearly drove me mad — a drumming that beat within her twice as fast as it ought to, vibrating like the wings of a humming bird.'

He experienced the same thing I had, hearing Evie's heart, but ... wasn't there more? Wasn't there something else that triggered him?

I read on, scanning as fast as I could, right up to the moment he stalked the high walls of her father's kingdom the night he gave in to the darkness.

I pictured him scaling the walls of the short tower he described as the moonlight shined on his back, fueling him, strengthening him. He recalled the sound growing louder, those hummingbird wings inside her.

She slept beside a dragon in the form of a man, one whose size alone would have ordinarily sent him scurrying to the shadows for safety, but tonight … tonight, nothing would stop him from seeing to it that she breathed her last breath.

I skimmed faster, bypassing words like *'hungry'* and *'savage'*, searching for answers, clues as to what, besides her heartbeat, made him snap. There had to be more.

The moment he snatched her from the warmth of her bed, from the arms of the dragon I knew to be Liam, he leapt from the tower with her gathered beneath his arm, landing on the grass below as she cried out in the night. The next segment was vague, and I could only guess it was because, at the time of this writing, he was sober, no longer drunk with whatever venom flowed through him that night. Remorse had set in. He didn't want to detail what it was like tearing her apart. Didn't want to recall what her blood tasted like sliding down his throat.

I slammed the cover shut and only now realized how rapidly my breaths came. There was nothing. Not a single clue as to what made him do it. Nothing I hadn't already experienced — hearing her heart, the rage, the blackouts.

So, was it random?

Would I strike out of nowhere just because?

The journal hit the ground with a thud when I tossed it away. Frustration spread throughout my limbs and I fought to quench it. Anger made me do things I wasn't proud of. I couldn't afford to let myself go there tonight. Roz would be on her own out here if I couldn't keep it together.

It was no longer just about me, about the consequences *I'd* face. It was about her, too.

I breathed deep, swallowing the rage. The only thing that came of reading my grandfather's account of that night was an escalated sense hopelessness. It was time to accept that my issue might be irreversible.

Unavoidable.

Would staying away even make a difference?

Based on my grandfather's journal, he traveled from Italy to Ethiopia to fulfill his duty. *Who's to say I wouldn't black out one day, only to discover I'd traveled back to Seaton Falls and followed in his footsteps?*

The outlook was grim. Even more so than I already realized. The dark cloud that hung over my head just seemed to grow more and more every day.

And now I was more certain than ever ... there wasn't anything I could do about it.

Chapter Eight

Nick

The sound of metal being stricken by another solid object startled me awake.

I darted from our tent to find Roz plucking pieces of ravioli from the dirt. Glancing around, it was easy to see she'd accidentally dropped the pot with her dinner in it. It landed on the log we dragged over for seating. The food and pot were still steaming, so I guessed she might have burned herself and somehow knocked it over.

"Sorry, I woke you," she apologized. "I was heating it up when my stomach started churning again and, when I came back, it was smoking, and I wanted to catch it before it burned, but ..."

She stopped speaking as I stooped to help, eying the wasted food where it lie in the dirt. I guessed she had a similar thought to mine, that we couldn't exactly afford to waste anything.

"I'll take it to the stream and rinse it. I don't mind eating it without the sauce," she mumbled.

I looked her over, the weariness in her eyes, the way she held her stomach while she cleaned up her mess.

"Still not feeling any better?"

She shook her head. "Been up half the night tossing my cookies," she scoffed. "I thought I was better, which was why I was trying to eat, but ... the smell got to me and ... long story short ... there may or may not be vomit behind that tree."

I glanced that way, making a note not to venture in that direction.

She grabbed the last of the ravioli and placed it in the pot with the rest. With a heavy sigh, she took a few steps away from camp.

"Where are you going? Shouldn't you be lying down?" I asked. She was so weak she could hardly walk upright.

"I need to rinse this. We don't have anything to waste."

She was right about that, but I wouldn't let her walk all that way.

"Here, I'll do it. Just go back in the tent and get some rest. I think we still have a can of soup. When you're ready, I'll make it for you," I offered, deciding the sauce-less, dirt-bathed ravioli would have to be mine. There was no way she'd keep down anything solid.

Reluctantly, Roz nodded, handing over the pot.

"Be back in a bit."

I trudged through the low brush and twigs that marked our path to the stream. I had no idea how to take care of a sick person, but would do my best to make Roz comfortable until it passed. Before now, I didn't even realize a supernatural *could* get sick.

Apparently, I was wrong.

Dipping the stuffed noodles in the water, I covered the pot with my hand to strain it. Two more times and it was good enough for me. Back at camp, I'd reheat them and they'd be good as new.

Well ... kind of.

On the walk back, I had time to think, time to reflect on the discovery I made the night before. It was still unsettling that there were no answers, and that my only option was to accept it.

Accept that I'd be a killer.

Accept that who I was becoming—the thoughtless, selfish guy who'd willingly seek to end another life—was who I'd be from here on out.

Once, my biggest gripe in life was that no one understood me, that my future in college football was mapped out for me. What I'd give to have it all be that simple now. What I'd give to go back to having petty, teenage problems that could be solved with a simple conversation.

If I'd known then how easy I had it, you couldn't have *paid* me to complain.

Our tent came into view and I had a fleeting thought; that now would be a great time to go over Roz's head to contact her father. She wasn't doing well out here. It'd be easy to tell him where we were, and he could come for her. While I was sure it would take a while for her to forgive me, it'd be worth it to know she was safe.

I dropped down onto the log again and stared at the trees because there was nothing else to stare at. If starvation didn't kill us, boredom would. And now, with Roz down, I had no one to talk to either. Going back to my grandfather's journals was out of the question, for a while anyway. Within them was reality—my reality—and I didn't feel like facing that just yet. I needed a break from it all.

I'd just gotten settled when the tent unzipped behind me. Roz came tearing out of it with a hand tightly clasped to her mouth. She made it to a tree a little further out than the last and I turned my head, not wanting to see whatever she barfed up.

Seemed she was getting worse.

And there was nothing I could do about it.

I turned. The tree had her mostly hidden, but I saw enough to deduce she was weak, resting her weight against the massive trunk for support. She couldn't keep going like this. Especially seeing as how she was only here because of me.

I glanced around at our sparse supplies and breathed deep before turning toward her again. What we had, versus what we needed, simply didn't add up.

Each step looked like it drained her energy. When she got about halfway, I stood to walk her. Surprisingly, she accepted the help as I draped an arm around her shoulders, taking on her weight. We said nothing, probably quiet for two different reasons.

Her—sickness.

Me—guilt.

Holding the flap of the tent, I watched Roz ease inside. She just about collapsed on her sleeping bag the second she reached it. I glanced back at the log I just stood from, and then at the frail girl who could barely walk on her own.

I abandoned the log and laid beside my friend.

I wasn't cold, so only rested on top of my pallet right beside Roz's. I was wide awake and felt fine, but didn't want her to be alone. Would she have minded the solitude?

Probably not, but still. My presence was about the only thing I had to offer.

"Everything hurts," she moaned.

I turned toward her, resting on my side now as I took note of her labored breathing.

"I thought we were invincible." This time, I was pretty sure she meant it as a joke, but there was little to no inflection to her voice. I guessed it would've taken too much energy.

"Is there anything I can do?" It seemed like a silly question, seeing as how she knew resources were limited.

Her brown hair shifted when she shook her head. "No," she sighed. "I just wanna lie here."

She reached to cover her shoulder when a breeze penetrated the thin material of the tent. But I beat her to it, pulling the edge of the sleeping bag to her neck. Only, my hand didn't move. I left it lingering there on her arm long after I should've moved it. She was completely still, like she wasn't even breathing anymore as the contact seemed to resonate with us both. Reluctantly, I pulled away, folding my arms across my chest.

"You, uh ... you think it's the flu?" I stammered, hoping she didn't read too much into that last gesture — me touching her for too long.

"Maybe," she shrugged. "I don't think I've got a fever, though."

I started to touch her forehead, but thought better of it. It was probably for the best that I kept my hands to myself.

"Just get some rest," I suggested. That was always my mom's solution when I didn't feel well, and it seemed to help.

Roz nodded and took a deep breath. "Okay, but don't let me sleep all day. I hate that because it throws off my schedule."

Smiling a bit, I agreed. Seemed silly to worry about keeping to a schedule out here in the middle of nowhere.

"I'll wake you in a couple hours," I promised.

With that, she settled her head against the bundle of clothes that took the place of a pillow, and I watched over her while she slept.

Well ... for half an hour, at least.

The moment she started snoring, I took off, leaving our camp to prove something to myself.

That I'm not a terrible person.

That I was still capable of making good decisions.

That I still knew right from wrong.

The trek out of the woods was only easy because of my abilities. I was quicker on my feet than the average person, able to leap over fallen trees and stray stones instead of tripping over them.

The clean lines of rooftops came into view quicker than expected, but I was glad for it. The faster I could do this, the sooner I could get back to Roz. If she woke up to find that I'd left, she might panic, and in her condition, she didn't need to get worked up about anything. So, the plan was to get into town, do what I had to do, and then get back.

I caught the eye of every local I passed. They stared like I was some feral caveman who'd just emerged from the woods.

Actually ... I could totally see why they'd think that.

I wasn't filthy, but definitely looked like I'd been sleeping outdoors for some time. My hair was a mess and I hadn't shaved since we left the motel. Bypassing their dirty looks, I thanked my lucky stars this town was stuck in the dark ages when not everyone had cell phones and tablets for communication. It meant some still used payphones, and I was glad for it.

Holding the receiver to my ear, I panted while searching my pockets for change I knew I wouldn't find there. If I'd overthought this trip, I probably wouldn't have made it, which was why, when the thought hit me, I just left—not worrying about the fact that Roz shouldn't be alone, not worrying about the fact that I had zero money.

I just needed to get here.

"Here you go, son," A white-haired man said as he dropped fifty cents into my palm. He must have seen me tugging at my empty pockets.

"Thank you, sir," I barely got out, scrambling to get the change into the machine. Then, I dialed a number from memory, one I only knew because, as a firefighter, Richie was all about safety and had stuck a magnet to the fridge years ago. Apparently, it stuck with me.

"Seaton Falls Police Department," the woman answered.

Bracing an arm against the ridge of the rectangular phone box, I breathed wildly, praying this was the right thing to do.

"Officer Chadwick, please."

God, please let him be available.

I had no other number to reach him. No more money to try again.

"May I ask who's calling?"

"Nicholas Stokes."

When the woman said nothing, I got the distinct feeling she knew exactly who I was, which meant she was likely a lycan and had heard of the things I'd done. The Council made it a point to place lycans in high places should there ever be a need for a cover up or to protect our secret. My grandfather's journals went into great detail about it. The lycan government was far more organized, ran far deeper than anyone might have thought.

"One moment, please," the woman said, her tone short and cold this time.

At least I knew my name was at least as tarnished as I already believed.

"Yes? Hello?" Officer Chadwick answered in a rush. It became abundantly clear he'd been on edge since his daughter went missing. I was sure hearing from me made him assume the worst — that something had happened to Roz and she was unable to call.

I guess that kind of *was* the case.

"Is she okay?" was the next question that flew from his mouth, letting me know I assumed right.

"She is," I blurted, forcing myself to be a man despite how easy it would have been to cower, to slink back into the woods and hide from the world. Hide from him. Hide from my problems.

Only ... I couldn't.

Because this wasn't about me.

"Roz doesn't know I'm calling you," I shared. "She'd probably kill me if she knew, actually."

There was an uncomfortable silence on the other end of the line as Officer Chadwick's mood shifted from concerned to angry. Most likely just at the sound of my voice—the kid responsible for his daughter running off without so much as an explanation as to why.

The best course of action was to get straight to my point.

"She needs to be home," I forced out.

"Tell me something I *don't* know," he scoffed. "Only, she seems to be under the impression that *she* can't come home because of *your* mess."

That stung a bit, hearing those bitter words slide off his tongue, knowing I could never make this right. Probably not with *anyone.*

I bridled the guilt that crept in and stayed the course. "I know you want her back in Seaton Falls and I want to help."

Silence.

Several seconds later, Officer Chadwick's voice returned to the line and he seemed calmer now, less ready to rip my head from my shoulders.

"What's your plan?"

I closed my eyes and breathed deep. "I was thinking that, if you get her a ticket, I can make sure she gets to the bus."

I heard his computer boot in the background.

"I'll need to know where you are, so I can access the nearest bus station online." He mashed keys on his keyboard quickly as I assumed he was logging in. "And you really think you can get her to come back."

My chest throbbed when I thought of what it might cost me to convince her, but it had to be done. She needed a doctor. She needed her bed. She needed her dad. I simply couldn't take care of her the way she needed to be. Especially while she was so sick.

"I'm sure," I sighed.

He typed some more, and I prepared my mind to give him our location — the one thing that had kept me from being tossed back in a cell ... or worse.

"So," Officer Chadwick went on. "Where are you two?"

I breathed deep and gave him the name of the town. "Brandonburg, Louisiana."

He typed at light speed again, not saying a word as he searched for the station, I guessed. There was more to this, the hardest part, but it took a moment to get up the nerve to say it. However, I had to. It was the only way I could guarantee Roz would go.

So, as quickly as I could, before my nerves got the best of me, I blurted it. "Sir ... please make that ... *two* tickets. The only way Roz will go home is if I go back, too."

He was quiet and I knew it had nothing to do with not wanting to cover my fare. If I had to guess, he knew only trouble awaited me if I went back to Seaton Falls.

Which also meant he most likely knew I wouldn't have done this for just anyone.

His daughter was important to me.

"Consider it done," he finally stated.

And ... just like that, I sealed my own fate.

Chapter Nine

Evie

Hilda huffed when I slammed her book shut and raced downstairs to answer the door. Today, the others returned to Seaton Prep. Meanwhile, I sat cooped up in Hilda's study where the most success I had all day was making one of the rings glow a strange shade of green before giving myself the world's worst migraine.

Needless to say, I couldn't get to the door quickly enough, looking forward to hearing how Beth's day had gone. Seeing as how mine wasn't exactly exciting.

"Hey!"

She seemed surprised I was so happy to see her. Especially when I took her wrist and snatched her inside. Her attention was only on my odd behavior for a moment, though. As soon as she stepped foot in the foyer, her mouth fell open at the sight of this place.

An awestricken, "Wow, " echoed in the wide-open space.

I closed and locked the door behind her.

"My sentiments exactly," I replied, still not over the fact that this was, technically, my house. A dozen people could have easily lived comfortably in a place this size, which meant the five of us barely took up any space in it.

"So, how was it?" I asked, referring to her return to school.

She shrugged, and it wasn't lost on me that she bore that 'I could take it or leave it' expression of hers.

"Mostly everyone I'm cool with was at Damascus, too, so that made for somewhat of a lackluster homecoming." After speaking, she eased her backpack off her shoulders and placed a set of keys in the side pocket.

"I see somebody is back on four wheels," I said with a smile.

"Parents didn't have much of a choice, seeing as how Roz is still M.I.A. It was either give the car back or drive me around everywhere. And *that* wasn't happening, so …"

She concluded with another shrug.

I'd been trying to steer clear of anything that might remind me of Nick these days—like now, as I acknowledged how Beth's parents' decision related to Roz, related to Nick. When I *did* think of him, it always resulted in anger and the urge to burst into flames again, letting my dragon spring forth. I fought the feeling even now.

"So, we wolfing out, or what?" Beth asked with a smile, glancing at the time on her phone. "We should start sooner rather than later so we have a chance to chill before training tonight."

I'd hoped we would ease into this whole … wolf thing. To be honest, I wasn't ready. I had no idea what it would feel like and I'd just gotten the hang of accepting my dragon … now this.

I faked a smile. "Sure."

Before giving me a chance to back out, like I fully intended to as soon as I found the words, Beth grabbed my hand. She led me toward the back door, headed for the woods, I imagined.

"Have fun and keep the barking to a minimum. I'm trying to catch a nap." Liam's voice inside my head was a welcome surprise—lingering sarcasm and all.

"Ha-ha, funny guy. Don't forget ... I do bite," I replied, traipsing behind Beth as we bounded through the kitchen on our way.

"I seem to recall you being the one who liked to be bitten, but I think I could get into it." As usual, his words brought heat to my neck and face. With Beth so close, I could only hope there wasn't redness to match.

"On that note, I'm out." I tried not to grin as I forced him back into his own head space, thinking of lying beside him while he rested. Actually, I could think of a *million* things I'd rather be doing besides this. Yes, I wanted to see and hang out with Beth, but I would've preferred chatting over mugs of hot chocolate.

It's true what Liam said, I did prefer my dragon form to my wolf. But both were me, half of the same whole.

"Ok, so I'm guessing that, by now, you know we can't shift with our clothes on," Beth announced, reminding me of yet another reason I hated this.

I gave a tense nod and she smiled.

"You'll be warm," she promised.

I hadn't even thought about the eight inches of snow the storm dumped on us the other day. Being cold wasn't an issue.

"We probably shouldn't do this right near the house," she laughed. "I don't know about you, but the fewer people who see me naked today, the better."

I agreed, and we ventured toward an old shed that looked like it'd been here since the beginning of time. Today, it sat empty with Liam's truck parked in front of it. Out of view of anyone in the house who might be near a window, Beth gripped the lapel of her Seaton Prep blazer and I went for my shoes first. Soon, our clothes were in a heap, resting on a table we cleared of snow.

I breathed deep, watching it thicken in the frigid air. Using my arms and hands, I covered my important parts to make this ... mmm ... *marginally* less weird. Beth did the same. My skin was only dotted with goosebumps for a moment, because as soon as I was able to call my dragon forward, I used the technique Liam had shown me before flying to warm myself. My veins glowed orange and it was like standing in front of a fireplace.

"Okay, first things first. Today, let's look at shifting as an incentive for not standing in front of your best friend naked, so the sooner we get this party started, the better," she joked, dispelling some of the awkward energy that crept in when the last of our garments came off.

"Agreed."

"Good. So, I'll shift first, so you can see what the transformation is like, and then you give it a try."

I nodded before holding my breath.

Here goes nothing ...

Beth dropped to all fours and bursts of air puffed from her nostrils. At first it looked like she was simply resting there, but then ... her spine thickened, and the notches of bone began to grow larger beneath her skin.

I stepped back at the sight of it.

At the sight of my friend morphing into a beast.

At the realization that ... I was next.

She was always small to me—my own above average height making her seem even smaller. But now, her slight hands and feet grew as the shifting bone made them into something else altogether. Where there were once nails, there were now claws.

Another step back.

Joints twisted and turned, forcing her limbs out of place as she gritted through it all. I had to imagine it was painful, but she didn't make a sound. Blondish-brown fur began to cover her and the small figure that I once observed on the ground was now a massive wolf that made me shudder. I'd seen Nick and his brothers as wolves, but hadn't gotten the chance to watch them transition from men.

Her underbelly moved rapidly with each breath she took, and I had no words. Gleaming, yellow eyes stared back at me, and when she dipped her nose with a nod, I knew she was saying it was my turn.

I blinked at her, unsure of where to even start. I imagined it couldn't have been much different from accessing my dragon, so I gave it a try.

Closing my eyes, I focused on the dormant primal side where I always found my dragon. Only, this time, I was looking for the wolf. I breathed deep, trying to sense her.

A few days ago, Hilda suggested part of the reason I felt inadequate was because I *was* inadequate. Essentially, she stated that I felt like I was only half of a whole because I kept the other half locked away. Thinking about it that night, I called Beth. She was the only wolf I trusted to help me, and I didn't want to let either one of us down.

I searched the darkness, still only sensing my dragon. She was powerful. Perhaps so powerful she overshadowed the wolf. That's when it dawned on me that, while accessing her abilities to keep warm, I may not be able to tap into my *other* abilities.

So … I had to let her retreat, feeling the cold pricking my skin like a thousand needles. It wouldn't last long, only until I shifted.

Beth dipped her nose again, encouraging me, and then turned the other way for the sake of privacy when I dropped my hands, clenching them.

Where was she … the wolf?

A low, guttural growl surprised me at first. Until I realized where the sound came from … *me*. It vibrated energy through my entire body—every limb, my bones, my soul. I found her.

I pushed, bringing her out of hiding as I welcomed her in—the one thing she was waiting for.

At the first snap of my leg, I cried out as pain ripped through me, stealing my breath, my thoughts. I'd never felt anything like it. My dragon was still present despite being in the shadows now. She signaled to Liam and I felt the instant the pulse left my chest, reaching him within seconds. As soon as it did, he was there, inside my head, but silent. He couldn't see through me, but he could listen. And right now, I was screaming out in agony when my shoulders shifted out of socket.

Hot tears slipped down my cheeks and I wanted it to stop, wanted it to all be over, but I knew I had to endure this. If I was ever going to feel complete … this hell was a part of the process.

I panted, feeling my insides move out of place, organs getting out of the way as my ribs expanded outward. I was brought to my knees and I barely even noticed the cold through the pain. My neck snapped and cracked as it lengthened and doubled in width. Dark fur cloaked my arms and my nose became snout-like. I could hardly hold a thought in my head. There was so much to take in—and not just the constant burning and aching. My senses, they were heightened in such a way that it overwhelmed me. The white of the snow blinded me now as my vision superseded anything I imagined possible. And the smells—everything had a scent all its own. Everything. It was like sensory overload.

Liam came in stronger now, but still said nothing. I focused on him, pushing everything else aside as my body turned into something else altogether. I thought of flying with him, being held tight to his chest while the world disappeared beneath us. For a second, I let it all go, everything but that moment we were weightless.

It became clear he'd come to me for this reason, to distract me. To calm me.

I'd given up trying to stand. I lie there in the snow, staring at the contrast of my black fur against the brilliant white covering the ground. I was exhausted and couldn't quite get my bearings straight, couldn't quite grasp the idea of being so much larger than just a moment ago. It was disorienting.

Slowly, Beth approached, her blondish fur quivering when a brisk breeze moved between us. She sniffed the air, the nostrils of her dark snout flaring. I lie there on my side feeling like I'd just gotten run over by a steamroller. Her paw nudged mine and she stared in such a way I guessed she was wondering if I planned to get up. If I'd been able to speak, I would've told her I wasn't sure I could.

Liam was gone now, which meant my dragon had settled. As the seconds ticked past, the sharp jolts plaguing my extremities faded until they were gone. That's when I lifted my head, blinking as I waited for my eyes to focus. Fuzzy light in the distance became sharp lines and I could see details so far away.

A rabbit. He was at least half a mile from us, but I could see his whiskers twitching from here.

Beth nudged me again and I sensed she was impatient with excitement. I pressed a paw into the snow and put weight on it, and then the other three. I was up on all fours and felt sturdier than expected. Beth gestured her head to the right and I guessed she wanted to go that way. I took a step toward her and she began to head east. How I knew it was east, I couldn't explain. It was like some sort of internal compass. I didn't have that as a dragon. The only thing similar to this sensation was what kept me aligned with Liam. It didn't matter where I was, I felt the magnetism pulling me in his direction.

He was my soul's due north.

Beth picked up speed, glancing back every so often to make sure I kept up. I did, following in her tracks. My lungs swelled with each breath, expanding so much more than usual, telling of their capacity. Despite my size, each movement was sleek, calculated, efficient.

Like a hunter.

Our brisk run turned into a full-on sprint. Trees whizzed past and there was no fear of collision, because I saw every obstacle miles before we came to it. I felt ... untouchable.

Beth glanced back again and I was right on her heels. She ran faster and so did I, topping out at a speed of what I guessed to be around sixty to seventy miles per hour, slightly faster than in dragon form. However, the ability to fly made up for the discrepancy.

As we ran, there was a pivotal moment where I identified with this side of myself, accepted I was as much *this* being as I was a dragon, and I embraced it. Acknowledging that I was more brought my sense of self into alignment and I had to wonder if Hilda had been right.

Before finding out I was a supernatural, a huge hole hollowed out my soul. Embracing my dragon filled it in, as did opening up to Liam. Slowly, but surely, I was finding myself. And now, the void inside me was disappearing.

Hilda may have had a less than stellar way of conveying her thoughts, but I appreciated it. She was honest with me in ways others weren't. She didn't treat me like a child and had never once tiptoed around my feelings. If she had, I wouldn't have made so much progress. No, I still couldn't cast a spell to save my life, but I was getting to know the true Evangeline.

And that was, quite possibly, the most important thing of all.

Beth veered right and I knew she was circling back. I could have, honestly, run forever, but knew we needed to get prepared for tonight's training. It'd be more of what we learned at the facility, but the stakes were higher. We were, essentially, unprotected as a clan and the race to prepare for the future was even more pressing.

That old, rickety shed on the edge of our property came into view. It was only now that I realized how far we traveled so quickly. We slowed and I felt my heart race inside my chest when the rush of adrenaline began to dissipate. Beth huffed for a second and I would have smiled at her if I'd been able. She'd just done me a huge favor, introducing me to my wolf.

I gathered my clothes in my teeth and went around to dress beside Liam's truck, giving Beth privacy, something that hadn't been an option when we shifted. I dropped my things in the snow and panted while trying to figure out how to change back. You'd think it would have been simple, but …

Breathe.

Focus on the wolf.

Make her submit.

Slowly, I felt my bones shifting back into place. Still painful, but nothing like when I turned. Finally, I was me again. Naked, cold, me.

I reached for my shirt and stood upright. When I did, my dragon stepped forward and my veins glowed to bring me heat. Her return also brought with it a stronger sense of Liam, prompting me to look up, barely able to see above the hood of the truck. However, my view of the house was clear enough to see I had an audience of one.

"Is this payback for when I wandered inside your head after your shower?"

I laughed, remembering that night. It was one I thought of often, no matter how hard I tried to forget. It was several months ago, around the time I finally accepted that Liam wasn't just a figment of my imagination. Still, despite how much time had passed, the visual of him standing in that mirror ... before he had a chance to dress ... it was seared in my brain.

Every.

Single.

Detail.

Warmth spread through me at the thought of it, but this had nothing to do with my dragon. It was all because of Liam.

"If it makes you feel better, I can't see lower than your shoulders," he promised with a slick grin, sipping from a bottle of water.

I stared at him through the pristine glass, knowing his inability to see more of me hadn't been for lack of trying. It was my understanding that, once, we were wild together—all heat and passion. All the time. I couldn't imagine it'd been easy for him to suppress that now. In fact, little by little, it'd become more difficult to contain.

For him.

For me.

It was mostly lingering glances saturated with need, but he'd gotten bolder with his words, the thoughts he let me hear.

Whenever I imagined being with him in *that* way, it always made me mindful of the symbol of our union—the bracelet that signified we were mated centuries ago and, technically, still were. Taking my jeans from the snow, I slid the bracelet from the pocket and back onto my wrist. Our commitment was one Liam upheld even after my death, long before he had any hope I'd return.

His loyalty was something I didn't, and probably never would, understand.

"So, how was it?" he asked.

Shrugging before slipping my feet into my shoes, I answered, *"Different. Shifting sucked, but the rest was pretty cool."*

"Good. We'll talk when you get inside."

He dismissed himself quickly, which was strange. Or at least it *seemed* strange before I noticed Elise had approached him. Her expression was dim, which meant it was likely something else had gone wrong.

The usual.

Behind me, snow crunched beneath Beth's boots as she came close. I tore my eyes away from Liam and Elise conversing and focused on Beth. Well, I *tried* to anyway.

"You survived," she grinned. "How do you feel?"

"A little sore, but I think I'm okay." I rubbed a tender spot on my shoulder, vividly recalling the way it shifted out of place. Chances were, it wouldn't hurt long with the rate at which we healed.

"It won't always be like this. First time's the worst. And I hear, eventually, the pain disappears altogether."

Thank God for that.

Curiosity got the best of me and I glanced up toward the window again, noting the tension in Liam's brow. Tension that hadn't been there a moment ago. And now Dallas was standing with them, too.

"Everything okay?" Beth asked. She must've read my expression.

I met her gaze again and faked a smile, but when she didn't smile back, I knew she wasn't buying it. I stopped pretending.

"I think something's going on," I confessed. "Whenever they have these little powwows without me, it's usually because things have gone to crap and they're trying to figure out how to shield me from it."

We walked toward the house, making slow strides up the porch steps.

"That's not the worst thing in the world," she replied, but didn't understand what it was like being tiptoed around all the time, treated like a child when you definitely weren't one.

I shrugged, but didn't share my thoughts aloud.

We were quiet a moment and it seemed the woods became quiet, too.

"You think it's got something to do with Nick?"

This time, a long breath puffed from my lips. "Could be that," I replied. "Could be *anything*."

Which was true. Any number of things could have gone wrong.

"Have you ... heard from him?" There was a smidge of hesitation when she asked.

Beth was well aware of the bad blood between Nick and I. When I brought her up to speed, I brought her up to speed on everything. Not leaving out a single detail because, next to Liam, I trusted her most of all.

"No. I think he knows better than to call me. We have nothing to say to each other."

My chest clenched tight and I hated the ball of mixed emotions I carried for him. The romantic ones had completely faded, but I still cared. Not to mention, a small part of me still mourned the friendship I believed we could have had if the chips weren't stacked so high against us. Once, I believed a kind heart beat within him. Now, after he so willingly sacrificed Liam, after he recklessly called on the witches without thinking of who else it could affect, who else it could hurt ... I only saw him as cold.

Liam hated him, yes, but Nick was still breathing. He could have easily gone over the heads of those who argued to keep Nick alive if he really wanted to. Including myself. But he kept his word.

Was he perfect?

No, far from it.

But, despite the darkness shrouding Liam's past, he was innately good. Right down to his soul. He'd only ever taken two lives in cold blood — Nick's grandfather and his mate, but his pursuit of them was to avenge *my* death. The others had only been casualties of war. Even if his darkness made him more willing than most to fight.

To kill.

But he'd never intentionally set someone up to die.

Not like Nick had willingly done.

And, for that, I could never forgive him.

"Well, whatever it is, I'm sure Liam will see to it that things don't get out of hand." She smirked before adding, "It's not every day a girl gets to say she has a dragon warrior at her disposal."

I smiled, too, but it felt weak as I considered him putting himself in harm's way for me. He'd already done so more times than I could count.

Glancing up, I found his gaze already locked on me as Elise continued to address him and Dallas.

Something was definitely wrong. If I wasn't sure before, with that look set in his eyes … I was positive now.

Chapter Ten

Liam

Proud ... that's how I felt when a loud thud echoed off the trunks of surrounding trees. That sound meant she was making progress.

She'd taken down Chris, a sizable lycan, with little effort. They paired up this time, and I kept an eye on them in case he got too rough. It didn't take long to realize I had no reason to worry. Evangeline was holding her own.

At the sight of the poor kid laid out in the snow, in shock, Dallas passed me a sideways glance, holding in a laugh. Chris smiled as he stood again, shaking snow from his clothes ... and possibly shaking off a little embarrassment, too. He gestured for Evangeline to come at him again, and she did without hesitation. Just like I taught her.

Beneath the canopy of branches, the light of the moon glinted off fresh fallen snow. We had to meet here — out in the woods, away from humans who might hear or see — to continue with combat training. The Council was smart. They knew now was not the time to let these kids get soft, was not the time to drop our guard. Things were relatively quiet for the time being, but that could all change in the blink of an eye.

"Looks like we've got company," Dallas said, nodding toward a mass of shadows weaving its way through the trees.

The atmosphere itself seemed to grow silent. For a moment, the only sound to be heard was the whistling of the wind as it swept through. It was quiet despite there being hundreds here, all with eyes set on three hooded cloaks that came into focus. The same three hooded cloaks most had never seen outside the confines of the chamber beneath the town library.

"Elders," Dallas grumbled. As dragons, we had a natural dislike for all levels of lycan government, mostly because of our history and the part they played in leading charges against dragons. It'd take him a while to understand that, here in Seaton Falls, an alliance existed. An alliance that came to be because of Evangeline.

Most forced themselves to turn away, but their sparring efforts had clearly weakened as they half-focused on the tall figures coming nearer. Baz was at the lead as the others followed — two more Elders, and two new witches. They were a stoic group, bringing with them a chill that seemed to surpass the already frigid, winter temps. The new witches didn't wreak of death and evil quite as boldly as the others, but I still didn't trust them. Considering what I knew the others were capable of. Apparently, Baz had learned his lesson as well, instead choosing two whose hearts were slightly less dark.

A deep, gravelly voice brought my attention to Baz when he came to a stop beside me. I glanced at him for a moment, noting the hint of withered, white flesh and hollowed cheeks hidden in the shadow of his hood.

"Liam," he said in greeting.

I nodded once before turning my gaze back toward Evangeline. He did the same, watched her. Beside me, I felt tension rolling off Dallas' body in powerful waves. Elise and I had discussed the arrangement we had with the Elders of Seaton Falls, but he trusted them about as much as *I* did upon first meeting them. If I'd been able to tell him to relax, I would have.

"It appears our queen is learning rather quickly, is she not?" Baz's words boomed from beneath his cloak. He spoke quietly, but the depth of his voice made it impossible to whisper.

I nodded, shoving both hands in the pockets of my jeans. "Seems like."

He was making small talk and I *hated* small talk. Besides, it wasn't fooling me anyway. Elders didn't simply decide to leave their quarters. Especially not for minor gatherings like this, a training session for their young clan members. Myself, Dallas, Elise, and the many *other* seasoned shifters scattered about, could've handled this without their presence.

They were here for a reason.

To spy?

On assignment from the Council? Possibly even the High Council?

I decided to wait Baz out, mostly ignoring him and the others as we stood, watching. I focused, instead, on the shifters' stances, looking for those who needed correction, making sure none of the sparring got out of hand. If Baz wanted to discuss something, I'd listen, but I wouldn't volunteer information.

My silence made it impossible for him to stall long. My guess? He'd suddenly grown tired of standing here, pretending to be interested.

"Are we free to discuss ... *personal* matters?" When he asked, a long gaze was cast toward Dallas. A long gaze Dallas returned with a hard stare of his own.

I nodded, hoping to dispel the hint of aggression I sensed thickening in the air. "He's aware of everything," I answered. "He's a trusted friend of Elise's."

Evangeline caught my eyes as soon as I finished speaking, and I knew she was at least curious as to why the Elders had come. But I would've gone as far as to guess she was *more* than curious … she was concerned.

The talk I had with Elise and Dallas this afternoon had most likely raised her suspicions. She was observant and likely sensed we were discussing something of a serious nature. There'd been no time to explain because Beth stuck around until it was time for training and rode here with us as well. So, now, I was sure this unscheduled visit seemed incredibly sketchy in Evangeline's eyes.

Maybe … because it was.

A thought entered my head. One that seemed counterintuitive at the time. I'd fought so hard to protect her, to shield her from truths I considered grave enough that I should bear them on my own.

But I made her a promise.

She wanted to be revered as an adult, and rightfully so. Still … that didn't make this easy. The last thing I wanted was for her to feel unsafe, or to make an already difficult time even *more* difficult. But … she had as much right as anyone else to know what we were up against now.

Maybe *more* of a right than anyone else.

After all, everything came down to her.

Fighting my own instincts, I opened my thoughts to her, allowing her to hear everything *I* heard. Whatever Baz said from this point forward, Evangeline would be privy to the same information.

"Can I assume you've heard the news?" Baz continued on, asking in that slow-dragging voice of his. The sound of it inside her head had Evangeline's attention, too. She put up a finger, asking Chris to give her a sec, and then stepped off to the side to listen, I guessed.

"Depends on what you're talking about," I finally replied, keeping to my decision to not offer up information. Although, I would've bet money Baz and I were thinking of the same, ridiculous situation.

Ridiculous because, if it'd been up to me, if I didn't think Evangeline would've hated me after, it would've been rectified a long time ago.

"Nickolas has returned," Baz clarified.

I nodded and, on cue, Evangeline's eyes landed on me.

"I made it a point to speak to you in person, per our agreement," he added.

He swore to me that he'd keep me in the loop when it came to Evangeline, her safety. I respected that he kept his word.

"We had suspicions Officer Chadwick had been in contact with his daughter, Rozalind. So, once we had confirmation that this was indeed the case, we took matters into our own hands."

Dallas and I both turned toward Baz, knowing there was some hidden meaning beneath those words, but I didn't ask questions. My only concern was what the next course of action would be.

"The officer's daughter fell ill suddenly, which left Nicholas no choice but to come out of hiding. Two bus tickets were sent to bring them back here to Seaton Falls, and we're expecting both to arrive in a matter of hours."

"And this guy, Officer Chadwick, just surrendered this information about communicating with his daughter without being ... *coerced* in that fun little way you all like to do?" Dallas asked, not bothering to hide the cynical smile that sprang free. "I mean, you've gotta get use out of these witches somehow, right?"

He was clearly no stranger to the particularly sadistic brand of torture only a clan witch could inflict.

Baz studied Dallas a moment, and then chose to answer his initial question.

"Officer Chadwick did play a part in helping us bring the two misfits home, but I can assure you there was no ... *'surrendering of information'*. In exchange for my word that his daughter wouldn't face any consequences upon her return, he was wise to cooperate in a much earlier phase of our plan."

Tension spread across my brow. "What's that mean?"

"Rozalind's *'sickness'*," Baz started, "was the result of clever conjuring by our witches." I couldn't see his face, but he was smiling. I knew it. There was a sickening pride he felt for manipulating his own people.

I chose to ignore it and asked for clarity. "You made her father help with that?"

Large shoulders shrugged when he explained. "His only role was to bring us an item of the girl's, so the spell could be cast. Other than that, he merely awaited a phone call," Baz explained. "Although, I'm sure he wasn't expecting that phone call to come from the fugitive himself."

Yeah, he was definitely smiling under that shroud. You couldn't convince me otherwise.

"Despite Officer Chadwick describing the nature of the relationship between his daughter and young Nicholas as mere *friendship* ... it's become apparent that he seems to hold some level of affection for her."

"Figures," Dallas chuckled. "Women make you do stupid things at *any* age."

"It was his concern for her wellbeing that made him come out of hiding, made him surrender himself to escort her home safely," Baz explained further.

Listening to him speak with such cold indifference solidified my theory that he held very little regard for his people. But that had nothing to do with me. I only had one question for him.

"What's this mean for Evangeline?"

Dallas crossed his arms over his chest, just as interested in hearing the answer as I was.

"Her safety is now, and has been, our number one concern. We'll handle this case like we would any other. A summons will be issued to the Stokes residence and Nick will be expected to appear come nightfall tomorrow."

"And if he runs?" I countered.

"He won't get very far," Baz assured us. "We'll have a team on him the moment he steps foot off the bus. He'll be unaware of their presence, of course. The delivery of the summons is simply customary. He's been away from his family for a long time," he explained. "And, depending on the outcome of his trial … it may be the last time he sees them for a while. Maybe forever."

Another fact about lycan government was that, while they pretended to operate with fairness and dignity, they were cutthroat.

For a moment, I almost regretted letting Evangeline in. With her emotions so raw, so open … she'd cast a wall up wherever Nick was involved. But because I knew her, because I knew how compassionate her heart was, this couldn't have been easy to hear.

Nick had violated several cardinal laws within the lycan system. They'd never take into account that he was most likely ignorant to his offenses before committing them. First, he took it upon himself to summon the clan witches, and then went on to use them for his own, personal business. According to their law, only Elders and members of the Council had such authority.

His second offense?

Endangering the life of the queen. Even if only inadvertently. No, he couldn't have predicted that Evangeline would become directly involved, but this was the way of his people. He was once considered an asset, but he was now just as expendable as everyone else under the umbrella of the Seaton Falls clan.

There were a slew of minor infractions that would've most likely only gotten him a slap on the wrist, but coupled with everything else … it didn't look good for him.

Officer Chadwick was right to protect his daughter by any means necessary.

"And you'll be pleased to know we've had the Stokes household under surveillance for several days now," Baz offered. "We've even got a team monitoring all incoming and outgoing communication."

"Is this because the missus was getting lippy?" Dallas quirked.

Baz hesitated, but then responded to the less-than-elegant question. "Precisely. We took her threats quite seriously. The moment she alluded to her intentions to *'go above our heads'* we set a plan in action."

Without spelling it out, it was clear the Elders took this threat to mean that, if there wasn't news about her son soon, Mrs. Stokes planned to do whatever it took.

Even if that meant presenting this matter to The Sovereign.

Typically, he wouldn't have been interested in trivial clan issues, but if she mentioned Damascus … that could potentially not only expose the facility, but expose all the secrets so many fought to keep hidden.

My only hope was, for all the Elder's effort to bridle Mrs. Stokes tongue ... they weren't too late.

***

Evie

Tonight should have been a good night.

I conquered my first lycan shift, spent time with Beth, and kicked Chris's butt during training.

But things had taken a turn in the last half hour.

The truck rocked Liam and I back and forth as we ambled over the snow-covered roadways, heading home. My thoughts were muddled, clogged with too many emotions to list. To name a few, I was worried, scared, and confused.

Nick was on his way back into town or had already made it, for all I knew. While I wasn't afraid of him per se, I no longer trusted him. He'd shown me the darkness he was capable of, and that was enough for me.

So ... why was I worried about him?

The things I overheard through Liam's thoughts, the things the Elder said ... there was no telling what fate, or punishment, awaited Nick. He was not at the top of my list in terms of my favorite people, but that didn't mean he deserved to suffer.

To die.

At the thought, I reached for Liam's hand, needing to cling to him for comfort. The ways of the supernatural world were quite different from the natural. Because of our abilities, we were held at a higher standard. I guessed it was because the probability of us doing more damage and causing greater destruction was greater, we had to be punished more harshly. But it still seemed cruel.

Especially when I took into consideration that Nick had only given himself up because he cared about Roz.

Once, I pegged him as selfish for his willingness to cause me grief just to satisfy his hatred for Liam. But what he'd done for her ... it was one of the most selfless things I'd ever seen. He knew things could, and probably would, get worse for him once he came home, but he willingly surrendered.

For her.

Only love would make a man risk his life to save another. Glancing at Liam, I had a full understanding of this. He'd put himself in harm's way on my behalf more times than I could count, so I could only imagine a similar sense of vigilance in Nick's heart when it came to Roz.

Even if he hadn't fully accepted it yet.

"This doesn't feel right."

Liam glanced over when I spoke for the first time since being let inside his head. Without asking, he knew what I referred to.

"There's nothing you, or anyone else, can do."

My knee bounced up and down as frustration set in. "I'm not willing to accept that. Maybe if I go to the Elders on his behalf I could—"

"Absolutely not." The words left Liam's mouth with such ferocity I was shocked. Stunned to the point that I didn't immediately have a response.

I blinked at him as it set in that he'd all but forbidden me.

"You can't tell me what to do," I countered, turning to face the window as I slowly pulled my hand from his.

Hadn't I already made it clear that I wasn't a child?

Children didn't have to worry about the things I had to worry about, weren't faced with the responsibilities I'd soon face. I wouldn't bear the burdens of being an adult, but experience none of the benefits. The days of me being pushed around ... by *anyone* ... were long gone.

A sharp breath left Liam's mouth and he spoke far more calmly now. "I didn't mean it that way."

"He saved my life once during the earthquake," I blurted, recalling the details of the day disaster struck Seaton Falls just this past year.

"I would've been crushed inside a building had he not come for me," I added.

Beside me, Liam was silent for a moment, taking in this newly-revealed information. The truck's headlights illuminated falling snow and I stared, just as quiet as a parade of thoughts stampeded through my head. Thoughts like how, at the time of the quake, I hadn't transitioned yet, wasn't invincible yet. Had Nick listened to someone telling him I wasn't worth saving ... I wouldn't be here today.

Liam shifted in his seat. "I didn't realize you'd been in danger," he admitted. "At that time, our tether wasn't as finely tuned as it is now. If something like that was to happen today ..."

His voice trailed off and I closed my eyes, breathing deep. "I know," I sighed. "But that's not the point."

There was a brief moment of clarity as I realized what I hoped to shed light on by sharing this experience.

"I only mean to say, if he thought enough of me to put his own life on the line, if he thinks enough of Roz to do the same ... doesn't that have to mean he's not all bad?"

I chewed the side of my lip to keep from crying. I wasn't even sure why I wanted to, but the stinging in the corners of my eyes meant tears were on the way.

The hand I'd just taken back was warm again and I didn't pull away, didn't miss the fact that I felt better when he held it.

"Evangeline ... I understand you feel like you owe him something," Liam sighed, saying these words despite them feeling unnatural to him, I'm sure. "But it's unwise to intervene in Council business," he reasoned. "Yes, they revere you as their future queen, but the operative word here is *future*. They're under no obligation to grant you favors," he clarified.

I knew he was right, about *all* of it, but I couldn't justify my lack of action with such flimsy reasoning. So what if they didn't listen to me. I still needed to try.

"I know what you're thinking," Liam said, cutting in.

"Actually, you don't."

He spoke tenderly despite my clipped tone, proving once more that he sees right through me when he blurted, "You blame yourself."

I said nothing, focusing my eyes as only a supernatural could, counting trees through the haze of falling snow. It was all I could do to distract myself from the reality that seeped in with Liam's words.

Very rarely was he wrong about me, so it came as no surprise that he was spot on even now.

I *did* blame myself. To a degree at least. This all boiled down to me.

I was the cause of Nick being the Liberator.

I was the reason he hated Liam, enough to want him dead.

I was the reason he so desperately sought a cure.

It was all on me. Had I not been born, Nick could have had a normal life.

"I don't want to talk about this anymore," I sighed, feeling those tears gathering into pools.

Nick had been away for so long—away from his brothers, his parents. Even before he and Roz had run off. And now, fear of the Council's punishment kept him away even longer. He was just a kid. It wasn't his fault he was more than human, but being more had damned him to a fate none of us could fathom.

I squeezed Liam's fingers now, suddenly over the brief bout of defiance that momentarily made me crave distance. He wasn't my punching bag. Yes, he was strong physically, emotionally, but I had no right to lash out. Especially knowing he only wanted what's best for me.

"I'm sorry," I uttered softly.

He didn't respond, just lifted my hand to press a kiss to the back of it. I knew I'd been forgiven even before I realized I'd been wrong.

"I'm worried for him," I admitted, never concerned Liam would misinterpret my feelings. My whole heart was his, and there was never a reason for him to doubt it. He knew these sympathetic thoughts toward Nick were innocent.

"He's doing all of this because he cares about Roz," I went on. "Will the Council take that into consideration? Would they allow me to speak on his behalf?"

I never thought I'd even think to do such a thing. Not for Nick. Not with all he cost me.

Yet here I was, begging to save his life if it came down to it.

Regardless of the turn things eventually took with us, he was my first friend here. And that was real, genuine. I hadn't gotten over the problems that crept in these last few months, but I found it hard to believe he deserved to die because of it.

Call me crazy.

We pulled into the driveway, and before I could undo my seatbelt, my chin warmed at Liam's touch. He lifted my gaze to meet his.

"I'll do what I can."

There was such sincerity in his eyes, I didn't doubt him for a second. He didn't have to agree to this—especially since Nick had set him up, had nearly gotten him killed—but he was willing for me.

Because these were the sacrifices a man made for the one he loved.

My lips pressed to his. Every time I thought he couldn't get any better, any more right for me, he proved me wrong.

"Thank you," I whispered against his mouth, repeating myself just to make sure he knew the gratitude that filled my heart. "Thank you."

I wasn't sure if Liam's request would be enough to sway the Council, but it meant so much that he'd try.

Even if only for me.

Chapter Eleven

Nick

It would have been ideal to walk her to the door ... but she insisted I get out of there before her father saw me on their property.

Officer Chadwick hated me—of this I was certain.

I watched from behind a nearby tree as Roz was greeted with a huge hug that told of how deeply she was missed. She was taken inside where it was warm, where she could be cared for the way she deserved, where she'd be safe. These were all comforts I couldn't offer her.

Suddenly aware of how alone I was, how vulnerable I was, I ran to my grandfather's estate, the only place I could think to go.

My bags hit the ground with a thud as I fumbled along the wall, feeling for the switch. Once the place came alive with light against its dark fixtures, I breathed deep, letting the heap of emotions that'd been dangling over my head come crashing down. It would have been nice to go home, but I wasn't sure who might be looking for me. I couldn't risk anything happening to my family. For now, I'd hang around here until I figured things out, decided on my next move.

Everything that could have possibly gone wrong did. Roz getting sick was just the final straw. I was sure coming home was about the worst thing I could have done right now, but we were out of options. Besides, I was sick of running. Whatever consequences I had to face ... I'd brought it on myself.

Showering ranked so high on my list of things to do, I could hardly focus on anything else—even eating. I scarfed down a pizza I left in the freezer when I stayed here around Christmas. It wasn't all the way cooked when I pulled it out the oven, but I didn't care. I wanted to get something in my stomach, but mostly I wanted to get clean.

I wasn't sure which I enjoyed most—the hot water or getting to shampoo my hair with real shampoo for a change. Since leaving the motel, the stream near our camp had been me and Roz's only means of getting clean.

Well ... clean-ish.

I stood there, beneath the stream of piping hot water until it ran cold. Toweling myself dry, I stared at the reflection in the mirror — at the dark mop of hair that hadn't been cut in months, at the scruff on my face. I looked like someone nearly twice my age, but wouldn't bother trimming or shaving until tomorrow.

Or the next day.

Maybe.

Content to sport the caveman look for a bit longer, I stepped back into the master bedroom. However, the moment my feet left the cool tile, touching carpet the next instant, I knew something was off. Sensed it.

I wasn't alone.

There were traces of others' scents in the air. No, they weren't in this room, but they were definitely in the house.

Quickly and as quietly as I could, I slipped into sweats from a drawer I claimed while staying here before. I'd left things behind in just about every room, making this house feel more like mine than anyone else in the family. No one spent as much time here as I did. Especially lately.

My steps were light as I eased out into the hallway. Clenching my fists at both sides, I put one foot in front of the other. I wished I could have nailed down one scent, but there were so many, mingling with one another, making it impossible to identify them individually.

Or maybe ... I couldn't identify them because they weren't familiar to me.

Maybe they were strangers, lycans from the Council who'd come to detain me.

At that thought, I froze in place, one foot on the stairs, the other in midair. Every light I'd turned on when I came in was out now, casting the entire first floor in darkness. I paused and listened harder, hoping to get a location on at least one.

Nothing but silence.

"Who—who's there?" I stammered, feeling the erratic throb of my heart against my ribs.

I could hardly catch my breath, so I chose to hold it. Doing so would also keep the intruders from knowing how freaked out I was, but ... I was definitely freaked out. In fact, I'd just made up my mind to sprint down the stairs and make a run for the front door when a figure emerged from the shadows.

"Don't even think about it, kid."

The voice ... I recognized it.

"Richie?"

He stepped into the light and that's when I saw the others, dark silhouettes all over the foyer. I counted five.

The next second, the chandelier at the foot of the stairs shimmered with light and I laid eyes on the last faces I expected to see here tonight—all three of my brothers, plus Lucas and Chris.

My heart rate slowed and I clutched my chest, easing down to sit on a step.

"Did we scare ya?" Kyle asked, grinning big. Of *course* he got a kick out of this.

"The theatrics were my idea," he bragged. "Seemed only fair after you had us terrified these last few months, thinking we'd lost you."

His smile faded a bit and I had nothing to say to that as I imagined what I'd put my family through.

I locked eyes with my friends, and both wore a mix of relief and anger on their faces, which I *also* understood. I'd left abruptly with no word and they hadn't heard from me since. They were upset and I couldn't blame them.

I pushed a hand through my hair and breathed deep.

"Guys, I'm—" The words wouldn't come, because there was nothing I could say to make up for the things I'd done. There was absolutely no excuse. For any of it.

"I'm sorry." That was all I could force out, hoping that, somehow, it'd be enough.

Richie lowered his gaze to the tile and nodded. "We know, kid."

He was always so hard to read, was always pretty monotone, so I couldn't gage whether his response was one rooted in sympathy or sarcasm.

"We thought they'd been lying to us," Lucas chimed in. "We thought they took you and just didn't want to tell us. It was hard to believe you'd run off like that without warning again," he added. "You had to have known you could talk to us, right? About whatever was going on?"

I felt sick to my stomach, facing them all at once.

"It was more complicated than that," was the only answer I could give without going into detail about what I am, what my destiny is said to be. That'd be the only way to explain why I'd gotten so desperate. Desperate enough to be fooled by the witches into doing their dirty work. It was never about helping me. They used me to get to Liam, fed off my hatred for him.

Chris shook his head. "Nah, you gotta give us more than that," he demanded. "It's coming up on three months since you left. Where have you been?"

I breathed deep. "Nowhere really. Cheap motels and outside once we ran out of money."

They were all silent.

"You guys have to believe me, I would've told you everything if I could have."

"You told Roz," Lucas cut in, poking holes in my excuse.

He was right. She *did* know everything, all my secrets, but that was different. However, I knew they'd never understand *how* it was different. I didn't even fully understand it myself. Things with her had changed, evolved into something completely different altogether, but I didn't want to think about that right now. My head was cloudy enough.

"Let's lay off him a bit," Richie cut in, saving me from having to explain things I couldn't. "We're just glad you're home."

My eyes lifted when he said that, the first welcoming thing I'd heard since this conversation began. Kyle made his way up the stairs to where I sat first, bringing me in for a rough hug. Then Ben and Richie. Chris and Lucas were the last and I knew it'd take a little while for them to understand it all, but I made myself promise I'd tell them everything as soon as I figured out how.

They each settled on the stairs around me and I asked the big question. "How bad do Mom and Dad wanna kill me?"

Richie chuffed a short laugh. "Let's not ruin the moment."

I nodded, deciding to leave it alone for now. If I had to guess, they'd most likely ground me until I turned thirty, and I couldn't fault them for that. I screwed up. *Big* time.

But my next thought wasn't of whatever punishment my parents had thought up, it was of whatever punishment the *Council* had thought up.

With a sigh, my hand slid down my face. I was exhausted, but more worried than anything else.

"So, you came home for Roz, huh?"

I turned to Ben when he asked, and then nodded. "Yeah. Didn't have much choice. She came down with some kind of flu, and it just kept getting worse and worse."

I caught a strange look being passed between my brothers. "What?"

It took a moment for any of them to respond, but then Richie spoke. "We don't get sick," he explained. "We're immune to any and everything you can think of. Especially a virus as weak as the flu."

My brow tensed. "So ... you think she was faking?" I pulled together all the details, how weak she was, how she couldn't keep anything down.

Richie shook his head. "Not at all, but I *do* think the Council played on your feelings for her."

That statement ... *'feelings for her'* ... it made me uncomfortable, but I kept it to myself. That wasn't what I needed to be focused on.

"You think *they* made her sick?"

Richie nodded again. "Well ... I think the witches did."

I was silent.

"Pretty sure they used her to flush you out into the open," Ben added.

My thoughts reeled. This had all been a setup. They knew I wouldn't let Roz suffer.

The sound of a paper crinkling brought my eyes to Kyle as he pulled something out of his pocket.

"Until this came, it was only speculation," he explained. "But now, we're *sure* that's what happened."

He handed the paper over and Ben spoke again. "They already had this drafted and delivered a couple hours ago."

My bus hadn't even gotten in a couple hours ago, which meant ... they were expecting me.

"What is this?" I asked, turning the paper over in my hands, knowing I could have answered my own question if I'd just look inside. But fear stopped me.

"A summons," Richie sighed.

I couldn't lift my eyes to look at them. Their expressions would only make this more real, seeing the worry I was sure resided there.

"It's just for a hearing," Ben said, trying to ease my mind I was sure, but it didn't work. Being summoned by the Council was a big deal.

I clenched the paper in my fist. "When?"

"Once members of the High Council make it into town," Kyle answered. "Tomorrow."

Tomorrow.

"It says you're supposed to arrive alone, but we're going with you," Richie cut in.

"No."

Every pair of eyes was set on me.

"What do you mean *no*?" he snapped. "We're not letting you face this alone."

"And I'm not letting anyone else suffer because of me."

My gaze landed on Richie as soon as the words left my mouth, and a familiar sensation hit my chest. It was the same sensation I felt the day I showed up for the meeting at Officer Chadwick's, right after so many young lycans shifted in one night. Angry, Richie had done his best to force me out, wanting to shield me from a reality I'd already begun to see the full scale of. I understood what this feeling was now.

As our pack's alpha, he was pulling rank.

A sharp pain seared through my skin like a hot iron, his attempt at forcing me to submit. Only, it wasn't working like last time. Dead-set against the idea of him or anyone else tagging along, I pushed back. Slowly, surely, the burn subsided, and my will was my own again.

Confusion crossed his face when I made my point clear. "I'm going alone."

Ben passed a discreet glance Richie's way, but said nothing.

With that, the atmosphere thickened and the mood shifted.

"Suit yourself." I stared at the back of Richie's head as he trudged down the stairs. Like usual, my defiance rubbed him the wrong way.

"Just understand what you'll be walking into," he called back, his hand already on the doorknob. "There's no guarantee they'll let you leave once they have you."

No guarantee they'd let me keep breathing once they had me.

I swallowed hard and then gave a nod. One that exuded false confidence. "Understood."

His gaze remained locked on me a moment longer, maybe waiting for me to change my mind, but that wouldn't happen.

I made this mess and no one else would pay for it but me.

Chapter Twelve

Liam

Only for her.

No one else could have talked me into being here, in the Elders' chamber, pleading the case of someone I'd imagined killing a hundred different ways.

He'd been back in Seaton Falls just under twenty-four-hours and the quick summoning made it clear they were eager to deal with him. Possibly because of all the trouble he'd caused.

Baz was silent, his milky-white eyes lingering on careful penmanship scrawled across a sheet of paper. *Two* sheets of paper—a letter Evangeline had written, listing the reasons she thought Nick's life was worth sparing. At her bidding, I supported her plea by adding my two cents, asking the Elders to have mercy on Nick, as much as the Council and High Council would allow.

Baz spoke for the two seated beside him, like always, and I didn't miss the hint of amusement in his tone.

"When we discussed young Nicholas' fate months ago ... were you not eager to have him put to death?" he asked. "And now, you're requesting that we show him mercy this evening?"

I knew how ironic this was.

"It isn't *my* request, per se. I'm only here on Evangeline's behalf."

"I see." He nodded slowly. "She's quite compassionate," he noted, reading more of her words. "And persuasive."

He'd get no argument out of me on that one.

There was a long bout of silence while he thought, possibly considering Evangeline's plea. However, I had little hope they'd allow her wishes to sway their decision.

"I'll present it before the Council and High Council once members arrive shortly, but I make no guarantees. As you well know, we take behavior that threatens the safety and balance of the clan quite seriously."

I nodded. "I do."

"Then, please explain this to Evangeline ahead of time. It's better she be prepared for the worst outcome tonight, because ... this isn't likely to go in her favor."

There was nothing more to say. In so many words, Baz made it clear they had no intentions on giving Nick a light sentence. I had a mix of comfort and uneasiness about it all.

Comfort knowing Nick wouldn't be able to hurt Evangeline.

Uneasiness knowing her soft heart would be broken if he received the severest punishment. Despite her ill feelings toward him. She had the presence of mind to see past how he affected her personally, and considered others—his family and friends, and even Nick himself.

But Baz was right; it'd be best to prepare her for the worst.

This thing could go either way.

***

Evie

There would be repercussions for sneaking off alone while Liam was gone, but I had to.

I had to see for myself.

Warm, yellow light beamed through large windows where the blinds hadn't been shut. The sun had just gone down, so I guessed they hadn't gotten around to it.

Thank God they hadn't gotten around to it.

I watched them from the rooftop of a family's home who hadn't yet returned for the night. Perched there, I had a clear view of my parents, of the love and closeness I had only dreamed about lately. They looked so happy. So blissfully unaware.

"I'm still here," I whispered.

Only to myself, because telling them wouldn't even matter.

They'd long-since forgotten me.

Mom reached across the table with a laugh, swiping food from Dad's chin. Tonight was family date night, and from what I could see, removing me from the equation hadn't changed things all that much. They'd likely just come in from a movie, and per our tradition, they were ending the night with pizza.

I missed them so much I ached all over just thinking about it. They were missing a third of their trio and didn't even realize it.

Wetness slipped down my cheek and sizzled from the fire blazing just beneath my skin. It kept me warm, seeing as how I'd wandered off after the dinner Elise prepared—no jacket, no phone. Just this emptiness I tried to keep to myself.

I was drawn here similarly to how my core was magnetized with Liam. I simply couldn't keep my distance. It killed me being in the same town, but having to stay away. So, tonight, I found a way to be with them while still only existing on the fringes.

Like a ghost.

A twinge in the center of my chest prompted me to stifle the tears pooling in my eyes, because I had company — the kind that panics when he can't find me. The kind that used a handy tether that led him straight here. My skin tingled with awareness as Liam drew closer, still hidden under the darkness of night, but I now heard snow crunching beneath his boots.

I'd climbed a nearby tree and walked a branch tightrope-style to get on this roof. It was a less than graceful performance I was glad no one witnessed but me. Now, putting me to shame, Liam burst into the air just like the night we flew, only with far more control as he landed gracefully beside me. His footing was so sure. A far cry from the slippery dance I'd done over ice-covered shingles twenty-minutes ago.

"Show off," I smiled, wrangling in the emotions I allowed to surface when I was alone.

He filled the space to my right, and to my surprise, I wasn't chastised for running off on my own. He didn't waste breath pointing out all the reasons this was an awful idea.

He just … sat.

I inched closer to his side, slinking my bare arm around his. Our combined light was mesmerizing, a network of glowing veins that ended where my fingers tangled with his. My cheek pressed to his shoulder and I breathed deep, keeping my eyes on my parents, accepting the fact that I was an outsider.

A car passed on the street in front of the house and my eyes followed it until it came to a stop in the circular drive next door—the Stokes' home. The entire first floor was lit and the car that just pulled in, joined three others. It looked like the entire family was there.

All except Nick.

Tonight was sure to be a somber one for their pack. I knew this to be a fact without seeing any of them face-to-face, without having to guess. As I sat here watching Kyle jog to the front door, I knew Nick was with the Council where his future hung in the balance.

I couldn't turn away now, wondering if the letter Liam had just delivered for me was enough. Wondering what would happen if it wasn't. The Elders respected me, but they didn't respect me nearly enough for my words to change their minds. Still, I had to try. I couldn't sit by, knowing it might have mattered if I spoke up. So, despite it likely being a futile effort, I wrote the letter.

Now, all we could do was wait.

"You did everything you could." Liam's voice touched my ears and the rest of the world took a step back. "Baz gave his word that the Council, and High Council, would take your thoughts into consideration."

The High Council—a combination of several clan's oldest lycans who'd been groomed to uphold their law to the fullest.

Yeah ... they'd take the letter of a fretful teenage girl *real* serious.

I kept my doubtful thoughts to myself for fear of what might happen if I released them into the atmosphere. It may have been superstitious, but I couldn't afford to jinx this situation any more than it already had been.

"Thank you for going," I replied, squeezing his fingers a bit. "I know you hated being there, but ... you went, and I won't forget it."

He nudged me a bit before placing a kiss on top of my head. "You're welcome."

When there was no more movement at the Stokes residence, I turned toward my own again, just as Mom moved to the sink to wash the few dishes they dirtied. My father flipped through mail while they laughed at each others' jokes, shared about the day both had at work. I could almost guess the conversation because it was always the same.

Not redundant, just ... comfortingly familiar.

More words moved into my hair and I tilted my head some to listen.

"I told you it was Ivan who did my tattoos, that we were the only two who mastered the technique, but I never told you how we ended up in Egypt where we learned."

I lived for these moments, being told about my past, my family. Liam had my full, undivided attention.

"It was never a mystery where I came from, but I didn't know much about my past other than being the product of rogue dragon shifters who'd made a game of leaving human women for dead."

I remembered the story. Liam's mother was the victim of an epidemic spreading throughout Egypt centuries ago. Human women were ravished by these shifters, and then, because their bodies weren't made to handle birthing super-human children into the world, they died after delivering, thus creating an explosion of feral dragons.

It was my father's duty to put a stop to it, and during that journey, he found and spared Liam, making him a part of our family.

"Yes, you told me that part," I said softly, eager to hear what he'd share next.

A surge of air filled his lungs and his shoulder moved with it, shifting my body because my weight mostly rested on him.

"The part I *hadn't* shared yet was how that stayed with me, how it lingered in my head that I didn't belong with your mother and father."

My brow tensed as I thought about that. He'd never shared that he felt displaced, and I guess I didn't consider it because, to me, he was always so focused. I can admit it was sometimes hard to see past my own hurt to grasp the bigger picture, but Liam always seemed so ... *together*. It never even crossed my mind that we had so much in common. That he, too, had dealt with the emotional stirring of being adopted.

Heat pulsed through my palm when I held his hand tighter.

"It hit me out of nowhere right after my first shift at twenty — this unshakable feeling of being a fish out of water," he explained. "Most of your brothers were like you, favored the gifts of their dragon more than those of the wolf, but it was never far from my mind that we were different, that I didn't quite belong."

A long breadth of silence passed between us and I couldn't believe I missed it, couldn't believe I hadn't seen that same distant look in his eyes I sometimes saw in my own.

"It was Elise who suggested I go to Egypt, to find myself," he shared. "Of course, being overprotective, she made me take one of your brothers," he added with a smile. "So, with her and your father's blessing, Ivan and I left. Didn't come back for six months."

"And did you find yourself while you were away?"

He shrugged and one corner of his mouth turned upward. "That voyage made me aware of many things."

I turned, letting my eyes settle on his face, shimmering silver beneath moonlight.

"You gonna keep me guessing?" I pressed, smiling a bit.

A hint of nostalgia softened the stern lines of his expression as his gaze landed on our matching bracelets.

"It made me painfully aware of where home truly was," he breathed. "I enjoyed learning about my people, enjoyed learning their ways, but more than anything, I wanted to get back to *you*."

He always said exactly the right thing at exactly the right time.

My heart fluttered.

"Were we ... together that early on? Right after you first shifted?" I asked.

Liam shook his head.

"No, far from it," he laughed. "I was willing to own my feelings long before your stubbornness would allow you to admit you needed anyone other than yourself."

I had to laugh. I didn't think of myself as being that way *now*, but if I had to guess, I wasn't as cold as I may have seemed back then either. There was a small part of me that naturally preferred to conceal my emotions, but it was my mom, Rebecka, who taught me it was okay to feel.

So, I guess I *was* different in some ways.

"How'd you do it?" I asked with a grin, leaning into his side again.

"Do what?"

"How'd you knock down *The Great Wall of Evangeline*," I teased.

A soft chuckle wrapped in a deep, velvety voice warmed my soul when it left his mouth. "Lots and lots of hard work," he joked. "But it was well worth it."

I was glad to hear he felt that way.

"Tell me about the day I finally came to my senses." Those were the perfect words. A girl *had* to be senseless not to see Liam for what he is. Myself included. In *both* lifetimes.

He laughed again before sharing. "Well … I wish I could tell you we had a fairytale beginning, but it wasn't anything like that. In fact, I distinctly remember you once referring to me as *'the most pompous, insufferable bastard you ever had the pleasure of slapping'*."

He laughed, but I didn't. Actually, I was kind of mortified.

"Was I really that terrible?"

When he caught his breath, he answered. "Nah, you were no more snobbish and entitled than any *other* princess."

I cringed at the thought of speaking to him that way.

"But I always saw through it, saw your big heart through all the ice." His chest vibrated with another deep chuckle. "Even when you were telling me how much you hated me, or how overprotective I was, I saw it."

"Saw…?"

"This," he clarified. "Our future."

I had to laugh. "So, even through the rudeness, and the insults … you knew we were meant to be."

He nodded as if he saw nothing wrong with anything I said. "Absolutely. I've never wanted anything unless it was a challenge."

And I guess I gave him that and *then* some.

"I'm pretty sure my immunity to your callousness was why your father assigned me to you, to serve as your warrior," he went on to explain. "You went through five in one year and, eventually, he got sick of searching for new, trustworthy shifters to fill the role. Next thing I know, he came to me with the proposition. And because I knew you were mine from the beginning, I didn't hesitate to accept." His smile grew. "You, on the other hand, weren't quite as easily convinced."

"We couldn't have *always* been at each other's throats," I commented, feeling confused. If I was close to my brothers, I had to have been somewhat close to him as well, seeing as how we were raised together.

"We definitely had our good days," he explained. "But … I can own that I was at fault for some of the bad ones."

Curiosity was eating me up inside. "Meaning?"

"I hold on too tight," he admitted. When I didn't dismiss the claim, he looked at me and laughed. "Stating the obvious, I know. Let's just say not much has changed there. And let's *also* say you're much more gracious about it now than you were then."

I smiled against his shoulder. "You still haven't said how you changed my mind."

I didn't care that it wasn't some fairytale, didn't care that the story seemed to involve at least *some* measure of me cursing him out, I only cared that we ended up here.

"I was supposed to escort you on … an outing," he said vaguely, leaving me to guess what he could mean. But then, he made things crystal clear. "Your father arranged for you to court the son of a Duke. They were lycans, but only other supernaturals were aware."

I choked out a laugh, thinking of how many social cues I miss on the regular. Thinking how, once, my summer goal had been to learn how to burp the alphabet. Thinking how I had a reputation around my house as being a 'snorter' if I laughed too hard. So, me? Courting the son of a Duke?

"True story," Liam smiled. "You two weren't allowed to leave your family's property, so he took you for a walk through one of the gardens. I had to stick close by, of course."

I tried to imagine it, Liam sitting idly by while I walked hand-in-hand with someone else. It reminded me of his first meeting with Nick. Who would've thought we lived through that twice?

"The guy spent the whole time trying to outsmart me, trying to lose me so he could be alone with you, but he had no idea how persistent I can be."

Those lips of his spread with a devilish grin after he spoke. Those lips I wanted against mine even now as he shared long-forgotten memories locked somewhere within me.

"Eventually, he gave up and settled for sitting beside you on a stone bench near the castle wall. And I held my post despite the hatred and jealousy eating me alive from the inside out."

"What'd you do? Rip his throat out?" I teased, knowing that was his kill of choice.

He grinned again. "If doing so wouldn't have sentenced me to death, I'm sure I would have."

"What happened next?"

He thought back. "Well, he played it cool for a bit, but then got the bright idea that this was a good time to kiss you … and I guess we could consider that my breaking point."

I was almost afraid to ask.

"Or … maybe we'll say that was his *jaw's* breaking point," he corrected. "Thus, earning me the title of the most pompous, insufferable bastard you ever had the pleasure of slapping."

Holding a hand over my mouth to stifle a laugh. "I really slapped you?"

He nodded. "Yup, and it was a good one. My cheek stung for hours."

It was so hard to imagine us as anything but loving and affectionate toward one another. No wonder the indifference I first showed toward him wasn't a deterrent. He'd dealt with much worse from me.

"Did you get in trouble for hurting him?" I asked.

He shook his head casually. "Not much. Your father lied to the Duke, told him he'd deal with me that evening. Basically, it just earned me an hour long lecture."

My teeth dragged along my bottom lip as I zoned out, picturing it all like a movie playing inside my head.

"And all this led to me finally accepting my feelings for you?" I asked a bit skeptically, failing to see how it all came together.

I glanced up when Liam didn't answer right away. Scrubbing a hand down his face, grazing his low-shaven beard as a smile ghosted on his lips. I was dying for a response.

"It did," he went on. "I went to you later, hoping to apologize."

"And ... did you?"

His lips quirked a bit and I felt my heart flutter.

"I did," he teased, being cryptic again. Maybe on purpose. "And you forgave me." I blinked at him when he added, "Actually, if memory of that night serves me well ... you forgave me *three* times."

Heat spread across my cheeks and I breathed a deep, quivering, "Oh ..." as realization set in.

There was no need to guess what he meant.

An electric pulse vibrated from my core, through my limbs just at the thought of ... *forgiving* him.

"From that point, your father no longer had an issue finding a warrior who could put up with you, because I was permanently on the job." White teeth flashed when he added, "You might say I was the best you ever had."

That heat in my cheeks spread down my neck as I deciphered yet another double-meaning.

As if taking things slowly with him wasn't already difficult enough ...

My house went pitch black and I focused there again, on thoughts of a life that seemed so distant now. Liam's arm moved to my shoulders and he held me close. Having him here, talking me through this moment, was exactly what I needed. As I guessed, my parents made their way upstairs for the evening, I stood. My eyes lingered there for a moment, on those dark windows, and I decided to find a positive takeaway from all this.

They were alive.

They were safe.

They were happy.

Liam's story stuck with me, namely the part where he traveled home to find himself. He returned to Bahir Dar with a sense of closure that went beyond seeing himself mirrored in his people. He had closure because he realized the word "home" was relative.

My parents' memories would never be restored, and I had to accept that. But, thanks to Liam, I still had family.

I still had love.

Chapter Thirteen

Nick

I remembered the first time I wandered down to this chamber, the night our clan stood up to the Elders, demanding answers. Tonight, my visit served a very different purpose.

Tonight, the only question I sought an answer to was whether I'd again see the light of day.

I came alone, wanting to spare my family the pain of seeing me being taken away. It was no secret the Council had a zero-tolerance rule when it came to jeopardizing the safety of the clan, risking exposure. I later discovered it was also against the rules to fraternize with clan witches without the consent from the Elders.

I'd done all three, and to add fuel to the fire, I inadvertently endangered Evangeline's life, whom the Council regarded as their queen.

In short, I jacked this up about as much as anyone could possibly do. If there was an award for royal screw-up, I'd win gold, silver, *and* bronze.

My arms ached where two giants gripped them. They showed up at the door of my grandfather's estate to escort me to the trial. I suppose lycans in my position typically tried to run, but they wouldn't have any trouble out of me. I'd done enough running, and at the end of the day, the Council knew exactly how to make me come out of hiding. All it took was endangering the life of someone I cared about. This time, it was Roz. Next time, it could be any one of my friends or family and I wouldn't risk it. They were all-seeing and all-powerful, so the best chance any of us had to exist in peace was if we submitted.

So, I submitted.

Heavy chains were clamped to my wrists when we came to a stop at the foot of the long, descending staircase. Like always, the only source of light came from torches placed intermittently in holders along the stone walls and pillars. This place always held a sinister air to it, but now, as I awaited the Council's decision, it seemed darker still.

"The Chancellor will be out in a moment. Don't move," one of the giant lycans ordered as he attached my chains to a pillar. The chains were spelled, bound with magic, making it impossible to break free.

There were others here. Three. All in chains, all with the same frightened, desperate looks on their faces. When I tried to imagine what this experience would be like, I never even considered anyone else being stupid enough to piss off our supernatural government.

Clearly, I was wrong.

Then again, it was likely they'd only committed minor offenses, small things deemed criminal by the Council.

More rattling chains dragged across the stone floor behind me. The four of us who waited suddenly turned, taking in the site of another figure, a weak man; one who could barely stand on his own. More of the giant lycan guards brought him closer, into the light of a nearby torch, and it was then that I took in the sight of him.

Naked, shaking, covered in dirt and deep, bloody gashes. It was impossible to tell what caused the wounds—his own actions or the guards as they rounded him up—but deciding why he was so groggy took little thought.

A witch.

I'd never seen this one before, but guessed she was among the Elders' replacements, seeing as how I watched the others lose their heads and burn to death.

Courtesy of Evangeline.

She appeared to be young, no older than her mid-twenties, but I guessed that was nothing more than illusion.

As the man stood and the guards held him upright at either side, she kept a hand to the chained lycan's back, using her magic to subdue him. They continued forward, and so close, I recognized his face. His name escaped me, but I knew he was a senior my freshman year, a member of Kyle's graduating class.

I watched as they bypassed the pillar beside me. Instead of linking him to it like the rest of us had been, they proceeded on toward the long table where the Council would soon be seated. As soon as I thought of them, the sound of screeching, metal hinges filled the hollow room.

Shuffling feet and dark robes.

Each of the twenty or more seats were filled and the already silent room became even quieter.

It was the sound of uncertainty.

The sound of fear.

My heart raced and my wolf tried to burst free. However, but the magic spelled around my wrists made shifting impossible, leaving me in physiological limbo. The bones that broke and repaired themselves as I shifted, cracked one by one, sending searing jolts shooting through every muscle, every limb, and then stayed that way, ready to shift.

But magic forbid it.

I wanted to cry out in pain, but knew it'd be in my best interest to show some semblance of control. I needed to reverse this, needed to send the beast within me a signal to calm him.

Closing my eyes, I breathed deep and searched for a thought to take my mind off the threat I sensed all around me now that the Council was among us. Perhaps it'd just become real that, on this day, my life could end, sending my beast into survival mode.

Think, Nick. Think.

These lycans needed to know I wasn't just some uncontrollable freak of nature. In fact, I hadn't had a single blackout since leaving the facility. I'd gone over the possible reasons for this about a million times. And each of those million times, I was forced to admit that only one new factor had been introduced.

Roz.

We were together around the clock, and any other incident in which I'd lost time, I was alone-either in my room at the facility, or at my grandfather's estate. But once she was with me, it stopped.

Revisiting a theory I'd come up with late one night, I focused on her. Maybe she was the key to subduing me.

She called several times since we arrived home roughly twenty-four hours ago. I didn't answer, but did text to let her know I was okay. She didn't know about tonight, though. I kept telling myself that was because I didn't want her to worry, but … being honest, I didn't tell her because I was afraid she'd show up, putting herself in harm's way once again.

For me.

We were beginning to evolve. Thinking back, I believe the change started a while ago — before I was ready to accept it — but it was directly in my face now. Yes, she was a friend, but … if I was being honest, she'd been more than that for quite some time. I felt things for her a guy doesn't really feel for a friend.

Back when we still felt like normal teenage kids, Lucas and Chris suggested she was into me, but all I saw was the smart-mouthed sophomore who could never leave well enough alone. When I looked at her lately, I saw so much more.

A beautiful girl with a beautiful soul to match.

Slowly, gently, my fractured bones mended themselves and the pain evaporated like it never existed. I could focus again, blinking my eyes as a surge of air filled my lungs.

The man was called forward, the one with all the gashes.

Jared Spencer.

He ambled toward the Council's table and, again, the witch kept her palm to his back. I wondered if he'd been brought here filthy and unclothed to humiliate him, but, when his trial began, his story started to unfold.

I scanned the panel of Council and High Council members as one dressed in a navy cloak read the case aloud. The variation in color set them apart from lower-level Elders in red who were *also* seated among them. The one who read fell silent, studying the stack of papers for a long stretch of time before lifting his gaze again.

Without guessing, his presence alerted me right away as to who he was. This had to be the Chancellor a guard mentioned.

"Am I wrong to assume this is exactly the outcome you sought? Wrong to assume you were hoping to one day stand before us, a pitiful sight and embarrassment to lycans everywhere?" His deep voice rattled loose stones that'd fallen from the aged pillars.

"When one bridles his wolf to the point of the beast breaking free of his own volition," he went on, "it is, typically, either the result of negligence or stupidity." A long stare lingered on Jared, the lycan in question. "So, which is it, Mr. Spencer? Are you negligent or stupid?"

I hadn't forgotten what my brothers told me when I first shifted, that not doing so often enough would make you morph out, and the punishment for such a thing was death.

Did they really think this guy let that happen on purpose?

However, to my surprise, he nodded.

Two of the others being held like I was, turned to stare at one another in disbelief.

"It's true," he admitted.

A quiet murmur surrounded the Council's table as different ones reacted to the confession.

"If choosing not to shift, if choosing to be human isn't possible, then ... I've got nothing to live for."

The one seated in the center, holding Jared's file, didn't move as the chatter around him continued. He stared from beneath his hood's shadow and I imagined the look of disgust that likely lingered there.

"You have nothing to live for," he repeated, still gazing at Jared.

Jared's chains rattled when he shifted his bare feet over the cement floor.

"Because I don't want this," he said, staring at his shackled hands with conviction. "I don't want to be … a monster."

My brow quirked at those words, hearing someone voice aloud a thought I'd had myself. While most embraced lycanism as a gift, there were the small few of us who saw it as more of a curse.

Jared's views, clearly, aligned with the minority.

The room was quiet again, and I was aware of each breath that left my mouth, wondering if my brothers had been right. Wondering if death was truly the only outcome.

"Very well then." I stared as the Chancellor stood, the hem of his navy cloak dragging the ground as he rounded the table, lessening the distance between himself and the pillars where the rest of us stood waiting.

Eventually, he came to a stop before Jared. Only now did I realize how much larger these lycans were than the rest of us—who were quite large already. These members of the High Council were as foreboding as the giants who brought us here.

"In accordance with the sanctions of this sacred Council, it is with great sadness that your journey must end here. At all times, it is our duty to protect our clans. On this day, it has been decided that you, Jared Spencer, have knowingly committed an offence that threatens the safety and secrecy of our species. Do you have anything to say for yourself?"

I listened to the cloaked beast's speech and felt the cool indifference in his tone. While he spoke of sadness, there were no traces of that emotion in his words.

"No, sir," Jared trembled.

"Very well then," the beast said once more, giving those of us who looked on no warning before revealing a sharp, pointed blade that he'd hidden in his sleeve. The tip of it disappeared in the side of Jared's neck, shoved violently into his flesh.

Sound gurgled from his mouth as he instinctively reached for the guards, looking to hold on to someone as his last seconds of life ticked past. The Council member stepped back to avoid Jared's touch, staring down on him when his knees hit the cement with a loud, jarring thud. Blood poured from his mouth and wound, painting the floor a macabre crimson.

He was fading too fast. With how quickly we heal, it should have taken longer for him to die, but when his limbs went still, I knew the blade had been laced with magic.

Just as cold as the speech he delivered, the Chancellor handed the dripping blade to a guard who wiped it clean, and then placed the weapon back in the Chancellor's possession.

As he returned to his seat, the now lifeless lycan was dragged off into the shadows.

"Nicholas Stokes."

The other three who were to stand trial shifted wide-eyed gazes in my direction.

A key clanked in the lock securing me to the pillar. The guard returned it to his pocket before yanking me toward the Council's table. While my case was silently looked over, I closed my eyes, deciding that I'd accept my fate and take whatever I had coming to me like a man. A solid minute passed and I opened them again, seeing that the one who'd just executed a man right before my eyes held a paper in his hands — one on lined, notebook paper, written in blue ink. My brow tensed, not remembering anything but typed documents in Jared's.

The paper lowered and the Council member glared at me. Well, at least I *think* he did.

"You've been rather busy, I see."

My stomach sank and I didn't respond.

"Several counts of recklessness that would justify being sentenced to the same fate as Mr. Spencer," he added, causing me to wince.

Swallowing a lump in my throat I reminded myself of the promise I'd just made a moment ago, that I'd take this like a man.

"I'm aware, sir," I choked out, feeling the familiar sting of bile in the back of my throat as my stomach churned.

"Do you have anything to say for yourself?" he asked. "Any … colorful excuses to offer for this elaborate mess you've created? Anything to add that might change our minds here tonight?"

I thought about that, aware of the amusement in his tone when he posed the question. He may have thought my youth made me ignorant, but I knew this wasn't possible. There was no talking them out of adhering to their strict laws and subsequent punishments.

It was written in stone even if I wouldn't let myself accept it until now.

In this spot, standing in another man's blood … was where I'd die.

"No, sir," I forced out, sounding far more confident than the pile of mush I'd become on the inside.

"Very well then," he said in the same monotone he'd uttered those very words to Jared before ending his life.

In similar fashion, he rose from his seat and made slow steps around the table. My heart was in my throat as I wished I *had* said more. Even if it wouldn't change things, I should have prepared *something*. Seemed a shame for me to die like this with not having thought of last words.

With not having said goodbye to Roz.

The sickening feeling spread within me, and in that moment, not reaching out to her was my biggest regret. While I still believed she would've done something stupid and gotten herself involved in this in some way, not admitting to feelings I kept under wraps seemed like a tragedy.

But here I was.

Facing death.

"In accordance with the sanctions of this sacred Council, it is with great sadness that your journey must end here," he recited. "At all times, it is our duty to protect our clans. On this day, it has been decided that you, Nicholas Stokes, have knowingly committed an offence that threatens the safety and secrecy of our species. Again, I ask, do you have anything to say for yourself?"

I froze, paralyzed by fear and something else I couldn't place at the time — incompletion. My life was ending like an abrupt, mid-sentence cliffhanger. The finality of it rendered me speechless again. Another missed opportunity to give my final words.

When I failed to reply, a metallic glint caught the light of a nearby torch and I glanced there, to his shriveled, white hand. He held the blade, the one laced with magic, the one that would pierce my throat, resulting in my untimely death.

He stepped closer and my knees felt unstable, like they'd give out beneath me.

Take it like a man, Nick. Take it like a man.

I braced myself, anticipating the sting of the blade breaking skin as I squeezed my eyes shut. But … that sting never came.

"You deserve to bleed out at my feet."

The coarse words took me by surprise and my eyes popped open.

So close, I could make out his features, although just barely. His face was what nightmares are made of.

Death.

He looked like death.

I was so startled by his appearance that I nearly missed what he said next.

"Lucky for you … someone of importance doesn't see you as a *complete* waste of skin." The words came out like he was smiling, amused by my shock, my fear.

"I—I don't understand."

He stepped toward his table again, grabbing the sheet of paper I'd seen him reading a moment ago. The one someone had written by hand. When he turned to me again, he said two words that made everything come into perspective.

"Our queen."

Evie.

She'd written the letter?

"And, if I've read your file correctly, one of your infractions involved an act that endangered her life," the Chancellor muttered, beginning to circle me several seconds before going on. "How gracious of her to submit such a … *moving* letter on your behalf."

My mind raced, stopping at every one of my infractions, everything I'd done that brought me to this point—facing my own death. I, according to our laws, had *earned* this.

But ... she saved me? After everything I'd done? After everything I cost her?

The Chancellor stopped in front of me again and I got another darkened glimpse of his face, as if the first hadn't been enough.

Stepping closer, he whispered. "Since the first time your name was mentioned in my presence, since I first came to know *what* you are ... I've been against letting you live," he confessed with so much conviction it surprised me he hadn't persuaded the others to side with him.

"You're a maverick," he added, annunciating every syllable as he spoke them into my ear, keeping these words between only he and I when adding, "And there's no place for mavericks in our realm."

I breathed deep, but never spoke to defend myself.

"Nevertheless," he sighed, stepping back and allowing the volume of his voice to carry again, "my peers have decided to vote on the matter, and to my dismay, you'll live to breathe another day."

Relief swept over me and I nearly passed out from breathing so deeply, staring at the blood beneath the soles of my shoes. The blood of a lycan who hadn't been so lucky. A lycan who didn't have connections to a compassionate, selfless girl named Evie.

Adding to the apology I owed her was a huge thank you.

"However," the Chancellor crooned, turning on his heels to face the rest of the Council as he addressed me once more, "your deeds will not go unpunished. Death is not the *only* way to settle your debt." He whirled, and I imagined a grin on that terrible face of his when he added, "I'm sure you've realized by now, we're quite a clever and innovative species."

Curiosity and dread both filled me at the same time.

"I'm sure you prepared your family for the possibility of never returning home after your trial, and you were right to do so."

That churning in my stomach was back as I stared, waited.

He stepped close again and, upon breathing one word, my knees nearly buckled.

"Exile."

Exile.

"Nicholas Stokes, by the power vested in me as Chancellor of this, our sacred Council, I hereby sentence you to a life of hardship among other criminals like yourself." The words left his mouth in slow, satisfied waves. "We may have agreed to let you leave this room alive, but … I'm sure you'll soon realize we've only prolonged the inevitable."

One of the guards that held me in place snickered and a chill rushed up my spine at the sound of it. This decision brought them all so much joy, knowing I'd suffer.

"Our verdict is just, and it is final," The Chancellor said in closing. "Good luck," he added with amusement. "You'll certainly need it."

Chapter Fourteen

Evie

"The Isle of Rayma."

Hilda casually chomped down on a grape after answering my question. I asked where Nick would be sent when the High Council banished him in a week. I got all the information I could from Beth when she called first thing this morning to inform me of the verdict, but the information she had was limited.

According to Hilda, this island was hidden somewhere in the Indian Ocean and had been heavily spelled with magic by a chosen few, powerful witches, including herself, many centuries ago. The worst of the worst dragons, lycans, and witches were put to death, but those who were deemed too dangerous to maintain a life among their clans and covens spent the remainder of their days on The Isle of Rayma.

Hilda stared. My eyes were fixed on the arm of the couch where I sat, but I could feel the heat of her gaze.

"If you ask me, you shouldn't *care* where they're taking him, only that he'll be far, far away," she added.

Over the past few days, she'd made it clear she didn't support my decision to write the High Council. In her opinion, Nick ought to lie in the bed he made. I begged to differ. Had he messed up? Absolutely. No one felt the effects of his actions more than me, but did I think he deserved to die because of it? Absolutely not.

However, I seemed to be alone in this opinion.

Not even Elise sided with me. And Dallas being one to abide by a very black and white, eye-for-an-eye moral code, I wasn't surprised he disagreed as well. Liam only held his tongue because we had already discussed it and he knew I felt very strongly about this.

It was quite possible I'd regret sparing Nick later down the road — if the day came that he'd fulfill his destiny — but for now, I felt compelled to do what was right. Not what was easy.

"I need air," I sighed, standing from my seat.

Even in this ginormous house, the walls could still close in on you in times like these.

"The books will still be waiting when you return," Hilda replied, making it clear that my unscheduled break wouldn't get me out of work. Even though *these* books had nothing to do with spells or sigils. Turned out Hilda was just as vigilant about me focusing on my *general* studies as she was about me grasping the concepts of magic.

I rushed down the carpeted, attic stairs and quickly crossed my bedroom, bursting out onto the attached balcony. Hopefully, the cool air would clear my head.

Nick being exiled was better than being put to death, but … he still stood to lose so much. Keeping him from his friends and family wouldn't make him a better person, wouldn't teach him how to control whatever changes had made him so irrational lately.

Listen to me … worried about him losing his family when, a short time ago he cost me my own.

Was I being stupid? Was it ridiculous to consider his *feelings and his loss … when he so callously ignored mine and went after Liam?*

The answer came swiftly and I didn't question it. The words were my mothers, and she lived by them. In situations like these, she'd say: "Never base your *reaction* off someone's action." To her, a person's true character was revealed when they either took or passed on an opportunity to seek revenge.

I didn't really care too much what *others* thought of the decision, but I made the choice I could live with. The one that wouldn't keep me up at night. The one that wouldn't make it hard to look at myself in the mirror after.

But he was still in trouble.

I leaned against the railing, staring out at the stark-white, snow-covered terrain below, at the twinkling flecks that shimmered in the early morning sunlight.

Still, I felt trapped, like I needed to break free.

Glancing over my shoulder to make sure no one was watching, I turned toward the trees lining the edge of our yard, the first line of foliage before stepping out into miles and miles of woods. And it hit me.

I wanted to run.

Not as my dragon … as my wolf.

There were no witnesses, so … I went for it. After setting my jewelry aside and draping my clothes over the rail, I shifted, leaping off the edge before I raced off into the woods of Seaton Falls on my own—no one watching, no one listening, no one worrying. It was just me.

Beth was right about the pain—about there being less of it each time. I'd transitioned into my wolf much more quickly now that I was familiar with it.

Mounds of snow flattened beneath my large paws as they burrowed deep with each step. Thick, dark fur kept me warm, and my keen vision gave me a clear view for miles ahead. I intended to keep running until I trekked at least twenty of them.

This, shifting into a wolf, hadn't been at all what I expected. I mean, yeah, the initial pain was something I could live without, but running so freely, transforming into such a formidable creature … it was invigorating.

My spirits rose quickly, thinking over Nick's fate. Exile. It was a bitter pill to swallow, but far better than the alternative. I had to let that be my comfort. Otherwise, the sadness, the finality of it all, would have consumed me.

The last interaction we had was amidst a dark, tragic time. No words were exchanged, but … I hated him then. Time and acceptance had been the only thing to change my heart, but it had indeed changed. I wanted nothing but the best for Nick, regardless of our history. Regardless of our inability to coexist without hurting one another.

There was some measure of regret that we hadn't been able to find common ground before now, but at least he knew I fought for him. So, if he wondered if I still hated him, hopefully that gave him his answer — he was forgiven.

At the sight of a swiftly moving shadow to my left, my head pivoted that way as I ran, only spotting trees and large stones that marked the terrain. Moving at such high speed sometimes made the peripheral view distorted while what lie ahead, directly in my line of site, was like watching the crisp, high-definition picture of a brand-new TV. I turned straight ahead again and thought of Roz of all people.

How would she cope with Nick being taken away?

I sensed something brewing between them quite some time ago. Mostly, the interest seemed to be on her side, but, hearing how Nick risked his freedom to bring her home ... I knew my assumption had been wrong.

He felt something for her, too.

I put myself in her shoes, trying to imagine what a mess I'd be if something were to happen to Liam. Even thinking about it made me sick to my stomach. I'd never survive it. She and I weren't friends. Actually, I was pretty sure she disliked me because of the past I shared with Nick, but I'd reach out to her anyway. Even if only to extend my condolences and to let her know I'd done everything in my power to help him. It might not make a difference, but I'd visit her anyway, once the wound of losing him wasn't so fresh.

Another shadow.

I turned again, scanning more carefully this time, lifting my eyes to the towering branches above me, but still ... nothing. I was alone out here.

I kept running, faster, harder, as a surge of adrenaline coursed through me.

There's nothing, Evie. If there was, you'd sense it.

Somewhere not too far away, I heard the rushing water of the falls and had my bearings once again. My internal compass was thrown off during the momentary bout of panic, making me aware of how important it is to stay focused. I sniffed the air, detecting hints of pine and moss despite the cold. Willing myself to relax, I took in the beauty around me as a thought set in.

I was equally as fond of my wolf as I was my dragon.

Another difference between *this* me and the *old* me.

I'd taken a step as the story Liam shared on the rooftop came back to me. However, I didn't get to revel in the sweetness of how we came to be. This thought, and the short-lived comfort that accompanied it, were stolen from me the moment I grasped on to them.

The peace I found was snatched away at the feel of a powerful bite to my hind leg. Pain seared the limb and spread like venom, filling me completely. I cried out and it was a blood-curdling sound, one that ricocheted off every tree for miles before boomeranging back to my ears.

I fell onto my side, unable to move forward. I reached toward the wound with hands, not paws. I'd begun to shift back to my human form. Warm stickiness met my fingertips. Blood. Lots and lots of blood. My fingers traveled lower as I clenched my eyes tight when tears spilled from them. A thin stick jutted out from my flesh and I willed myself to look, forcing my senses to align—sight, touch. Focusing through the pain, reality came flooding in.

There was no bite.

There was only an arrow.

Someone was out there.

Afraid, naked, I slinked across the snow-covered ground until I could brace myself against a nearby tree, my eyes darting in every direction. I saw no one, but the evidence of not being alone was sticking out of my leg. It was hard to hear the sounds around thanks to my ragged breathing. I couldn't control it. Whether the cause was fear or agony … I was losing it. My hands shook and I panicked, accepting one glaring fact…

I'd never felt more powerless in my entire life.

A branch snapped, then another, and despite my eyes revealing nothing, I knew I was surrounded. That's when I felt it—the thin, invisible thread that linked me to Liam vibrated. If he hadn't *already* felt the twinge, he would in a second. But I didn't want that, didn't want him walking into … *whatever* this was.

Unaware.

Unprepared.

Warm air cascaded over my lip as I breathed deeply, thought quickly, scrambling to access the rational side of my brain despite my senses betraying me as I huddled.

Think, Evie. Think.

It started as one thought and it linked to another. I followed each prompt blindly, knowing I had no other plan. Mustering as much courage as I could, I wandered inside Liam's head, doing all I could to hide the distress in my tone.

"Sorry about that," I chirped. *"I went out for a run and tripped. Everything's fine,"* I lied, watching as red streams trailed down my leg before staining the surrounding snow.

"You're sure everything's okay? … Because it sure doesn't feel like it."

He must have still felt me, because of the pain. More tears moved down my cheeks as I struggled to cast up a veil between myself and him. It was the only way to block him out, the only way to keep him from coming to me.

"Mmm hmm. Everything's all good. I'll be home in a few."

There were a few seconds of silence on Liam's end as another branch snapped to my right.

"Hurry back," he said gravely. The very next second, I forced myself out, knowing that if I lingered in his thoughts too long, he'd see through the lie I'd just told to keep him out of harm's way.

My cheeks puffed out when I breathed deep, glancing down at my leg again, taking in the sight of the weapon used against me by an unknown assailant. I'd heal, but only if I could get this thing out.

Another deep breath as time wound down. I could feel them closing in on me, whoever watched from afar. I gripped the shaft, and after accepting that this was the only way, I yanked the arrowhead back through my leg, taking with it chunks of my flesh.

I cried out again. Long and desperate as I slumped onto my side. I clutched the wound, but it did nothing to quench the pain. It was then, in the haze of agony and disbelief, that I saw it—a ripple in the air, similar to heat rising off pavement on a scorching hot day. Only, last I checked, we had single-digit temperatures across Michigan today.

Suddenly sober and alert, I panted, following the breach in a perfect circle, roughly a few hundred feet in diameter with me at the center. It was closing in, darkening as the sound of snow crunching beneath the boots of a hundred or more. Slowly, as I focused, figures began to emerge from the distortion.

There were so many of them. All staring. All with malice in their eyes. Several carried bows and arrows, and other various weapons, but there was no sign of which was responsible for my injury.

They observed me like an animal on exhibit. I covered myself, squeezing tight into a ball as much as I could to hide my bare flesh from them. I studied each face, maybe searching for one I might know, but these men were all strangers to me. Large, ominous strangers.

Among them were a few women dressed in familiar garb. I recognized them as witches right away, and likely the cause of the invisibility cloak that protected their group a moment ago. All witches, Hilda aside, chose the macabre attire and most had a distinguishable scent. Or, rather, their *magic* did. The ones I'd taken down at the facility wreaked like these did, but Hilda's scent always reminded me of fresh herbs.

Hilda ... I should have stayed with her, should have just ... finished my lesson.

More tears.

More regret.

I was terrified.

The tight formation of lycans was impenetrable. I'd never be able to break through, not with my leg injured. And I could try to fly away, but they'd probably shoot me with another arrow if they sensed I attempted to call up my dragon.

I was trapped.

There was a sinister charge to the air, unlike anything I'd ever felt before. It was a strange mixture of dread, oppression, and evil. The weight of it was stifling.

A near-constant, chilled breeze had whipped through the woods all morning, but now, as the seconds ticked past, it was as though we existed in a cone of silence, cut off from the rest of the world as I turned toward another set of footsteps. These were slow, calculated, and for reasons unknown, they terrified me.

"Step aside."

The words, spoken in an impossibly deep baritone and laced with a thick accent I didn't immediately recognize, shook me to my core as I searched for whoever grumbled them. With military precision, the circle parted like the Red Sea. I blinked and breathed wildly, desperate to know who was coming forward. As the crowd moved and shifted positions, I caught sight of something.

A robe—long, dark fabric that dragged the snow as he crossed it.

As he came closer, another lycan flanked him to the left, one who stuck close, leading me to guess he must have been second in command. My gaze rose to take in the sheer size of him, this man who issued the command that moved his men almost instantly. There were only two things that inspired that sort of obedience, either loyalty or fear.

I took a guess at which of the two motivated the lycans that surrounded me.

The buckles of his boots rattled as he moved closer, only stopping when he stood within arm's reach. I trembled, but did all I could to hide how inferior I felt.

"Get up," he seethed, his lips barely moving with the words.

A hard stare hadn't left me since I first spotted him. That stare was filled with hatred that defied reason. After all, we were strangers.

"Get ... *up!*" he boomed. At the sound of it, birds that perched in surrounding trees fled in a dark, squawking cloud.

Oh, how I wished I could have taken flight with them.

The bloody leg throbbed beneath my weight. It was with the aid of the tree I sought refuge beside that I was able to stand. My arms were all I had to shield my nakedness from the crowd, from the hungry eyes that did little to conceal the brood's thoughts.

Breath puffed from the man's nostrils and I forced my gaze to stay trained on his, doing all I could to ignore how his protégé ogled with little discretion. I gritted my teeth and bridled the urge to gouge out his eyes with my fingernails.

My senses aligned, taking note of the keen power struggle that ignited between myself and the robed one the moment I was on my feet; the moment we were eye to eye. I recognized it right away as supernatural. It was my wolf who'd risen up against his, threatening to bear her teeth. There was no doubt in my mind he felt it too.

Whoever he was.

The features of his thin, stoic face were partially hidden behind a dark mustache and goatee. Beneath a black, brimmed hat, hair the same inky black fell well past his shoulders. I'd never seen eyes like his — so cold and unfeeling.

Like he was dead inside. These were the eyes of a madman.

He leaned closer and I stiffened, holding my breath as he sniffed me, like the animal I sensed him to be. I felt violated, *angry*, being forced to stand before them like this.

"Well, what have we here?" A sinister grin spread across his thin lips. "It appears my little informant, and one very gullible Council guard, weren't wrong after all. Not only is Seaton Falls among the many clans withholding a portion of the tariff … they've managed to keep quite a few pertinent secrets from me as well."

At those words, at the sense of entitlement laced within them, awareness filled my senses. I knew exactly who he was.

He had a name — Sebastian De Vincenzo — but to most, he was simply known as the Sovereign.

He turned, facing the one I wanted to blind. Realizing his protégé's attention was focused solely on me, on my nude body, Sebastian cleared his throat before calling him by name.

"Easy now, Blaise," he snickered. "You may have bitten off more than you can chew with this one. She's no ordinary wolf." There were traces of a warning in the statement.

A low rumble in Blaise's chest signaled my wolf to respond in kind. She, nor I, were particularly fond of him. At the sound of her issuing a warning that came from within my chest, he smiled behind dampened lips.

"You have no idea who this lovely specimen is, or what she's capable of," the caped one warned.

"Maybe not … but I wouldn't mind getting better acquainted." Blaise took a step closer before Sebastian placed a hand to his chest, stopping him in his tracks.

"Easy now," Sebastian warned again.

I got the impression he spent quite a bit of time correcting this one's waywardness. With what little patience he seemed to have, I gathered they must have been close for him to put up with it. Maybe family.

"But you know I have a thing for the feisty ones," Blaise countered, narrowing his gaze toward me.

The crowd laughed and here I stood, on display, exposed. It would've been too much to expect even *one* to show mercy, to offer a jacket, a shirt. Listening to them, the cackling as a barrage of filthy comments flew from their mouths, I shrank into myself, wishing I could just … disappear.

Humiliated.

I felt humiliated.

"Settle down," Sebastian ordered, holding back a smile as he feigned decency. "There was once a time a man could lose his head for disrespecting this particular lycan," he grimaced, taking a step closer and another whiff of me. "Or … do you identify as dragon?" The question was laced with sarcasm as he tapped one wiry finger to his lips.

"…Dragon." The word left Blaise's mouth with just enough intrigue to suggest he hadn't sensed it before. "She's a hybrid."

I didn't like that this discovery seemed to only pique his interest.

Sebastian paced—slow, intentional steps as our eyes locked. When he stopped in front of me, the corners of his mouth tugged up. And at his sudden movement, I flinched, fearing he'd strike me or worse, but … to my surprise, I was wrong.

More laughter rang out—in part due to my reaction, in part due to the show Sebastian made of bowing before me. A blatant gesture, meant to mock my family's rank, my inherent title.

Still bent at his waist, he spoke, further shaming me with the words that followed.

"Gentlemen, behold. I present to you ... the mighty queen of the Bahir Dar kingdom."

My chest heaved with labored breaths, eyes stung with tears.

Some whispered, questioning whether they heard correctly. Some laughed, likely because nothing about me must have seemed very regal or stately at the moment.

"Settle down," he beckoned as his men roared. "I know what many of you are thinking." Those wiry fingers of his laced behind his back as his large boots made tracks in the snow. "How is this possible?"

The crowd was silent as he stopped before me again, that cold stare locked. "For many, *many* reasons ... this is an excellent question," he nodded. "How *is* this possible?"

A trimmer ripped through me, but I held my composure.

"Someone did this," he smiled, nearly whispering. But the expression soon evaporated as that deafening baritone shook the earth beneath my feet.

"Who had the unmitigated gall to defy my commandment?" he yelled.

No one spoke. No one moved. Maybe they, too, held their breath like I did.

A long, aquiline nose came mere inches from my own as he invaded my space, pierced the delicate cone of safety around me.

"Death," he whispered, sending the word scurrying over my flesh like a living, breathing thing. "Death awaits whoever did this."

I wanted to take a step back, but, at the feel of bark against my skin, I knew I was trapped.

Heat spiked through my limbs, warming my neck and face, probably reddening them as I continued to stare. The dread and evil I sensed were warranted. And now, I understood why my wolf was on edge.

"What do we do with her?" Blaise asked.

Sebastian thought for a moment. "Well … in accordance with lycan law, users of restorative magic are to be executed. And their subjects," he added, pointing toward me as his eyes gleamed with delight, "are mine for the taking, but … seeing as how I have no use for the girl, I suppose she'll be all yours."

Blaise couldn't have asked for a more satisfying answer. That disgusting grin was back. "And I happily accept your gift, Father."

Father. Now I understood.

The first step Blaise took in my direction was his last. His eyes rose to the sky just as the atmosphere above thundered. A streak of fire barreled toward us all, the site of which sent most scattering into the surrounding woods.

The ground quaked as a plume of snow rose several feet into the air, turning to steam in the heat of bright flames. My chest hammered, a fear-induced spike in heartrate. Not the same sense of fear that caused the others to flee as the meteor-like mass descended upon us.

No ... I was afraid because a dark tattoo inked the spine of the one who just landed on the ground before me, his knee and fist embedded in the dirt.

Without turning to face me, without asking who these people were, or why there was so much blood, Liam said one word that rolled from his throat like the calm before the storm.

"...Run."

I knew he meant well, but I had no intentions on following his order. Leaving him here was simply not an option.

"Careful, dragon. That advice will get you *both* killed," Sebastian grinned.

The next second, my waist was seized by one of his henchmen. In his grasp, I struggled to keep myself covered, fighting to maintain the last ounce of dignity this ordeal hadn't yet stripped away. The ongoing scuffle between myself and the brute had Liam breathing actual smoke from his nostrils as he panted, anger brimming from his core.

His jaw gritted, causing his words to come out hard, bitter. "Take your hands off her ... *now*."

Detecting the challenge in Liam's tone, the henchman tightened his hold, making a show of his strength when he gripped my arms and aimed to pry them away. He meant to expose me even more than I already was, most likely to further embarrass me, to show Liam who was in charge.

But, unfortunately for the lycan, Liam was in no mood for second warnings.

In a cloud of snow and fire, he was upon us. A violent snap and the restricting embrace of the henchman went limp. Then, the distinct thud of a body hitting the ground. Liam stood before me, clutching me as his warmth pressed to my chest, the solid mass of his body shielded me from the prying eyes of a hundred men.

Sebastian stepped forward, staring at his fallen soldier lying at Liam's feet. There was a brief flash of disappointment just before his gaze rose again. It settled on Liam. As Sebastian glared, I felt hollow inside when awareness filled his expression.

With one word, it became clear these two had history.

"Reaper," he seethed. "I should have guessed." Those long, fingers of his balled into tight fists at his sides. "Seems we have ourselves in quite the conundrum."

Liam ignored the solemn greeting and made a demand. "I won't discuss a thing until she's clothed."

Behind Sebastian, Blaise's eyes narrowed into slits as he glared.

A long, disinterested breath puffed from Sebastian's mouth and he turned, snapping his fingers at a lycan off to his left. "Shirt," he sighed.

Without delay, the lycan removed his black tee and placed it in Sebastian's hand. At the sight of the dark fabric soaring through the air when he tossed it, my heart leapt. With only a glance over his shoulder, Liam caught the covering and handed it over, spreading his wings the next second to create a shield between me and the strangers. Slipping it over my head, I was painfully aware of there not being much material, but at least I was covered. When I finished, Liam passed a long, hard stare my way ... and it made my heart race.

"Whatever happens, I need you to promise me you won't look back. I want you to promise me you're gonna run until you can't anymore."

What was he ... what was he saying?

There was no time to answer.

"Enough, dragon."

My hand warmed when Liam took it into his for the fraction of a second—a fleeting moment that made me grateful, and sad, and afraid all at once. Letting my fingers slip from his grasp, he turned toward the Sovereign and his army once again, wearing a disquieted expression I wished I could forget.

Because the sight of it made it feel like my heart was breaking.

Impressively broad wings retracted and disappeared beneath tanned skin. I discreetly placed a hand on his waist, taking slow steps until my chest was flush to his back, needing to be close as fear nearly strangled me to death.

"Unless you're a ghost, I suppose it's safe to say the report of my men was false. Last I heard, you were in pieces on the battlefield after the Lunar War." Sebastian paused to chuckle. "In fact, all this time, I was under the impression the set of wings hanging over my mantle belonged to you, the infamous Reaper." The last syllable dragged a bit as he scanned Liam.

"Guess you heard wrong," was all he said back, glancing to each side, making sure none of Sebastian's men had advanced toward us.

"Hmm ... and I supposed I ought to hunt down the man who sold them to me, and demand he return the $2.7 million I paid for them, plus interest, but ... it's neither here nor there," he shrugged.

That figure ... nearly three million dollars, it put into perspective the price Liam's reputation had put on his head. At the thought of it, I felt sick to my stomach.

"Besides, there's not much to fret about ... seeing as how I've stumbled upon something much more valuable today." His eyes landed on me, prompting my heart to race again as he stepped forward.

In response, heat rose from Liam's skin and I heard the crackle of embers bursting just beneath the surface. Sebastian heeded the silent warning with a grin.

"You're really going to make this harder than it has to be?" he asked. "By law, she is now a prisoner of my kingdom. It doesn't matter who she is, or who *you* are, rules are rules," he smiled. "And, seeing as how you were foolish enough to resurrect her, I'll bleed you to death right where you stand, dragon."

My brow quirked at those words. He thought Liam was to blame for my being alive. And, in true Liam fashion, he didn't correct that assumption. If I had to guess, he was well aware of the consequences that coincided with restorative magic. As Hilda once shared, and as the Sovereign reminded me today, this practice was punishable by death.

Sebastian took another step, and while Liam's attention was focused there, I was snatched from behind, lifted off the ground by a set of powerful arms. They squeezed until I couldn't get air into my lungs. I gasped, clawing at the attacker, but wasn't strong enough to break free.

Liam started in my direction, but halted when the sharp point of Blaise's knife pressed to his jugular. A trickle of blood raced toward his collar bone, and in that moment, as I focused on that red streak, the last grain of hope I clung to slipped through my fingers.

We were outnumbered, out of moves, out of time.

"I'm so sorry," I told him, slipping into his thoughts to get this out while I still could. *"I tried to keep you away from here."*

I never wanted this. Never wanted him to wind up hurt because of me.

He didn't waste time accepting my apology or saying things to make me feel better. Instead, he spoke from his heart, stating the one thing that mattered, what was most important.

"I love you."

I'd barely gotten a syllable out in response when a sudden turn of events stole my chance. Two large wings extended from Liam's back and the force of it knocked Blaise back several feet. While he scrambled to right himself, Liam turned the tables, switching roles, locking an arm around Blaise's neck. I wanted him to squeeze, wanted him to end his life right then and there, but … he didn't.

Instead he spoke.

"Let her go, and I'll let your son live." The offer was aimed at Sebastian, but Liam's eyes never left mine.

A tear spilled over my lower lid and I understood why he hadn't just finished Blaise off. He needed leverage, needed to create a cushion of time where none existed.

"Liam, no …"

He ignored me, forced me out as he stated his terms to Sebastian. "Let her go and I'll come with you without a fight."

I wanted to scream. Wanted to fall apart right then and there, but I was frozen in shock. How had it come to this?

Liam continued to hold my gaze as he sweetened the pot for Sebastian.

"I'm nearly as valuable a trophy as she is," he explained. "But … you and I both know I'm worth more to you," he went on, adding, "especially if you sell me off in pieces—my wings, my head."

The gruesome image he inflicted made my eyes slam shut, made my stomach swirl, nearly made me vomit. In a state of sheer disbelief, I tried to wake myself up from this nightmare.

"I'm willing to bet I can even get a pretty penny for locks of your hair," Sebastian remarked, speaking with the same chilled indifference despite the grave subject matter. "Or perhaps I might flay off your tattoos, seal them in jars, sell them individually."

Liam remained stone-faced, like this wasn't his life he bargained with. Like Sebastian wouldn't make good on all these promises and more.

I lost it. The contents of my stomach poured out into the snow as the henchman kept me locked in. A few on the outskirts laughed, of course, because that's what seemed to amuse this brood—the anguish of others, whether it be physical or, in my case, emotional.

Sebastian considered Liam's offer, tapping his chin while he thought. "I suppose I could agree to this if you're also willing to give up the name of the witches who assisted you with the spell."

"They're dead. The former three who were linked to this town's clan were the only others involved," Liam said convincingly. "Their names were Scarlet, Marin, and Lilith."

The lie seemed to hold. Sebastian was thoughtful for a moment.

"If you try anything ... *anything,* dragon ... I promise you that, on this day, Lake Superior will run red with your blood."

Liam spoke with so much bravery and boundless conviction. "If you let her go, I won't fight," he reiterated. "You have my word."

Sebastian was silent again. Eventually, a half-satisfied sigh left his mouth as he stared down on his son locked in a chokehold.

"Fine." His gaze shifted to the one who captured me. With a nod and a few short words, I was free.

I backed up, and much to Liam's dismay, I didn't run. I couldn't. I was frozen, knowing this could have very well been the last time we'd ever be face-to-face.

And ... I couldn't leave.

"Run, Evangeline!" he demanded, his voice booming a harshness I knew wasn't meant for me. He hadn't released Blaise yet, and likely wouldn't until I was out of sight, but ... my feet wouldn't move.

"Now!" he growled.

I back up, feeling the bark of a tree against my fingertips as I stumbled past it, barefoot. When I took another step, Liam nodded, making it clear he was pleased that I finally followed his orders, seemingly unaware of what this all meant for him. I clung to that last fleeting moment we stared, feeling robbed of physical contact, a chance to embrace him, kiss him.

Something …

My back was to the army now as I sprinted away like my warrior had commanded me to do. I went into his thoughts while I still could.

"I'll come for you," I promised. *"No matter what, I'll come for you."*

I expected to be scolded for even considering it, expected to argue all the reasons I was going to go over his head and do what I wanted anyway, but … there was no answer. Glancing back over my shoulder, I understood why.

Two of the Sovereign's witches rushed him, blowing a vibrant, purple powder into the air, letting it surround him. Within a fraction of a second, the light slipped from his eyes, his arms went limp, and his body slumped to the snow.

My feet continued ahead, but I was moving on autopilot as hopelessness ravished me like a predator.

For the first time in a long time, I was completely alone.

Chapter Fifteen

Evie

I ran in zigzags through the woods for hours, sensing Sebastian's soldiers on my heels each time I slowed.

Keep moving.

Keep moving.

You have to stay alive to save him.

Despite Liam's deal, it was obvious Sebastian simply couldn't pass up the chance to have us both. Still, the diversion had given me somewhat of a lead.

The sun was gone, leaving my wolf to race through the darkness by moonlight as I clutched the t-shirt Liam procured for me in my teeth. This chase was wasting valuable time, time I should have been searching for Liam. Time that gave Sebastian an opportunity to put hundreds of miles between us. But I couldn't focus on that, not on the fact that I had no idea where Sebastian intended to take him, couldn't focus on the fact that I was one person against an entire army. Neither of those things would stop me from trying. Neither would stop me from laying down my life in the process.

Going home was out of the question. With the lycans on my trail, I'd lead them straight to Elise, Hilda, and Dallas. I was on my own.

I slowed again, this time coming to a stop. I held my breath and listened, sniffed the icy air.

Nothing.

It seemed they had finally ended their pursuit.

I was painfully aware of time. It'd become a solid, tangible ball that sat in the pit of my stomach. Yes, time had suddenly become my enemy.

While I could, I shifted back to my human form and removed the shirt from my teeth, sliding it over my head. I'd shift into my dragon to search for a place to sleep. The only reason I hadn't done so earlier was because I wanted the

Sovereign's henchmen to have something to follow, something that would lead them as far away from my home as possible. So, I gave them paw prints, pawprints they'd see disappear here if they were still on the hunt, because I burst from the snow with flames engulfing me.

I was airborne and finally out of danger. For the moment anyway. I would, after all, be sleeping outside tonight, in the open, vulnerable. But I didn't even consider it an inconvenience. I'd do whatever it took to save him.

Circling the woods several times, I thought of a few places to hunker down, including the old, abandoned warehouse where I'd been to a party once. But then, that knot in my stomach ticked loud within me.

Tick tock.

Tick tock.

Tick tock.

I had to keep moving, had to find him.

When I landed, I had no real plan, only a destination. I needed help, direction, the guidance of someone who might be able to give at least *some* insight.

Baz … he was the only one I could think of.

A private, back entrance to the library led to the winding staircase of stone. I tugged at the shirt I wore, the only thing that covered me, and I knew what a pitiful sight I must be— half naked, dirty, and bloody. My bare feet were damp with melted snow, but at least gave me the advantage of being completely silent as I ascended, listening for signs that the Sovereign or his men had beat me there.

There was no noise in the dark abyss that awaited me at the foot of the stairs. Only the sound of dripping water as it echoed from some unseen source. There were torches lit, but far fewer with there being no meetings scheduled tonight. My heart raced with each step and I paused at the last, staring across the large, empty room.

Tick tock.

Tick tock.

There was no time for the childish fear that crept up within me, fear of the dark, fear of the unknown. I had too much at stake.

I stepped down and crossed the room, heading for the door behind the Elder's table. I'd seen them come from behind it when I attended a meeting, but had no idea what lie across that threshold.

Should I knock? Should I simply barge in?

I rounded the table, and just as I lifted my hand to bang against the dark, thick wood…

"Can I help you?"

I turned at the sound of Baz's gravelly voice as he emerged from the shadows, startling me. With a clear view of my face, recognition came shortly thereafter, prompting him to take quick steps forward.

"Evangeline?"

Panic swathed the sound of my name when he called out, only now confirming that it was, in fact, me. I couldn't blame him for not believing his eyes, given my appearance.

"What's happened? Are you injured?" he asked, gawking at the mix of blood and dirt that covered my legs, searching for a wound that had long-since healed.

"I'm fine—I'm fine," I panted, struggling to breathe after he scared me half to death. "But Liam isn't," I added in a panic, feeling my hands begin to shake as those words caused reality to set in.

A gentle touch went to my shoulder. "Slow down," Baz crooned. "Tell me what's happened."

"They took him!"

He lowered his hood and gazed at me with confusion in those milky-white eyes of his.

"Who?" he asked with a compassion-laden tone, far different from that with which I heard him address others.

Every limb shivered with terror at the thought of losing Liam.

My voice was quiet and strained when I uttered the name of the man who'd taken the most important thing in this world from me. "Sebastian."

Baz froze like a deer in headlights. Processing the full breadth of this information, his hand fell away. His eyes wandered back to mine.

"When was this?"

I shrugged, scrambling for numbers, clues as to how long they kept me there, surrounded in the woods, how long I'd been running.

"Hours," I choked out, feeling warm streaks of liquid race down my cheeks. "It's been hours."

They could have been anywhere by now.

Anywhere.

Baz suddenly came to his senses and reached to console me again when I slumped against the wall, feeling like Earth was upside down. I suppose, for me, it was.

"How many were with him?" was the next question.

I forced myself to see through the haze of emotion to answer. "At least a hundred. And there were witches." I thought of how the brigade seemed to appear out of thin air and added, "*Powerful* witches."

Baz was silent as he thought. "I'll get my best men on this," he promised. "By sunrise, they'll start out to—"

"No."

At the sound of my voice, Baz fell silent, questioning me with his eyes. "No?"

While the ordeal in the woods had left me rattled, I paid attention to details. My mother—in one of her "stranger danger" talks when I was a kid—taught me to always be aware of my surroundings, to pay special attention to what was done and said in any instance that I felt my safety was threatened. Coming face-to-face with the Sovereign definitely qualified. As he spoke, certain statements stuck with me.

"No," I repeated. "Your guards have been compromised. I have no clue which one or how many, but I heard it with my own ears."

Baz seemed to stop breathing as he listened. "Are you ... are you sure?"

I nodded. "Yes. He knew I was here because of *'an informant'*, and the report of *'a gullible guard'* who I'm guessing contacted him after Nick's trial yesterday, sharing whatever information he gathered."

Baz shrank back a bit as his eyes searched the stone floor. "Then ... he knows *everything*."

I hated being the bearer of bad news, but we were *surrounded* with bad. Better to be aware than ignorant, vulnerable.

"So, we have to do this another way," I asserted, feeling my dragon step forth, clearing some of the emotional haze my human form was drowning in.

Baz lifted his eyes to mine again. "What other way is there?"

I swallowed hard and offered the only idea I had. "I'm going after him myself."

An incredulous expression graced Baz's face. "That's absurd. You can't—"

Cutting him off, I corrected the statement I hadn't let him complete. "I can and I will ... I have to."

He blinked several times, and searching for a way to stall, placed his hand on my shoulder again. "You need to rest. I'll have Gadreal draw you a bath. She'll also conjure clothing for you, and — "

"I don't have that kind of time," I snapped.

I couldn't expect anyone else to understand the urgency that ate me alive inside. There were gruesome images embedded in my mind. Images of that madman tearing pieces off Liam just for the fun of it, torturing him for amusement until he inevitably ended his life.

My resolve hardened and I swiped away a tear.

"I'm doing this," I made clear. "With or without anyone's blessing."

Baz passed me a knowing glance, understanding I couldn't be swayed, and then spoke a few last words.

"Then, if you cannot be reasoned with," he began, "I hope you understand why I have to take matters into my own hands."

Confusion caused my brow to tense just before a prick in the side of my neck sent me staggering. My legs ... they felt like jelly beneath me. The room turned dark, and within seconds, my eyes were fixed on the ceiling.

Baz hovered above, as did one of his witches, and then ... I succumbed to a deep well of darkness.

***

No traces of dirt and blood. My skin and hair both felt clean as I touched my head, feeling the fog beginning to lift.

Neither the clothes nor the shoes I wore were my own, but they fit. Being immune to magic, I guessed someone had actually taken the time to bathe me. Then, when they were done, dressed me in clothes that had been conjured. Just like Baz said they would.

I sat up with a gasp, suddenly aware of my unfamiliar surroundings. The elegant room was decked from floor to ceiling with rich, mahogany wood and deep-crimson fabrics trimmed in gold. A large bed topped with a pillow-soft mattress swallowed me whole, making my already weak limbs nearly useless as I scooted to the edge.

Where was I?

How long had I been out?

How long had I been out … that question made me frantic.

Tick tock.

Tick tock.

I raced to the door and pulled it toward me. Stepping out into a dimly lit hallway, I pressed a palm to my head, trying to get my bearings. The stone walls, torches, and dark fabrics made it feel like I'd stepped back in time, into a Medieval castle.

Stone walls … torches … the Elder's chamber.

I remembered.

Faint voices murmured from the left. I took a step that way. I needed to find a way out of here without anyone seeing, without them knocking me out again, without them costing me more time.

I pressed my ear to the door and listened harder, noting one of the voices was female.

"According to our laws," she declared, "any clan member can take it upon him or herself to bypass local sects of government to seek aid from the Sovereign should he or she feel justice is being obstructed, or if there's suspicion that local government has been compromised."

"Please, Mrs. Stokes, enlighten us as to how, in your opinion, we have been compromised?" The one who asked wasn't Baz, but his voice was similar in tone and depth.

Mrs. Stokes ... *she* was the informant Sebastian spoke of? She'd all but admitted it; however, I still couldn't conceive anyone in this town doing such a thing. Seeing as how they all seemed so well aware of the Sovereign's agenda.

"I've got reason to believe the Elders, the Council as a whole, have all conspired to overthrow the Sovereign," she rebutted. There was only false confidence in her tone, proving that not even *she* believed her excuse would hold up.

"And—"

When she tried to continue, the man interjected, his words dripping with disgust.

"Oh, please, Mrs. Stokes. Save your lies," he boomed. "No one here is ignorant enough to believe you actually *support* the views of Sebastian De Vincenzo. Just admit you willingly endangered your clan to spare the life of that disgraceful boy of yours."

"Disgraceful?" she seethed. "What's disgraceful is your negligible plan to seat a *dragon* in the throne. As if their kind has ever been suitable to rule."

The sound of hollow wood scraping stone hit my ears — a chair being scooted back as someone stood.

"Mind your tongue, woman," Baz boomed. "I'll not have you speak of *your* future queen in this manner."

"She's got you all blind," Mrs. Stokes said incredulously, sounding like a woman who believed the entire world had gone crazy around her.

The echo of footsteps seeped through the door as I listened. She was coming closer, I could tell by how the volume and clarity of her voice increased when she spoke again.

"I'll have you know I took *great* pride sharing your plan with the Sovereign," she said, spouting a sinister chuckle right after. "The moment I went to that girl's parents and they had no *clue* who or what I was talking about … I knew you all and your witches had your hands all over this, knew I couldn't trust any of you," she added. "So, I did some digging myself, went through Nick's things and found notebook upon notebook of research and information, most of which centered around her — this … child you're reverencing as queen."

The Elders said nothing, just sat in silence while Mrs. Stokes' divulged more.

"My son may not have known who or what she was, but I did. Right away," she added. "And I knew it would've taken restorative magic to bring her back."

The other lycan, a member of the Council who'd lingered after Nick's trial I guessed, chuffed a long breath before asking a question. "And you truly believe our current ruler is more fit to meet the needs of our people than Evangeline?"

Without hesitation, Mrs. Stokes replied. "I'd pledge my allegiance to a lycan over a dragon any day. Hybrid or not, she's still one of *them*."

And there it was. Losing Nick, coupled with her prejudices against me, against dragons in general, had spearheaded a chain reaction. A chain reaction that resulted in Liam being taken.

This was all her fault. It was clear to me now. She, in her ignorance, in her grief, had called that tyrant here and gave up all our secrets.

"You foolish, *foolish* woman," Baz murmured.

I was done listening, done wasting time.

I burst through the door, no longer content to wait until they ironed out their spat. To me, it mattered very little how we ended up here. What mattered was what we did next.

The other lycan stood as I walked toward them. Baz sputtered, most likely searching for an explanation as to why he drugged me, but I wasn't interested, accepting the impromptu plan that developed along the way.

"I need Nick," I blurted, fully aware of his mother's eyes glued to me. "Since your guards can't be trusted, and because I'll be up against so many, I need his help."

Confusion crossed Baz's face. I knew what he was thinking, knew what *Liam* would be thinking if he'd been present to hear. He'd think I was crazy to suggest I embark on this journey with Nick—nature's kryptonite—but I think I made it clear how far I'd go. There were no limits when it came to Liam.

When my request wasn't immediately denied, Mrs. Stokes volleyed frantic glances back and forth between me and the two lycans. Her expression was riddled with desperation when she spoke, addressing me directly instead of the Council.

"Are you really this selfish?" she seethed. "Do you realize what you're asking? Do you have any idea the danger you'd be putting Nick in? He's not some pawn in your halfcocked plan. You can't just volunteer him at will simply because *you* don't value his life."

My fists clenched at my sides, but I said nothing. She had no idea how wrong she was; no idea how much I did, in fact, value Nick's life. Despite our differences, I'd willingly intervened when almost everyone else wanted him dead. It was on the tip of my tongue to share these thoughts and more, but I refrained.

I couldn't even look at her, knowing she would have loved having an excuse to launch a verbal attack. Doing so would've shifted the direction of the conversation and stall my effort to get to Liam. Nothing was worth that—not even the chance to put this woman in her place.

Ignoring Mrs. Stokes' protest, Baz glanced toward his comrade and stammered a few unintelligible syllables before speaking up.

"We, myself and the Chancellor, will need to discuss this with the others," he forced out, clearly stalling. I already sensed the hard *'no'* on his lips, although he hadn't said it. Stating that he needed to talk it over with the Council was merely to come up with a way to dismiss my idea, I was sure.

The Chancellor began sizing me up, and then addressed me for the first time. "Are you suggesting that you and Nicholas set out to retrieve this ... Liam that you speak of ... on your own?"

He doubted we were capable. That was clear. However, I didn't care a whole lot about his opinion.

So, with my shoulders squared, I nodded. "Absolutely."

There was a keen sense of Mrs. Stokes' eyes boring a hole through me, but I didn't shift my gaze, didn't acknowledge her.

Baz leaned in to whisper something to the Chancellor. Whatever he said, it brought a smile to the Chancellor's face.

"Is that so?" he crooned, offering Baz a surprised grin. "Reaper ... "

The name *Liam* he didn't recognize, but *Reaper* had definitely rung a bell. Hearing it seemed to have gotten Mrs.

Stokes' attention as well. I guessed she had a firmer grasp on supernatural history than the rest of this town seemed to.

The Chancellor stared at me long and hard. I held his gaze, making sure he knew I wouldn't back down on this. If they denied me Nick, I'd go on my own.

Bottom Line.

When a response didn't come soon enough for her liking, Mrs. Stokes interjected. "You couldn't *possibly* be considering the idea of sending my son to die beside this girl."

A thundering, "Silence, woman!" made my ears ring when the Chancellor yelled. His gaze lingered on her and it was clear his patience with her was running thin.

"I'll have you know," he stated in a much calmer manner, "had it not been for *'this girl'*, your worthless son would be smeared on the sole of my boot! So, if I were you, I would be careful to show some respect."

After a lengthy stare-down, the Chancellor turned from Mrs. Stokes and came closer, the hint of a smirk set on his lips. Three words fell from them and I exhaled with relief.

"I'll allow it."

"But, sir," Baz pleaded.

"Stop sniveling," the Chancellor barked back. "You and the *rest* of Seaton Falls ought to be embracing the fact that we've been graced with a future queen with such … poise, such … integrity."

With that same smirk, he walked a slow circle around me. "It's been quite some time since our people have had a ruler so fearless, one willing to lay down their life for the sake of another."

I breathed deep when he faced me again.

"Your bravery might just exceed your father's," the Chancellor added with a reserved smile as my expression went slack.

"You … you knew my father?"

His chin dipped with a nod. "We met on several occasions," he shared. "King Noah was a true man of valor."

My heart warmed. "Thank you."

Behind him, Baz lowered his head, most likely thinking of all the reasons this was a terrible idea, thinking of all the things that could go wrong, including Nick being triggered while we were gone. I thought of these things, too, but … the difference was … none of the possible outcomes that came to mind were worse than losing Liam.

Period.

"Every kingdom is only as strong as its leader, its foundation. So, it is my belief that, when you return, our people will be all the stronger for it," the Chancellor expressed. "Is there anything we can do to assist?"

I smiled, appreciating the offer. "Do you have any idea where Sebastian might have taken him? Any suggestion where I should start?"

He considered my words, locking his hands behind his back. I searched my brain for any hints, any morsel of information that might help.

"Lake Superior!" I shouted when I remembered something Sebastian mentioned. "He threatened Liam, stated that, if he gave him trouble, Lake Superior would run red with his blood."

With Seaton falls being located on the eastern most part of Michigan, and Lake Superior being on the northern shore of the Upper Peninsula, the statement struck me as strange. And now, it might have been a bread crumb, someplace to start my search.

To my surprise, the Chancellor smiled. "I might know where our dreadful Sovereign has gone."

I was anxious, chomping at the bit as he whispered to the witch, Gadreal, before she manifested a sheet of paper and a pen. The Chancellor turned to the table, and when he returned, had drawn a map. Tapping his finger near the shore of Lake Superior, he spoke.

"Mount Arvon," he stated. "A member of the High Council resides there and it's quite possible Sebastian and his men decided to set up camp on the property."

For the first time in hours, I felt hope.

"Thank you," I breathed, thinking better of my next action *after* I stretched to lock my arms around the tall lycan's neck. Certain it was *not* customary for someone of his caliber to accept hugs from teenage girls, I was surprised when his rigid body slowly submitted, giving in to my unconventional gesture. His thin arms returned my embrace.

Yes, this was my first time meeting the Chancellor, but I believed he could be trusted. And right now, I was incredibly grateful for how he stood up for me.

I released him, settling back on my heels. With the map in hand, I turned toward the door Baz had just opened, the one I assumed led to the cells where they held Nick.

"Queen Evangeline." At the sound of the Chancellor calling my name, I turned to receive his parting words. "You have our sincerest blessing."

Chapter Sixteen

Nick

Thump thump. Thump thump.

I'd know that sound anywhere. Evie was nearby, somewhere in the Elder's chamber, but I had no idea why. I chuckled as it crossed my mind that she may have come here to say she'd changed her mind about me, that she thought better of it and decided execution was a more fitting punishment.

But then I heard footsteps that got me up off the dingy cot I'd been given to sleep on. Moving closer to the bars of my cell, I watched as two dark, oblong masses on the cement floor, shrank to something resembling human shadows, and then she came into view. There was a brief moment when her eyes flashed toward mine, and I sensed the hurt still behind them.

Hurt I was responsible for.

Hurt that made her gaze shift away almost the instant it landed on me.

"Thank you," she said softly to the guard as he placed a key in the lock and turned it.

Confused, I watched as the door to my cell opened and the guard stepped aside. I wasn't sure if I was being let out, or if she was being let in.

"You're free to go," the guard grumbled.

"I — But."

"I'll explain," Evie said quietly, gesturing with her hand for me to follow.

We walked the dark, stone-covered hallway without words. I kept my eyes trained on the back of her head, wondering if I was dreaming this. The guard said I was free to go, but … I wasn't supposed to step foot out of that cell until I was transferred to the island.

We began ascending the staircase that led to the main level of the Elders' chamber.

"I need your help," Evie whispered once we were clear of everyone. She spoke urgently, like every second counted as the sound of our feet echoed with each step. "I know none of this makes sense yet, but I came to the Elders, and once I told them what happened, they've agreed to lift your sentence in exchange for coming with me."

Confusion made my brow tense. "Come with you where?"

A long sigh left her mouth and she stopped at the landing, facing me. Her gaze had warmed a bit and I was grateful for it—a sign she may have hated me a little less than I thought. She hadn't yet spoken, but I knew already that, whatever it was, she was desperate.

"He took Liam," she breathed. "The Sovereign and his men have him. They intend to kill him, and…"

The rest of the words seized in her throat, and of all the emotions I could have felt in the moment, I felt her sadness, her pain.

Our relationship had gone through so many phases—from shy strangers, to friends, to love interests, to enemies. For a long stretch of time, I hated Liam, hated what I thought he stole from me, hated that he somehow won Evie's heart completely when I never could seem to. Now, maybe as time had passed, or because nearly losing my life put things into perspective, those feelings of hatred had dulled considerably.

It didn't sting to hear that it tore her up inside having him taken. There was no malice in my heart, no thoughts of letting her fend for herself. I only wanted to help, only wanted what was best for her.

It wasn't lost on me that it took extreme compassion for her to request the High Council have mercy on me. She lost her family because of me. So now, I saw this as an opportunity to make sure she didn't lose anyone else.

Without hesitation, I nodded. "Okay, I'm in. Tell me what you need me to do and I'll do it."

She blinked with tears pooling in her eyes, maybe not expecting me to be so accommodating, but ... I owed this girl my life.

A distant smile tugged at the corner of her mouth and I returned the gesture. We hadn't had a chance to talk through or work through our issues, but I could only imagine time and experiences had changed her like they changed me. For the first time in a while, I had hope that we'd be all right. Maybe even friends again someday.

She breathed deep and those tears that pooled fell now. Swiping them away, she wrangled in her emotions, focusing on the task at hand again.

"We have to get moving. He was taken hours ago and I'm sure they've covered a lot of ground."

"How many were there?" I asked, remembering she said it was the Sovereign and some of his men.

As we approached the door to the assembly hall where I'd been sentenced to exile the night before, she paused, glancing over her shoulder before answering.

"A hundred or more."

I swallowed hard, fighting the next thought that came to mind — that the Council only agreed to let me accompany her because they knew we wouldn't survive it anyway. When I didn't respond, Evie pushed through the door.

Three sets of eyes met us when we entered. I hadn't expected to see anyone, but we had the attention of an Elder, the Chancellor, and ... my mother.

Tension spread in my brow as she rushed over. Gripping the scruffy beard I hadn't bothered shaving since Roz and I came out of hiding, she stared up at me with pleading eyes.

"What are you doing here?"

Ignoring my question, my mother's lips began to move at lightspeed. "Don't do this," she whispered frantically. Only she and I could hear her desperate pleas. "They're only letting you go because they want you dead anyway, Nick. First chance you get," she stammered through tears, "you run."

At those words, I glanced up to where Evie stood a few feet away, waiting as seconds ticked past, seconds I imagined to be agonizing as the life of the one she cared about hung in the balance. The goodness within her was impossible to miss, and ... I couldn't let that burn out. And losing him, Liam, would do just that.

My mother's complexion paled even more when I slowly moved her hands away, taking a step back.

"Mom, I have to do this. I can't turn my back on her," I whispered in response, hoping she understood. "Evie looked out for me when she didn't have to, and I owe her."

My declaration seemed to be a sobering moment for my mother, the instant she realized there was no talking me out of this. Clearing her throat, she blinked before giving one nod. I hoped she understood, but if she didn't, it wouldn't change anything.

"I'm doing this because you taught me to go the full distance for the people I care about," I explained.

I'd done some questionable things of late. Things I could stand to atone for. This opportunity to right one of those wrongs was a gift, a chance to prove to Evie, the Council, myself … that I might be redeemable.

"Then I guess it's settled."

I didn't miss the frustration in my mother's tone. Didn't miss that she both loved and hated that I'd become the kind of man who stood up for what he believed was right.

"I'll be okay," I promised, knowing I probably shouldn't have, but I'd do my best to keep my word.

We embraced again, and then I waited a moment while Evie conversed with the Elder and Chancellor in private. When they finished speaking, she gestured that it was time to leave.

"They're holding her here for a while, but she won't be punished," she said softly as we began our ascent of the long, spiral staircase that led to the library's back entrance.

I frowned, unsure of what she meant. "My mother? Did she do something?"

Evie took a few agonizing seconds to respond, but when she did, I felt my stomach churn.

"This was all her doing," she finally shared. "The Sovereign is here because of her."

Richie said she threatened to go over the Council's head, but …

"When they wouldn't give her answers about where you were and why she wasn't allowed to contact you, she took matters into her own hands. Apparently, they didn't realize she'd already been in contact. They thought they got out ahead of the issue, but she'd already set things in motion."

I wanted to apologize, wanted to say I was sorry for causing yet another problem, but it seemed like a moot point since the damage had already been done. The only thing to do from here was try to make it right.

"What's the plan?" I asked, knowing we were pressed for time.

Evie sighed and I could only imagine how she was feeling right now. "Well, for starters, I have to try and get to Dallas. I need him, but Elise can't know."

We finally stepped into the night air and the snap of cold air was enlivening. We trekked across the parking lot without coats as snow fell. Glancing at Evie's arms, her veins were aglow, surging with liquid fire. It was a dragon thing, I assumed. Meanwhile, I was beginning to catch a chill. Lycans ran warmer than humans, but we were only immune to it completely in our shifted form. However, I couldn't exactly shift right here in the open, so … I had to deal with it.

Evie glanced over when I tucked my arms inside my t-shirt. She didn't bother holding in her laugh. Reaching out, she gestured for me to give her my hand.

"I can keep you warm," she offered.

The second my palm was against hers, heat pulsed through me. Just like that, it was as though the seasons had changed.

I smiled. "Well, that's handy."

She laughed again. "Yeah, this whole dragon thing has its perks."

The brief spark of conversation died out quickly. It'd been months since we'd spoken, months since our falling out and everything that came after. I no longer had to wonder if she planned to hate me forever, but the air still needed to be cleared.

"Listen I …" The words got caught in my throat. There were so many things to apologize for, I honestly didn't know where to start.

"Don't," she sighed, staring off into the distance as we made it to the woods. "We have to keep focused, and … there's no point in rehashing the past."

But I disagreed.

"No, I need to say this," I countered. "If I don't, you'll keep thinking I'm oblivious to everything I did." I paused again, searching for the right words. "I just need to own it all."

And I did want that, to be free and clear of all my secrets. Not because it'd make me feel better, but because I realized how much keeping them in hurt the people I cared about most.

Starting with her.

"I was selfish," I started. "What I did to Liam ... I shouldn't have agreed to the witch's terms. I shouldn't have even contacted the witch," I corrected.

It didn't matter that I initially summoned Scarlet out of desperation, a deeply rooted desire to rid myself of the darkness. When she asked for Liam, I wished I'd been able to see beyond my issues with him to think of how losing him would hurt Evie.

However, acknowledging that it would hurt her would've required me to admit that she loved him. And she did.

"If I could take it all back, I would," I confessed.

She nodded, and I was sure she felt the sincerity.

"The part about your parents," I went on, suddenly speechless as shame washed over me. "Evie, I ... I had no idea."

She was silent. We both were.

I'd done so much, and in the spirit of being open about everything, I shared another concern with her.

"I don't know if it's a good idea for us to do this," I admitted. "Going after Liam ... maybe I should just go alone."

She turned to me, a frown pulling her brow together. "Absolutely not. I'd never be able to just sit around, hoping, wondering." She faced forward again. "I have to do this. I'm fully capable of defending myself."

She didn't understand.

"This isn't about you having what it takes to go up against the Sovereign and his army," I clarified, although that, in and of itself, was daunting. "I'm talking about me."

She turned again, blinking, but her feet never stopped moving.

Of all the things I revealed, this was by far the most difficult. "I'm changing, Evie."

The words tumbled out and I hated that there was so much truth in them.

"I … I lose myself sometimes, and when I come to, I can't remember anything. I'm scared that … one day, maybe soon, I'm gonna black out, and …"

I stopped there, unable to say the words, but she knew. Her gaze lowered as we stepped through snow that came halfway up our calves.

There was once a time that, when I mentioned the likelihood of me hurting her, she'd fight me on it, tooth and nail. She thought I was completely incapable. But now … there was silence.

I imagined her opinion of me had changed quiet drastically, considering the things I'd done as the darkness grew. It stung to see the blatant effects of that, but it was understandable. I'd shown her a side of myself she didn't know existed, and now she no longer thought of me as infallible.

"We'll just have to hope for the best," she decided, never even considering the idea of changing our course. If I hadn't known before that she was in love with Liam, I would have now. Her willingness to lay it all on the line for him spoke volumes.

We didn't speak much after that, thinking on all that lie ahead. Bright lights burned through the windows of a large estate that rivaled my grandfather's. I guessed this was her home now, seeing as how I made it impossible for her to return to the other.

Evie stopped and took a breath. "Okay, I have to get in there. Do you mind waiting here? I'll snag you one of Dallas' coats on my way back out," she offered.

I nodded, understanding it might not go over so well if she walked me through the front door. She took a few steps toward the tall gate surrounding the property when I had a thought.

"Actually, would you mind if I take care of something before we go? I can meet you at the falls in an hour."

Her dark eyes were set on me for several wordless seconds before it dawned on me she might think this was a ploy, a chance to run with an hour-long head start. I suppose I was responsible for her thinking that was the plan. After all, I'd built myself quite the reputation.

It took a moment, but she finally gave in. "Okay," she nodded. "One hour."

***

My clothes fell from my teeth to the snow before I shifted back, hiding behind a large tree on the edge of the Chadwick's property to slip them on. Staring at the patrol car in the driveway, I breathed deep. To get to Roz, I'd have to go through her father, and if I had to guess, he wasn't exactly fond of me at the moment. I was the reason she ran away, the reason she stayed gone for months.

Adjusting my belt after buttoning my jeans, I walked to the door in damp clothes, knowing I looked like I'd been locked in a cell for twenty-four hours. I didn't care though. As soon as Evie and I set foot outside that library, the only thing I wanted was to see Roz, to apologize for not having the balls to face her before my trial, for making her worry.

I knocked and then stepped back, shoving both hands in my pockets to keep them from shaking. Heavy steps approached the door, and as expected, I stared at the angry scowl of one pissed off cop.

I swallowed hard and didn't let his demeanor scare me off.

"Good evening, Officer Chadwick."

A sharply spoken, "What are you doing here?" was his returned greeting. He glared with suspicion, most likely aware of the outcome of my trial.

Yeah … this should be fun.

"The Council pardoned me," I explained, blurting the words when he reached toward his hip.

For his phone … or maybe his holstered gun.

"I'm only here for Roz," I added quickly. "Is she home?" I asked, feeling the tension between us thicken as each second passed.

"She is, and I intend to keep her here." The chill in his tone wasn't lost on me as we spoke through the screen.

I took a breath, wishing we hadn't gotten off to such a terrible start, wishing he knew I'd never do anything to hurt his daughter.

"May I speak with her? Please? I promise we won't leave the porch," I added.

Behind him, the gentle, rhythmic thud of a second set of footsteps made my heart race. There, over his shoulder, a head of long, brown hair peeked from around the corner. Realizing it was me, those deep, soul-stirring eyes of hers stretched as wide as they could go before she bounded toward the door, toward me.

Officer Chadwick grumbled as Roz pushed past him, ignoring the reminder he shouted at her back—that she wasn't allowed to have contact with me, that I wasn't allowed on their property. Yes, she ignored it all, and the next second,

I lifted her feet from the porch's wood slats, locking her in an embrace.

My eyes slammed shut at the feel of her in my arms — warm, safe. I honestly never thought I'd see her again. While I sat in that cell, thoughts of her were what kept me from losing it. She was the answer to the darkness inside me. Her light burned it away and kept me from being consumed.

Quiet sobs hit my ears as I held on to her, feeling the wetness of her tears against my neck.

"I never thought I'd see you again," she whispered, speaking my thoughts aloud. Her grip tightened and our hearts beat wildly — the center of her chest vibrating against mine.

Another heavy glare passed my way from Officer Chadwick before he slowly retreated, leaving Roz and I to speak in private. But I guessed he didn't go far.

"How are you … how are you even here?" Roz choked out, swiping her eyes with the sleeve of a fuzzy, blue sweater when I set her down again.

"The Council released me because I'm needed for a mission."

Roz frowned at that word. "What 'mission'?

"The Sovereign," I began. "He's taken Liam and Evie needs help getting him back."

The color drained from her rosy cheeks at the mention of the Sovereign. "You're kidding me, right? You're not actually considering this, are you?"

I took a breath, gathering my thoughts. "No, I'm not considering it. I've already made up my mind," I amended. "I cost her a lot, and … now I have to make this right."

"By dying?" Roz scoffed. "Because that's how this ends. You do know that, don't you? You've been given a second chance and you're wasting it. This is when you run, Nick," she rambled.

"I'm not gonna run." When I smirked, it nearly made smoke come out her ears.

"Are you seriously smiling right now? Are you insane?" she hissed.

I shook my head and an answer to that question slipped out before I could stop it, before I could rationalize how this was the absolute worst time to be so forthright.

Or maybe it was perfect.

"No, I'm not insane … But I promise I'll do whatever it takes to make it back," I assured her. "Because I want to make it back to you."

For the first time ever, Rozalind Chadwick was completely silent.

I stepped closer and pressed my palms to her cheeks, holding her focus. "You're right about one thing; this is my second chance," I added, agreeing with her. "And I won't waste another minute of it being afraid to show you how I feel."

I'd never been more brave or bold than I was right then and there. Maybe it was because so many near-death experiences in a row had taught me how precious time was and not to waste it. But I liked to think it was just that, for quite some time now, I'd been sure of how important she was to me.

We'd gone from being friends out of necessity, to actual friends, and now … we were something more. My mind drifted back to everything that'd taken place the last several months, and it was so clear; she'd been right with me through it all. Even at times when that couldn't have been easy, times when I didn't make that easy, she was there at every turn.

A sudden rush of awareness filled Roz's expression and I guessed it just hit her that I'd bared my soul. With her large, brown eyes fixed on me, I decided not to think so much for once and just … did.

I kissed her.

It didn't take me long to realize I needed it — the closeness, the reassurance. Fear kept me from giving in to my feelings for her as they grew into something more these last couple months. Before this, I'd been so concerned with ruining our friendship or hurting her, but … as her hands made their way to my waist, I was positive we weren't making a mistake.

Roz wasn't like most girls; she didn't scare easily. And considering the current state of my life, her strength was something I craved. I'd spent quite a bit of time focused on other things, other people, but all this time, what was good for me had been right in front of my face.

The kiss slowed, but I kept her close.

"Took you long enough," she whispered, smiling against my lips.

I breathed her in. "I'm sorry I didn't come to my senses sooner."

She leaned away, keeping her eyes trained on mine as I watched a range of emotion pass through them.

"I'd tell you I'm coming with you, but I know you'd never let me … and my dad would probably send out a search team to drag me back, kicking and screaming," she added with an eye roll.

A laugh left my lungs, puffing a cloud into the frigid air. "I'm glad you know not to suggest it."

She grinned again and moved her hands to my back. "You better come back to me, Nicholas Stokes. If you die, I'll kill you."

With a laugh, I pressed another kiss to her lips and felt more determined than ever to do just that.

"You have my word."

Chapter Seventeen

Evie

Beside me, Dallas checked his watch for about the tenth time in the last sixty-seconds.

"He'll show," I assured him, doing all I could to believe it myself.

Maybe I'd been naïve to think Nick would come back. I was asking a lot of him, asking him to put himself in harm's way for someone he once hated.

Or still did for all I knew.

The roar of the falls was usually calming, but right now, as I imagined the water rushing over the edge of the dam like time washing away, it unnerved me. I swayed back and forth as I searched the trees for a sign of life—a shadow, movement, anything to indicate that Nick was on his way. I had no clue what he ran off to do, but if I could bypass all Elise's questions and get Dallas here in an hour, he should have been able to do the same.

"We should get going," Dallas advised, feeling the same sense of urgency I did.

Our little family of five—myself, Liam, Elise, Dallas, and Hilda—was a bit of a mash up of species and personalities, but we *were* a family. It didn't surprise me that, as soon as I pulled Dallas aside and told him about what happened, he dropped everything to come with me. Now, as I stood here holding an extra jacket for a guy I was beginning to think bailed on me, I decided to just be grateful I didn't have to go it alone. Looked like it'd be me and Dallas.

"Okay." The word left my mouth like a weight, sinking to the snow with my hopes.

We turned, following the water's edge up the hill, headed for the road where Dallas parked Liam's truck. It was our only means of transportation, seeing as how leaving Elise without a vehicle wasn't an option. We packed the truck bed with the few supplies we could sneak out without Elise noticing, but we'd definitely be roughing it.

A sound behind us made my ears perk. Dallas didn't hear it, but I was sure someone was out there.

I stopped, turned, and felt my heart skip a beat when not one, but seven tall figures emerged from the trees. Tapping Dallas' arm, I was grinning from ear to ear. Nick returned, but not alone. He brought Lucas, Chris, Beth, and all three of his brothers. Our odds had just increased tenfold.

"You came back," I choked out, only now letting myself feel the despair of what it would have meant for us if he hadn't.

"I gave you my word," he reminded me.

I nodded, letting it sink in that that still meant something. His word.

Richie stepped up beside his brothers and aimed a thumb behind his shoulder. "We've got a couple trucks, loaded them with a few supplies and a ton of food for the ride," he added, making my heart swell even more the next second. "And ... thank you. For what you did for our brother."

Words of appreciation echoed among the group following Richie's words.

"We *all* thank you for that," Chris chimed in.

"Agreed," Lucas added.

"We're gonna help you get him back, Evie." My eyes lifted toward Nick when he spoke again. There was a sincerity in his gaze that I felt in my soul. "I won't let you lose anyone else."

Dallas squeezed me around my shoulders and Beth clutched my hand. I looked around at all of them, these people who stepped forward when they owed me nothing … I was moved beyond words. It was impossible to say if we stood any chance against the Sovereign and his army, but we had something they didn't have.

Heart.

And as for me, I was the most determined, willing to rush in with guns blazing because, as long as Liam was in danger, as long as I didn't have him … there was nothing left to lose.

***

We'd driven all night. Eight hours, to be exact. No one complained about bathroom breaks or stretching their legs, because the seven who chose to follow me into certain chaos understood time was of the essence.

We parked and waited for the vehicle ferry in the small town of Charlevoix. It would carry us across Lake Michigan to the Upper Peninsula, and from there, it'd be a rough trek inland once we'd inevitably have to abandon the trucks to ascend Mount Arvon.

And, hopefully, find Liam.

Beth and I sat at the water's edge, watching gentle waves lap against the dock. A lavender and coral sky had begun to replace dark blue as light flurries were blown from tree branches with each gust of wind. It would have been such a stunning sight, but here I sat, unmoved by the beauty surrounding me. It did nothing to lift my spirits as we waited, as we wasted precious minutes just ... sitting here.

"I'm gonna grab something to drink. Want anything?" Beth asked, her tone reflecting every ounce of her concern.

She'd stuck close since leaving Seaton Falls. Insisting on riding with Dallas and I, she held my hand the entire way, knowing I needed the contact, the reassurance. And now, she was still at my side, being the friend I was desperate for.

I smiled up at her. It was forced and weak, but it was a smile nonetheless. "No, but you go ahead."

It took her a moment to move, that sympathetic stare locked on me. But then, she stood, headed for the store across the lot. Of course, glancing back every few seconds like she feared I'd fall apart the moment she was gone.

I faced the water again, breathing deep. I still felt Liam. The connection had weakened significantly, but ... it was there. Every few minutes or so, I tried to communicate with him, to see through his eyes to get some idea of where he was being held, or what had been done to him, but there was nothing.

Just darkness.

It was hard not to think of what he'd gone through when the tables were turned so long ago, when *I* was the one who'd been taken from *him*. Every breath was painful, not being able to see or touch him, not knowing if this moment or the next was his last.

I'd looked into the eyes of the Sovereign, saw the wickedness within his stare. There was malice in his heart toward Liam specifically, and I knew he intended to make good on each and every one of his promises. To torture and maim him until his end.

Until death.

My eyes blurred with tears and I blinked them away, focusing on that invisible thread that linked me to him. It was of little comfort, but it was all I had left. He took my place, put his life in the Sovereign's hands to save mine, and I couldn't comprehend that kind of bravery, couldn't grasp how he could sacrifice himself for me.

Then … I considered this mission, and realized I was willing to do the same.

Rubbing both palms over my sleeves, embracing myself as I sat in the cold, I tried to keep it together. Crying and falling apart would do nothing but distract me. I had to keep a clear head.

I prayed Liam had worn the ring from Elise, the one that would be my saving grace should he … should he die before I could get there. It had the same powers as the necklace that'd been used to bring me back, and finding it might be the only hope I had left. However, with how the Sovereign spoke of Liam, like he was some rare, classic car whose parts increased in value with every passing year, I couldn't say for certain he wouldn't remove the ring before finishing Liam off, adding it to his own collection, or selling to the highest bidder. There were just so many ways this could go from bad to worse.

"Mind if I sit?"

I glanced up at the sound of Nick's voice and a warm smile came my way, one I thought I'd never welcome again. When I nodded, he settled into the spot Beth had occupied beside me. At first, he just rested there in silence, but eventually spoke, uttering the standard-issue question to ask someone in a situation such as mine.

"How are you holding up?"

I *wasn't* holding up, was the honest answer, but I had to be brave, had to keep as clear a head as possible.

"I'm just … anxious to get to him," was the answer I gave, checking the time again. What felt like hours ticking away had only been a few minutes.

Nick stared out at the water, thinking to himself before deciding to share out loud.

"I hope everything's okay when we get there."

I turned to face him, shocked by the kind words. It was no secret Nick and Liam were the polar-opposite of friends, but, as I took in the reflective expression Nick wore, I knew he was being sincere. Even if he only hoped for a favorable outcome for *my* sake.

I breathed a soft, "Thank you."

He nodded and seemed kind of lost inside his head for a moment. "I know you don't need my approval or anything like that, but … I get it. This thing between you and him," he expressed. "I get that it wasn't really a choice."

He was right about that; what I felt for Liam, was more of a need than anything else.

"That means a lot," I replied. "And I'm sorry if I hurt you in all this. If I'd realized how strong my bond to him was in the beginning, I would've been honest with you. I hope you know that."

He nodded again, this time before I even finished speaking. "I know," he said dismissively, seeming to harbor no ill feelings toward me, no bitterness concerning our past. "The heart has a tendency to do what it wants."

I turned again, noting something else behind his expression, something that actually made me smile a little.

"The heart has a tendency to do what it wants?" I said, teasing him a bit. "And … has your heart finally admitted it wants Roz?"

At the mention of her name, his cheeks burned red, a sight that made my smile grow even more.

"It's … we're exploring the idea, seeing where things lead," he confessed, but when I nudged his knee with my own, he shared more. "She's good for me. I can feel it. And I've never met anyone who can be a total sweetheart one minute, and bust my balls the next," he laughed. "Which I can admit I kind of need."

I laughed too, loving how happy he seemed. That was important to me.

"Have you told her how you feel yet?"

That redness spread even more. "Kind of," he confessed. "Right before I met you at the reservoir."

Now I knew what the important thing was he needed to take care of. It was sweet that, the moment he was free, he went to her. It said a lot about how deep his feelings ran.

"Well, I think it's great that you two figured things out," I stated. "She seems pretty cool."

"She is," he agreed.

We sat quietly for a moment, perhaps both thinking how things had seemingly come full circle.

"And thank you," he said next, causing my brow to tense with confusion.

"For?"

"Whatever you said to the Elders concerning my mother. You didn't have to ask them for leniency." His gaze lowered when adding, "I know she's responsible for this, responsible for what's happened to Liam."

In truth, I nearly walked out of the Elder's chamber without so much as a thought for the fate of Mrs. Stokes. It would have been so easy to leave that place and let her face whatever punishment she had coming, but I couldn't. Not with a clear conscience. She may hold hatred for me I don't understand, but she'd caused all this because she loved her family fiercely.

I could relate to that and couldn't say for sure I wouldn't have done exactly what she had.

So, before we left, I made certain they would only detain her until we returned, just in case this was a dead end and we needed more information, something she may have withheld.

"You're welcome," I finally replied.

Nick looked out on the water again, speaking his next thought aloud.

"So, this tether thing with you and Liam, how's it work?"

I was surprised he asked me to explain. Considering our history, his with Liam. This was proof of how far we'd all come, how much things had changed over the past several months.

"It's like ... we're always together. Like we're always holding hands, always linked," I clarified. My hand went to the center of my chest as I became more aware of that thread. "I can always feel him."

Emotion clenched my throat, but I wouldn't let it show on my face. The connection was becoming so weak, while it should have been growing stronger as we drew nearer. Something was happening, and I was too afraid to acknowledge what that something was.

Liam was ... dying.

I was sure of it.

It was a slow process from what I could tell, but he was slipping away from me.

My eyes settled on my bracelet, the one that matched his—a physical symbol of vows we made. While I couldn't remember saying the words, I felt the depth of our commitment at all times.

I belonged to Liam, and he belonged to me, but our tie stretched far beyond *'til death do us part'*. We remained as one despite my death centuries ago, and I'd honor him with the same commitment.

Should it come to that.

I didn't realize I was crying until Nick pushed a tear aside, and I didn't realize I needed a hug until he pulled me to his chest. Our differences should have made us mortal enemies, but you never would have guessed it by the friendship we forged.

It's funny how things that once seemed so big can be made so small in times like these, when a life is on the line, when someone you love was snatched away. I'd put so much time and energy into hating Nick after what he did, but now that we were here, it hardly mattered. He was stepping up, being so brave right now, I couldn't help but to let the last traces of resentment burn away.

A sight in the distance made me lift my head from his shoulder as excitement filled my heart.

"The ferry," I blurted, getting to my feet the next second. Nick stood too, and I signaled to the guys and Beth to get ready. We filed back into the trucks and got in line behind the other vehicles that would be crossing this morning.

Impatient, my fingers drummed against my thigh until Beth placed her hand on top of mine, calming me only a bit. I glanced at the clock on Liam's dashboard every few seconds as Dallas sat behind the wheel. This only made time crawl ahead at a snail's pace. Until now, I'd been hopeful it would slow down, but as we waited to board, it wasn't moving fast enough.

My other hand was clutched, and it wasn't Beth this time. I glanced up at Dallas to find a gentle glare trained on me.

"We'll find him," he said reassuringly.

"Yeah, but … I'd prefer to find him *alive*," I countered.

Dallas hadn't been there when Sebastian took Liam. He hadn't seen the gleam in that monster's eyes as he seized his new prize. It was one I'd never forget as long as I lived.

The line crept forward and, soon, we were headed across the water — still at a painstakingly slow pace, but at least we were moving, getting closer to our target. However, as we trudged ahead … the tie got weaker. There was a strange sensation within me I couldn't quite put into words. It was like … I sensed Liam's light burning out, that flicker of his dragon's flame within him that connected us. Closing my eyes, I held in another flood of tears. Even if it burned out completely, I'd still trudge ahead. Had to. I wouldn't believe he was gone unless I saw it with my own eyes. And, if that was the case, this quest would take on a whole new purpose.

It'd no longer be a rescue mission … my new focus would be to find and kill Sebastian De Vincenzo.

We departed from the ferry and headed inland as we followed the hand-drawn map with the aid of the GPS on

Dallas' phone. The terrain transitioned from smooth, paved roads to a single lane of dirt and gravel, inclining steeply every so often as we climbed, nearing the highest point of Mount Arvon.

My heart raced as adrenaline surged. I felt the excess energy building in my hands as the dragon within sprung to life, readying herself to do whatever it took to find and rescue Liam. She, like I, was frantic without him.

He told me once that I was never to run toward danger. Not even for him. He intended to spark an inward sense of self-preservation I seemed to be lacking at the time, but it never took. When it came to him, there was no task too great, no stretch of land treacherous enough to keep me from crossing it. He had to know his command would never hold up if his life was on the line.

The idea of embarking on this journey with Nick being an integral part of the plan would have set Liam ablaze. In his eyes, Nick was my most clear and present enemy. But I didn't care. As the biggest, strongest lycan I'd come across thus far, I needed him. If he was somehow triggered along the way, if he had one of his blackouts and ended up hurting me, I'd have to accept that. But what I could *not* accept was not doing everything in my power to save Liam.

Not doing everything in my power to bring him home.

Dallas' engine went silent and I watched from the rearview mirror as doors to the vehicles trailing us opened one at a time. The others emerged. We'd gone as far as we could safely on wheels. According to the directions, the Council member whose estate we were in search of wasn't too far away. Sebastian's men could be nearby and there was no doubt they were being at least *slightly* more cautious, considering they were holding a prisoner they deemed so valuable. It'd be too risky to rush their camp with engines roaring, so we moved ahead on foot, watching our surroundings.

Richie, Kyle, and Ben stepped forward with large, black hiking bags strapped to their backs. I stared, wondering if they misunderstood that we were only about an hour's trek from the estate, not a day or two. Kyle noticed the inquisitive look I must've worn and flashed a grin.

"You'll thank us later," he quipped, and I took his word for it. When he continued past me, I was about ninety-nine-percent sure I heard glass clanking against glass within his bag.

"Sometimes, you just don't ask questions," Beth joked as we moved ahead.

I'd warned of the witches, how they enabled the army to move through the woods of Seaton Falls undetected, unseen until they were good and *ready* to be seen. This was where the lycans in our group came in handy. Their sense of hearing was better than that of a dragon, and even my own as a hybrid. Every time they sensed something amiss, we slowed our pace a bit, waiting to move on once we were given the signal—a single nod from Richie, his pack's alpha.

I went over every possible scenario in my head, how we would approach, how we would get past the army, how we'd find Liam with my tether to him now so weak. It all came down to one thing.

Luck.

That's what this endeavor had been reduced to. I couldn't rely on my senses; they were overwrought with emotion. I couldn't focus a single thought without it somehow leading to how I wouldn't be able to move on without him. Inside, I was allowed to be a mess. But on the outside, I had to be the picture of bravery.

Liam taught me that.

"The Chancellor's sure this is where they took him?" Dallas asked.

The question made me smirk. "We come all this way and *now* you ask if he was sure?"

Broad shoulders lifted into the air and Dallas ran a hand through his sand-toned hair. "S'pose it just occurred to me to check."

Smiling as we trudged ahead, I nodded. "He was sure enough," I answered. "And now that we're close, now that I can feel him, *I'm* sure."

I kept to myself that if Liam were any further away, I wouldn't be able to sense him at all. The connection was so splotchy.

"So, we got a plan?" Dallas asked next.

"As good of a plan as we could come up with on the drive here," Richie answered. "Evie says there are roughly a hundred of 'em, and there are nine of us, so … as long as we can each take out twelve or thirteen of his guys, we'll be okay. It helps that we've got the element of surprise on our side."

"And Molotov cocktails," Kyle added with a huge grin, revealing a hint as to what those huge hiking bags they carried contained.

Bottles of alcohol.

"Fire's one of our biggest weaknesses," he shared. "Figured today would be a good day for Nick and I to see, once and for all, which of us has the better throwing arm."

"Dude, you're *way* past your prime," Nick assured him with a laugh. "Last I checked, my stats were killing yours."

"I just hope neither of you set *yourself* on fire," Ben, being the sensible one of the brood, mumbled under his breath.

"Either way," Richie cut in with a sigh, "We plan to take out a good chunk of 'em before we even get close. Then, whoever's left standing, we handle them."

He was so confident, so sure we could do this. Hearing him, I actually started believing it myself.

We walked those woods for an hour, wandering with my link to Liam and landmarks the Chancellor jotted down as our only compass. Eventually, we picked up on sounds other than our own feet crunching through the snow and the occasional gust of wind howling past.

There were voices.

Laughter.

Heat built within me at the sound of it, these men lighthearted and carefree. Meanwhile, Liam was barely clinging to life a short distance away. The closer we got, the louder *they* got, the more enraged I became.

The steep pitches of a sprawling estate came into view and we were still pretty far from the makeshift camp Sebastian's men had set up. Nearing the edge of the property, a few had been assigned to patrol the perimeter. As soon as we spotted them, we slowed our pace, crouching to keep ourselves hidden behind the trunk of a massive, fallen tree.

"What now?" Nick whispered, thankfully directing the question toward Richie, because I had no clue.

"We have to take these guys out before they alert the others. And it has to be done quietly," he added.

"I've got this one," Dallas whispered, keeping his eyes trained on the guard straight ahead. "Richie, Ben … you guys get the other two and make it quick. If they shift or howl, the others will know something's coming, and if that happens, we're as good as dead," he stated.

Ben and Richie nodded, spotting their marks as they lifted from the snow. The three shot out in all directions, moving with impossible speed. Within seconds, they were upon the unsuspecting guards, and with military-like precision, their necks were snapped just before their bodies dropped to the snow.

Dallas waved the rest of us ahead and we moved forward as a group again.

With the wind at our backs, and the height of the snow rising as we ascended the steepening slope of Mount Arvon, we pushed ahead, finally spotting the camp we first heard miles away. There were tents sprawled across the plot of land belonging to a member of the High Council, the only way he could accommodate his uninvited guests — the Sovereign and his men.

Bonfires had been lit around the camp. Nearby, damp clothes dried on lines, some cooked meat over the flames, others just sat close for warmth. But the one thing I *didn't* see was the Sovereign.

Of course he wouldn't be out here roughing it. If I had to guess, he and his witches were nice and cozy inside where he could keep close watch on his latest acquisition — *Liam.*

My stomach rolled and I felt anxious, ready to get to him, ready to look fate in the eye and dare it to try and stop me from succeeding.

"All right. There have to be more of those lycans wandering these outskirts and it's just a matter of time until they find us. So, we have to move quickly," Dallas explained, surveying our surroundings.

The prompt had Kyle eagerly lowering his bag to the snow. From it, he removed the first bottle, confirming what I already guessed. He placed it, and several others, onto the ground while Ben opened them. Next, Kyle grabbed strips of old t-shirts he'd cut up in preparation for this moment. He stuffed half inside each bottle, leaving the remainder of the swatch resting over the neck. After he got it all set up, he patted his pockets and a look of sheer dread filled his expression.

"Crap, I forgot my freakin' lighter."

My brow quirked as I stared at him, wondering if he'd forgotten there were dragons in the midst.

"I think we've got you covered when it comes to fire," Dallas chuckled. The next second, his finger glowed as a flame danced on the tip of it. Kyle touched the rag of the first bottle to it until it lit, handing if off to Nick. Then, he lit his own and there was no missing the excitement in his eyes as he turned to his brother.

"Ready?" he beamed.

"Watch and learn, big bro," Nick teased.

And then, in a display of the sheer strength these two possessed, those bottles whizzed through the air like screaming rockets, blasting two small groups of unsuspecting lycans. They went up in a beautiful, glorious blaze. I wasn't ashamed by the satisfaction that filled me as they ran and screamed in vain. No one could help them. In fact, the others purposely moved away to avoid the same fate. But that was impossible because, as they scattered, unsure of where the attack had come from, Nick and Ben fired off more, bottle after bottle, targeting the densest clusters of lycans until we'd taken out around fifty.

Seeing their numbers diminish so quickly made that sense of hope within me grow even more, spreading like sunlight on the horizon.

"Should we move ahead?" Kyle asked, aiming his question at both Richie and Dallas.

Richie surveyed the scene, the damage we'd done so far, how quickly the remaining lycans reorganized themselves as they scanned the woods for their attackers.

"Our best bet is to push forward as long as we can. Chances are, we'll only get one last round fired off before they nail down our location. So, make it count."

That was all his brothers needed to hear, each one taking a bottle this time, handing more to Lucas and Chris. They lined up their targets and cocked back, waiting for Richie to give the word. Dallas, however, had his sights set elsewhere, trained on something—a young girl with dark hair who trudged toward us. With fury in her eyes, she covered her head with the hood of a dark cloak.

"Time's up," Dallas mumbled under his breath, just before a command ripped from his throat and overshadowed Richie's authority. At the sound of a roaring, "Fire now!" the guys did just that. They launched the bottles, hurling through the air toward their intended targets.

My heart dropped as I watched, counting every precious millisecond as they passed. Watching the lycans scramble, they seemed so small now, so much less frightening than when they cornered me in the woods the day before. Then, I'd been alone and afraid. Now, with backup, the playing field was slightly less skewed in their favor.

Slightly.

My eyes flitted from the carnage unfolding outside the sprawling mansion of the High Council member whose land we so callously invaded. While I was sure he or she had no real part to play in Sebastian capturing Liam, nor in the decision for him and his men to stay here indefinitely, I still couldn't afford to care one way or another. These men, these monsters ... they deserved whatever they had coming to them.

I swallowed as the cocktails came within a few feet of the lycans—six bottles that, together, could have taken out thirty or more.

... *Could have.*

Had it not been for a small, pale hand lifting into the air. It was the witch. In an instant, the bottles slowed to a gentle stop, hovering in midair as our small group of nine stared on. The others were likely experiencing the same sense of dread *I* had way deep down in my gut. In that short time, a thousand thoughts passed through my head, but each one was washed away by Dallas' loud, booming voice when he yelled.

"Take cover!"

The warning came just before what looked like a storm of fireballs rushed toward us, the result of the six Molotov cocktails soaring back in our direction.

"Evie! Wings!" he yelled next, leaving me confused for only a moment before he leapt over the fallen tree that had once been our covering, moving *toward* danger instead of away from it. Ripping the shirt from his torso, large, flaming wings stretched from Dallas' back.

Like a shield.

And now I understood.

Warm breath puffed from my lips, crystalizing in the air as I snatched my shirt over my head — too little time to think, too little time to prepare. I stood beside Dallas, now wearing only my tank, bracing myself as the forceful thrust of my wings springing forth shifted my feet in the snow. Their bright orange light glinted off the sparkling white flakes that covered every inch of the earth for miles. The goal in mind was not to protect *ourselves* from the inevitable blast ... but to protect the others.

A rush of heat blasted Dallas and I from behind and my teeth gritted. Shards of the multicolored bottles we'd thrown were flung back in our direction at twice the speed, twice the intensity, breaking skin.

Dallas groaned at the feel of it as the seemingly unending stream of heat and glass surged against us. But we withstood the pain.

I caught a set of blue eyes as I blinked through the initial shock and sheer force exuded by the witch's maneuver. It was a show of strength that made our coming here resemble a suicide mission all the more. Nick's jaw clenched as he watched me breathe through the agony. The fire itself was of no consequence; my body absorbed the flames like a sponge in water, but I couldn't say the same for the glass. Long shards pierced my skin, sending warm trickles of blood streaming down my shoulders, back, and arms. I muffled a scream, holding it in as my dragon cried out from within, sending that familiar pulse from my chest, vibrating through an invisible thread. A sensation I knew would never reach Liam.

Not like usual.

Not this time.

"We have to move," Richie called out, motioning his hand toward a dense section where we could hide among the trees as we inched our way closer to the estate, closer to our intended target.

Closer to Liam.

My wings retracted, unharmed by the attack, but I couldn't say the same for my back. Dallas' had endured the same abuse and seemed to be unfazed by it. I felt no shame admitting he was stronger than I was. It was clear as he carried on as though nothing happened. Meanwhile, I was near tears.

But you have to keep moving. There's no time for crying. No time for pity.

Swiping at the water spilling over my lower lids, I hurried along with the others, praying for just one quiet moment to think, to figure out our next move, but that moment never arrived. At the feel of bark against my fingertips, I hid myself behind a massive trunk, one fifteen to twenty feet closer to our target. Nick ran up beside me, panting as his brothers, Chris, Lucas, Beth, and Dallas followed, crouching low while getting eyes on the witch again.

Standing there, staring at them all as they willingly headed into the lion's den with me, I realized this would never work. Now that one of Sebastian's witches knew where we were, our chances of getting inside were next to impossible. She'd already shown us how easily she could take out our group, all with one swipe of her hand. There was no way she would allow us to pass, no way we could get close enough with her standing guard.

So … I needed to get rid of her.

Breathing deep as I peered around the trunk that hid me, I spotted her among the mass of lycans that charged toward us. She came closer, no doubt plotting her next attack.

"They're coming," I panted. "Focus on taking *them* out while I take care of the witch," I whispered, moving my feet the second Dallas gave a confused nod. The next second, shirts and shoes were tossed to the snow as the lycans among us prepared to shift

I showed myself, facing the witch. Our eyes locked, mine with the one who stood by a day ago while Sebastian's men ogled me after cornering me in the woods, the one who protected these grotesque lycans as they brought Liam to this place to die.

Two burly beasts rushed toward me and I was startled by the lack of fear that rose within. There was never even a moment of doubt or worry as I stayed heavily focused on my target.

Dark fur filled my hands when I grabbed the first by his neck and slammed him against a nearby tree. Flames burst from my fingertips, igniting his entire body in a matter of seconds. I held him there, pressing him into the bark as he screamed and writhed, taking his last breath while I stared into his cold eyes.

A strange sense of calm rage filled me, helping me focus on the task at hand, making me fearless and yet level-headed at the same time.

The body of the lycan I'd taken on fell to the ground in a charred heap. I turned to handle the other, but Dallas beat me to it, wiping blood onto his jeans as more poured from an empty cavity in the beast's chest. A still-beating heart lie in the otherwise pristine snow.

My hands tightened into fists as I locked in on the witch again. A faint smile was set on her lips. There was no doubt in my mind that she could already taste victory with each step I took toward her. She, like every other witch I'd encountered besides Hilda, was drunk with power. Drunk with the knowledge that time was her only mortal enemy on Earth. It was the one thing her kind could not conquer, but even for that, they found a loophole by developing their codependent bond with the lycan race.

So, as far as she knew, she and others like her were infallible.

She stared with that sickening smile and a gleam in her eyes as she lifted both hands into the frigid air, no doubt feeling them pulse with dark energy, fully intent on wielding her magic against me.

Only to realize … it had absolutely no effect.

Wind whipped my cheeks as I charged toward her, full-steam ahead as my limbs blazed like the surface of the sun. I'd never moved so fast, not even as my wolf. Today, with so much on the line, my dragon's strength seemed almost too powerful to harness.

Falling snow evaporated like steam before touching my skin. The bewildered expression on the face of Sebastian's witch filled me with so much satisfaction. She'd never met a dragon like me, I was sure. However, as luck would have it, she would never meet another soul again … because I intended to destroy her.

The stench of evil filled my nostrils as I brought her feeble frame to the ground with ease. Soft flesh and a delicate neck in the bend of my elbow, I squeezed, feeling her windpipe constrict as I tightened my grip. The rage … it flowed through me and I felt high, intoxicated as life slipped from the witch's grasp. Hearing the last hiss of breath leaving her lungs, I let go, leaving her there to freeze in the snow, a reminder the lycans who fought on her side that our dismal numbers didn't mean we'd be easy to beat.

To my left, Beth and Chris were putting their training to good use. Three lycans lie dead in the snow while the two they tossed around like ragdolls staggered back to their feet. To my right, a large silvery lycan, one who dwarfed the others, unclamped his teeth to spit torn flesh to the ground before going in for another kill.

Progress.

We were actually making progress.

Locking eyes with another lycan, I stepped toward him, ready to put him down like we'd done to the others, but instead ... my body crumpled to the snow.

Chapter Eighteen

Evie

Dazed.

Blurred vision.

A dizzying sting that radiated from the back of my head.

I couldn't think or see straight. Couldn't form a single, lucid thought.

But I was sure I recognize a voice.

"Grab her arms and feet," he crooned. "I'm sure the Sovereign will be pleased to see he's got another dragon to dissect."

I still hadn't placed the voice, but those words were sobering, made the fog clear just a tad.

Dissect.

He said the Sovereign would be pleased to have *another* dragon to dissect.

Liam ... what had they done to him?

I squirmed, but my effort was in vain. Brief flashes of my surroundings made my heart race as I watched Dallas, Nick, and the others deep in the heat of battle. They were too preoccupied to notice I'd been hit, too focused to notice I was being taken away.

As my body was carried, we passed beneath naked branches that created a canopy above. They arched across the sky like bony fingers waiting to pluck me from my captors' hands.

What I would've given for that to have been true.

We were headed to the estate, no doubt—myself and the two who hauled me through the snow, the tall figure in a dark trench coat who walked beside us. I squinted as I fought to cling to consciousness, only now making out his features.

It was Blaise, the Sovereign's son.

Wet heat seeped through the back of my hair and I was sure a trail of blood had dotted the snow. I was losing consciousness quickly, but was determined to stay awake, determined to take note of the path we took. Thinking that maybe, by some small miracle, I might get free and would need to know how to escape.

Warmth and darkness were temporarily disorienting after Blaise pushed a heavy, wooden door ajar, letting the lycans pass through with me in tow. The stench of witches stung my nose and overpowered any other scent the home might have held. Dark stone walls I guessed dated back to the home's construction absorbed the light from a small lamp perched on a table.

"Downstairs."

I repeated that word over and over in my head.

Downstairs. Downstairs. Downstairs.

This door we'd just come through was near a set of steps, so if I could just make my way back to them, freedom was only a few feet away.

Don't forget. Don't forget.

My eyes drifted closed again and I forced them open when we began to descend. It was so dark, like we waded through ink.

Right turn.

Left turn.

Sound transitioned from echoing off the walls of a hollow, open space, to a confined hallway.

Keys.

A heavy door opening.

For a nanosecond, I was airborne, but then hit the ground with a violent thud. My body slid across the small room before my captors engaged a metal latch and walked away laughing as a scream spilled from my mouth. Remains from the glass bottles that had been hurled at Dallas and I were forced deeper into the skin. However, *that* paled in comparison to the surge of fresh pain that pulsed through my head when the wound beneath my hair struck the leg of a nearby chair. I whimpered as I clutched it, feeling the stickiness of blood coating my fingers. For a moment, the agony, along with the heavy sense of *defeat*, made me wish for death.

Where am I?

What will happen to the others?

How can I save Liam when I'm not even sure how to save myself?

The room spun and I lie there panting, working myself into a full-blown panic attack. My heart thundered against my ribs and I truly thought my lungs might explode. This was not the plan. Instead of rescuing Liam, I was now in desperate need of being rescued myself.

'*Brave on the outside,*' I said to myself, only finding the strength to think it when my lips failed to move.

'*Brave on the outside.*'

That was Liam's rule. I could feel whatever I needed to on the inside, but I could never *look* like I'd fallen apart.

And I definitely looked like that right now.

Forcing myself upright, I scanned the room as my breathing continued at an erratic pace. It was small, maybe ten feet by ten feet. A heavy metal door with a small barred window marked the only exit. Beyond it, only darkness.

Get to your feet.

I had to stand, had to fight through the pain — in my head, my back.

Get to your feet.

I'd never survive this if I gave in to the fear, the helplessness I felt.

If you can't do it for you, do it for Liam.

A deep breath puffed from my nostrils as I got my footing, shoving aside the fog and dizziness. With weary steps, I shuffled toward the door, letting my hands roam across it, feeling the lock that kept me prisoner. Although, I use the term *'lock'* very loosely. This thing was massive, a giant wheel I'd have to turn with the aid of another, and even still, it would have required some type of key.

I was stuck.

I braced my forehead against the bars on the small window looking out into the hallway. I sucked in a deep breath. It couldn't end like this. So many needed my help right now and here I was, stuck. An act of desperation, I shoved and pulled the door, hoping my increased strength would cause it to budge, but … no such luck.

What good was supernatural strength if it still wasn't enough?

Frustrated, a burn settled in deep within my chest, filling me with unspeakable rage the next instant. Heat seeped from my core and filled me completely as my dragon stood from her seat in the depths of my subconscious mind and stepped forth.

I felt her rage, her fury and embraced it.

Glowing streaks lined my arms as the veins there pulsed with fire. My fist drew back and slammed into the door, leaving a sizable dent when I pulled away. I stared at it and, realizing it wasn't indestructible like I allowed myself to think, I drew back and buried my fist in the metal a second time. The blemish on the door deepened and I stepped back.

The Councilman clearly had this room built for a reason. Maybe, at their level of government, there was always the threat of an attack and this particular member had decided to make himself ready. However, as a supernatural himself, he would have to have known this door would only hold for so long.

And that's when it hit me, that's when I remembered my one hidden ability that allowed me the element of surprise.

This door must have been spelled with magic, and I was the one being it didn't affect.

Hope nearly made me hyperventilate again. I moved close once more and touched the door, gauging its thickness, its density. It would take more time than I had to punch my way through, but ... there was another way.

Another ability Elise and her descendants possessed.

Staring at my hands, I observed the bright orange flames. And then, as I concentrated, the base of the dancing light began to turn that peculiar shade of turquoise — the hottest flames I was capable of producing.

This has to work.

Has to.

Shaking, and only half-believing this idea wasn't ridiculous, I placed my hand to the door, focusing all my energy on that spot, hoping the concentrated heat would be enough.

This has to work.

For a short time, I'd been able to block out that today's outcome depended most heavily on me. So many lives were in my hands right now. It wasn't far from my thoughts that the group who came with me today were loved by someone. Nick, his brothers, Beth, Lucas, and Chris by their parents. Dallas by Elise. They weren't disposable, which was all the more reason I had to try. I couldn't leave them out there fighting for *my* cause alone. I had to get Liam and then get back out there to help.

Had to make sure my quest didn't cost others the same pain I, myself, was trying to avoid.

I found the strength to burn hotter, watching as flames rushed from my hand to the door like a blow torch. The metal began to glow a deep orangish-red in the shape of my palm and fingers as I pressed harder, focused more intently.

At the feel of the material beginning to soften, I sucked in a breath. And then, when a small hole liquified, dripping molten metal onto the cement floor, I held my breath altogether. I only had the patience to wait until the widening hole was large enough to step through, giving no thought to letting it cool first. My only thought, only goal, was to get out of there.

Squeezing through as my flames extinguished, I glanced left and right, from one end of the narrow hallway to the other. I needed to get my bearings, needed to remember which way I'd find the exit. Being brought in dazed and injured meant I'd been in a bit of a fog at the time. Now that I was thinking more clearly, I couldn't recall.

My chest constricted again, tightening as I realized it wouldn't be as easy to get out of here as I thought. This house was huge, and with the sublevel basically being a footprint of the floorplan, it was huge too. I could wander around down here for a while and not be any closer to the exit.

Letting my shoulder rest against the cool, stone wall beside me, I forced my senses to sharpen—vision, smell, hearing.

And that's when I picked up on something that made me freeze.

The sound of shallow breaths. They were almost too quiet to hear, but I knew I hadn't imagined it.

Right.

I walked that way, toward the sound, feeling my heart race inside my chest with each step. There were other doors, other rooms, each with the same barred window at the top. I stopped at each, frantically searching. My hopes lifted at the idea of whose shallow breaths those might be, but I was afraid to think it was possible. The tie between Liam was so weak I barely even noticed it now.

But still, I searched.

Each room. Feeling the same sense of disappointment every time I stood on the tips of my toes and peered inside, only to find the space just as empty as the last. But then, at the moment I thought the sound might have just been a stray echo ... I spotted a figure. It was way deep in the corner, crumbled on the floor, but it was enough to jumpstart my doubtful heart.

"Liam ..."

His name left my mouth as a whisper. Not out of fear that someone else might hear. The fear I felt was at the thought that it might not be him. Or, if it *was* ... that I might be too late.

Frantic, shaking from head to toe, my hand ignited and I placed it on the metal door just like I'd done a moment ago. This time, I was smart, melting the space where the locking mechanism met the frame. It felt like it took forever for the steel to reach a hot enough temperature to soften, but eventually it did, the small patch I touched melting to the floor in a metallic puddle.

There was no need to climb through thanks to my last-minute idea. I only needed to reach inside and pull the door toward me. Standing there, with only a few meters between myself and the shadow in the corner, I was nearly paralyzed by that fear I tried to dismiss. In truth, it was beginning to overtake me.

What if it's not him?

What if he's dead?

What if the Sovereign has done heinous things to him, and what I'm staring at … is only remains.

A wave of nausea made my stomach churn at that last thought, at the idea of a being so powerful, so full of life and love, reduced to a heap of flesh after Sebastian had … *harvested* him for parts.

"Liam …"

My lips quivered as his name left my mouth for a second time, just as hushed and timid as before. Maybe even more so.

There was no answer and I willed myself to take another step. Stretching my hand forth, I ignited my fingertips to provide just enough light to see what was in front of me, not enough to give away my location too soon if someone decided to come down to check on me.

Another step.

Another vile thought of what I might find when I got closer.

And then … I saw something that made me stop dead in my tracks.

Blood.

Lots and lots of blood.

Some splattered on the walls, but mostly pooled on the floor near a dark boot that came into view. At the sight of it, I rushed ahead full speed until I was able to lay eyes on his entire body.

His bloody, beaten, broken body.

He would have fought them off. All of them. So I was sure most of this was the handy work of witches. Or they'd at least had a hand in rendering him helpless while Sebastian and his soldiers did this.

Tears blurred my eyes, but wouldn't fall because I'd suddenly switched over to survival mode. My thoughts were all centered around evaluating the situation and figuring out how to get us both out of this place. As I looked Liam over — the unhealed cuts and gashes, the swollen fingers on a hand I was sure had been broken. And that's when I noticed it; his fingers were bare. All of them.

They'd taken the ring, but left the leather band on his wrist because, to them, it held no value. No one but Liam and I knew that to be a lie.

A fresh surge of hatred and vengeance burst within my soul. For a second, I lost focus and could only think of how badly I wanted to kill all the ones who'd done this.

All of them.

The only thing I could do was get him out of here. He wasn't healing, which was another indicator of there being magic involved, so I had to take him with me as is, and would figure out how to fix him later.

Moving blood-soaked strands of his lengthy hair from his face, I touched a hand to his cheek, unsure of whether or not he even knew someone was in the room with him.

"I'm getting you out of here," I whispered, hearing the strained words leave my mouth as I forced my emotions into submission.

Putting myself between his body and the wall, I gripped him beneath his arms, turning him so it'd be easier to back out of the room. This was dangerous, and I was aware of the fact that I would likely be caught, but I wouldn't leave here without him. I'd rather die in this place than to make it out, knowing I hadn't done everything I could to save him.

Just like he would have done for me.

As I struggled to inch his weight down the corridor, I thought of how he ended up here, how he'd willingly laid down his freedom, and possibly his life, so I had even a *chance* of making it away from the Sovereign. It was this memory of his sacrifice on my behalf that made me fight harder, made me move faster.

He groaned as I tugged him and I was sure I was doing him more harm than good, but I couldn't stop. Blood soaked my hands and I had to set him down a moment to get a better grip before he slipped out of my grasp. Easing myself down onto the floor, I let his body rest gently on my legs. It was then that I felt it—two soft wounds in his back, side-by-side, leaking fresh blood onto my jeans. Breaths entered and exited my lungs rapidly again. I was positive I already knew what'd been done, but needed to see to be sure. Needed to see if the new measure of rage swelling within me was warranted.

His frame was solid and dense, so when I turned him, it was like shifting a semi-truck onto its side. But, eventually, I managed to lift him. Eventually, my suspicions were concerned.

His wings ... they'd been removed.

The wounds were jagged and ugly, a sign the makeshift surgeons had little concern for the condition they'd leave him in when their work was done. The Sovereign had done exactly what he promised, harvesting Liam's parts. If I had to guess, those wings had been rinsed clean of his blood and packed away neatly to be displayed the moment Sebastian returned to his own home.

My shoulders heaved when a flood of emotion powered through me with a force akin to that of a mighty, rushing waterfall. I could hardly control it, could hardly see straight through the fury within. Typically, my dragon was finely calibrated, in control in every situation in which she stepped forth. However, as I stared down on how they mangled Liam ... I felt her spiraling.

And there was nothing I could do to bridle her.

She got me to my feet, and this time, instead of dragging Liam in a painstakingly slow manner across the floor, I moved with ease. If I'd only been relying on my own strength, this would have been impossible. This was all her, my dragon.

We came to the end of another hallway and I went right, praying this was the direction I'd come from. Or, that I'd at least be able to find my way to the stairs again some other way. With each step, I felt my resolve strengthen. Making it out with Liam was the only option, so I had to keep believing this mission wasn't already a failure.

A slow creaking hinge made me stop where I was, freezing like a statue as I listened harder.

Footsteps.

Slow at first, and then picking up speed as they came closer. I panicked, but my dragon stood strong. Gently lowering Liam to the ground again, I turned to face the oncoming threat head on, prepared to fight whoever was coming to stop me.

My will was airtight, but … there was no guarantee I'd be any match for them. But there was no place to go, nowhere to run, so I did the one thing I could, what I'd been taught.

I would stand my ground and show no fear.

Liam wouldn't have had it any other way.

Chapter Nineteen

Evie

My heart had begun to beat double time as I stared at the corner, watching, waiting.

But then … I saw him, the one person I wasn't expecting.

Nick.

The relief that followed seeing him was dizzying. My body slumped against the closest wall as I caught my breath after holding it for so long. It was nothing short of a miracle that he found me. I sensed the lycans and Blaise had carried me quite some distance, and then to know exactly where I was in this massive, dark basement, composed of confusing, identical passageways.

And then I remembered his ability. Remembered how my heartbeat acted as a lighthouse whenever he needed to find me—a feature that was meant to be a curse, but at this moment, it was only a blessing.

"Come on. We have to get out of here. I wasn't able to get in without being noticed," he said in a rush, sounding winded, but not tired.

"The others ... are they okay?"

"We took care of most of the lycans, but it was only a matter of time before more of witches made their way out. I convinced Richie it was time for us to back off. Besides, there was no way we'd *all* be able to slip in, so I volunteered."

When he finished explaining, before I could even ask for help, he moved to where I laid Liam's lifeless body near the wall. Without a second thought about their past confrontations or the deep-rooted hatred between them, Nick hoisted Liam over his shoulder before taking me by the hand.

"This way," he urged.

Grateful to have him as a guide through the maze, I followed him blindly. We turned corner after corner, pausing at each to check that the coast was clear. When we confirmed that it was, we jogged to the next, moving us closer to our destination.

Freedom.

Soon, we came to a small corridor and it flooded with light, illuminating the stairs we'd been searching for. My pulse quickened, vibrating behind my ears. The hope of making it out alive became so real I could taste it, could feel my spirit begin to lift.

It lasted a moment, that feeling.

Only fading when a foreboding silhouette blocked the light, cutting Nick and I off from our exit as we came to a stop halfway up the stairwell. One silhouette became four and I focused my eyes through the sudden burst of light. Blaise and two lycan soldiers flanked Sebastian as he stood front and center, staring the three of us down while I'm sure Nick felt our chance slipping away just like I did.

"Well, what have we here?" Sebastian crooned, the soft, melodic tone of his voice contrasting such a tense standoff. His features were sharp and only added to the general darkness of his presence.

Nick and I both watched, calculating what his next move might be as we backed down the stairs slowly, keeping our eyes trained on Sebastian. Within a few seconds, we were back where we started, in the basement once more as the four who blocked us began their descent. The little progress Nick and I made had been erased. Just like that.

"What should we do with them?" It was Blaise who asked, waiting for his father's response with that inherited darkness in his eyes.

Sebastian was thoughtful for a moment, maybe running through all the possibilities, the many tortuous ways he could end us all. When he settled on a conclusion, a bored sigh left his mouth.

"Get the dragons back to their rooms. Kill the lycan and bleed him for the witches," he ordered, speaking about our lives as though they were so incredibly disposable, like we were nothing. I suppose, to him, we *were* nothing.

Blaise and the soldiers started toward us, prompting Nick to lean in. The words he spoke were faint and rushed, but I understood his warning when he issued it.

"I'm going to fight them without shifting," he whispered. "But just in case I can't control it, keep away from me."

A grave look came my way and I questioned why he would plan to fight them—those formidable men who made for even deadlier lycans—without shifting. But then I remembered. Lately, he hadn't quite been able to control himself, didn't quite trust his own judgements. I recalled the video footage I was shown of him leaving the facility in a trancelike state, unaware of his actions.

He was doing this for me … because he didn't want to accidentally hurt me.

Slowly, with a gentleness I didn't expect, he eased Liam down onto the ground. He was surprisingly sympathetic to those tender wounds on Liam's back, sympathetic to my sensitivity regarding how he was handled. There was no time to express my gratitude, but it was certainly felt.

When Nick stepped up, I grabbed Liam beneath his arms and pulled him back into the shadows, respecting Nick's warning, but knowing he'd need my help. I couldn't keep a safe distance and just … watch.

There was no time to be so careful.

I went to his side the next second and he glanced my way, realizing I wasn't going to stand by and let him face this on his own—in *any* form he took. Not after he'd come all this way to help me. Not after he stepped up when I needed him most.

The ice between us had completely thawed. The hatred and frustration I allowed myself to feel toward him faded into nothing as we stood side-by-side, possibly facing death together.

That sadistic grin on Sebastian's face spread as he realized Nick and I wouldn't go down without a fight.

"Very well then." The words left his mouth laced with intrigue and amusement. With one glance, a silent command, his soldiers both donned wicked grins, and then shifted.

Fragments of their dark clothing fell to the floor like black petals of some ghastly flower. Muscled, fur-covered limbs swelled to the size of tree trunks before my eyes, and I'd never seen a lycan transition so quickly. Then again, I'd never seen any shift who were as old as these soldiers. They, no doubt, had centuries of practice.

Bearing long, razorlike teeth, there was a challenge in their gazes. With heaving shoulders and chest, Nick readied himself for this inevitable fight. One that, if lost, would mean this had all been for nothing. One that, if lost, would mean the vision Hilda said the Oracles had of me reigning … was false.

It was clear that these prophecies were provisional. That was the word she used. Meaning, what was seen could be altered, affected by my actions, or the actions of others. Simply because the Oracles saw me seated as queen, didn't mean that couldn't change.

Right here.

Right now.

Another signal from Sebastian, and beside him, Blaise removed an expensive overcoat, making a show of setting it aside to avoid having it damaged. With the garment out of harm's way, he violently jerked his neck, from one side, and then the other, readying himself to act on his father's command. The dark eyes that had been set on mine began to glow an eerie yellow and the room went silent. In an impressive display of power, Blaise kept his wolf bridled, allowing it to emerge only so much before stopping the transition cold. His arms, shoulders, and neck grew to nearly double their size, tearing the seams of his shirt as dreadful teeth protruded from his mouth. Tightly stretched skin with blue veins bulging beneath it made a breath hitch in my throat.

A living, breathing nightmare.

My hands tightened into fists at my sides, clenching as I fought against intimidation, fought against the sense of this fight being over before it even began.

Nick and I were outnumbered, and these lycans had things on their side we couldn't fake.

Experience.

Skill.

I didn't turn toward Liam, but was aware of him, feeling my heart race as his life faded with each passing second. The corners of my eyes stung with desperate tears as I, no doubt, stared at the very men who had mangled him. The sense of urgency to get him some sort of help weighed heavy on me, although I didn't have much hope there was anything anyone could do.

But, even if there *was* something that could be done ... these four presented an obstacle.

One I wasn't sure Nick and I could overcome.

The soldiers hadn't moved to pursue us yet, but made a point of flashing those deadly claws. It was clear they could barely contain the urge to rip Nick and I to shreds.

My dragon stepped closer, into my consciousness, but didn't force her way out. I got the sense that she, that primal side of me, was still reeling from the state in which I found Liam. Their history — the one she forged with his dragon--was long and so intricately knitted. It made it impossible to imagine life without Liam present, impossible to imagine going on if we didn't *both* walk away from this alive.

Within me, a burn fluttered inside my chest. It was her, a sign of the seething rage that somehow surpassed fear and all other emotions.

A low hum vibrated in Nick's chest—a growl, a threat to those who cornered us.

Tension rose, thickening in the air as it reached boiling point. Time slowed. My thoughts became singular, focused in ways I'd never experienced.

A deep, surge of air filled my lungs, and by the time I released it again ... all hell broke loose.

In a flash of dark fur and luminescent, yellow eyes, a body hurled toward Nick, knocking him off balance, slamming his back to the unforgiving, cement floor. I watched in horror as those sharp teeth punctured soft flesh. Blood pulsed from Nick's arm, and when he yelled out, his voice didn't even sound like his own. It was otherworldly, primitive.

His body was nearly vibrating with rage as he struggled to subdue the powerful lycan who pinned him down. If he would only have shifted ... the fight would be fair, and he'd stand a chance, but ... he refused.

As long as he was in control he'd refuse.

... which meant I had to do something.

Sebastian and Blaise stood by, watching with excitement in their eyes. To them, this was merely entertainment. For us, it was the fight of our lives. The second soldier stood by, awaiting Sebastian's command, so I took advantage of their clear underestimation of us, of our willingness to lay it all on the line here today.

I was on the lycan within seconds, gripping his waist, tearing him away from Nick. Yes, I'd just made *his* problem my own, but it was all I could think to do to help him. The soldier was massive, solid enough to derail a train if he stood in the way of its destination.

A heavy arm came down on my back, pushing those glass shards in deeper, but wincing, nearing tears … I wouldn't let go. I squeezed even though my fingers began to slip where they locked around the wolf. I squeezed even though my instincts told me to let go and run.

Nick stumbled to his feet the moment I lost my grip, but he was stopped dead in his tracks, slammed down again when he turned his back to rush to my aid. The second soldier had him this time. He wouldn't make it to me.

I couldn't hold on another second. I was out of options, out of strength.

But as far as my dragon was concerned … we were just getting started.

Heat filled my limbs, and then flames. The stench of burning fur—disgusting as it was—was the best thing I'd smelled in forever. It was the smell of progress, the smell of the playing field leveling itself off, the smell of one of four lycans quickly becoming a nonfactor.

The cry for help coming from the soldier I clung to exploded in my ears first, followed by the sound of footsteps approaching from behind.

And then … the *last* sound was a quick, desperate warning from Nick.

There was no time to react to his voice, only time to turn just as a shadowy figure encroached. A jolt of electricity pulsed through my body. First, a jarring pain like nothing else I'd ever felt. Then, I was numb. Feeling returned pretty quickly and I managed to open my eyes, staring into those of Blaise in all his hateful glory.

The shock put me on the ground. All I had was a fuzzy image of him hovering above, clutching the tool used to subdue me—a long stick with electrical currents rippling and surging between two metal prongs on the tip. It resembled a cattle prod, but I guessed with a much higher voltage.

The crackle of flames searing the remains of the soldier's flesh were disorienting when I didn't hear movement, but then I noted his lack of screams as well. It became clear he'd succumbed to the fire.

Blaise glanced that way, too, where the fallen lycan must have taken his final breath on the ground.

"Get up," he seethed, still not placing his gaze on me.

I didn't move. But it wasn't fear that kept me lying there on that floor. It was defiance. I hated him—what he'd done to Liam, his smugness.

Wrangled into submission on the ground, Nick fought to throw the soldier off his back. All the while, keeping his eyes on me, unable to hide his concern. I imagined him at war within himself, knowing how much more helpful it would be if he'd shift, but also knowing how it would increase the risk of him losing control.

I didn't envy the decision he must have been at odds to make.

"Get up!" Blaise boomed.

This time, his command came with another shove of that godawful stick to my side.

I cried out as electricity ripped through me like an angry tide. My body slumped to the ground and the human side of me wanted to obey, wanted to do as this monster asked so he wouldn't hurt me again.

My flames extinguished against my will as I struggled to lift my head again. It became clear to me this was Blaise's goal. His method of torture taught me something about myself, pointed out a susceptibility to electricity. It was as though my shifter was forced to stand down.

At the site of her fading into the background, at the sight of the bright glow that lit this space a moment ago going dark … Blaise smiled.

"That-a-girl," he crooned, those words sparking more fight in Nick. A quick glance that way revealed that he was losing the battle to bridle his wolf.

And if that happened … everyone in this room might be in danger.

"Stand. Up," Blaise hissed between clenched teeth.

One last show of rage from my dragon drew reckless words from my throat, words that were sure to provoke Blaise to take further action.

But … I couldn't stop her.

"And if I don't?"

My heart raced at the sound of my voice, at a question that breathed fresh anger into Blaise's lungs. His brow twitched, probably asking himself if I was stupid or crazy.

If he'd asked, I would have told him both.

An incredulous laugh chuffed from his mouth when he turned to his father, maybe shocked I hadn't yet learned my lesson. But when he turned back to me … it was with the fires of hell burning in his eyes.

The sole of a heavy boot slammed my chest. Sharp pings of pain scattered across my scalp where a wound had just begun to heal. With the sudden burst of fear that shot through me, another sensation pulsed as well … that invisible thread.

That useless, now dormant, invisible thread.

Once, there would have been someone there to respond to the distress signal my dragon had just put out. Someone would have come to my rescue. But not today. Today, Nick and I were on our own and I accepted that we would die here — wanna-be-heroes who failed halfway into their mission.

I lie there, staring at what I could see of the ceiling through the fog of pain and darkness. The last image I would ever see hovered above me—a smiling sadist who'd get so much joy out of ending me today.

His boot now shielded my view, and as badly as I wanted to shut my eyes to block out the horror, I couldn't. I felt compelled to see everything as it unfolded.

Power built in Blaise's thigh and he breathed deep to put as much might as he could muster into stomping me, but ... light.

Through the haze I definitely saw light.

Maybe I was delirious.

Maybe the light was similar to what others saw when the moment of death was upon them.

But then, there was that look on Blaise's face, the one that let me know I hadn't imagined it.

I didn't understand.

The condition I found Liam in, the deep gashes in his back ... it *should* have made what I saw next impossible. But right before my eyes, sheathed in flames ... were wings.

I thought, for sure, these monsters had taken them.

I hadn't even had a chance to gage whether this was real when one cut through the air sideways with unimaginable speed, slicing Blaise's throat with scalpel-like precision.

Stumbling back, Blaise clutched the front of his neck as blood seeped between his fingers, from the corners of his mouth. He could only gurgle a few syllables as his eyes stretched wide from fear, perhaps even more in shock than *I* was to see Liam standing.

He was weak, he was bleeding from too many places to count, but ... he was standing.

My heart, it raced.

It raced like mad.

Strength came out of nowhere and I got to my feet, unable to take my eyes off him, still wondering if this was real. These hours that passed while I thought I'd lost him for good ... they felt like I'd died on the inside. Like I'd completely withered away to nothing but a hollowed-out shell. But now ... seeing him, I wanted to wrap myself in him and never let go. I wanted to pretend we were out of danger, that we'd already won, but I knew better than to let my guard down so soon.

He taught me that.

Sebastian called the soldier off Nick at the realization he no longer had the upper hand. At his command, the lycan obediently rushed forward to retrieve Blaise, bracing his staggering body to pull him out of harm's way.

Tension in this now small space rose to heights that didn't even register—as Sebastian weighed his options, as we weighed ours ... as Nick stood and Liam suddenly became aware of him.

For now, *that* was a secondary issue.

I went to Liam's side when the adrenaline rush faded, and weakness returned to his knees. His arm was practically limp when I tossed it over my shoulder, letting most of his weight rest on me.

From where he stood, Sebastian snickered, seemingly in limbo someplace between accepting defeat—however temporary it may have been—and contemplating one last move to finish us off while he had the chance. However, Blaise's vulnerability was too great to ignore, forcing Sebastian to retreat, quickly fleeing down one of several dark corridors hidden among the shadows.

The air was still so charged, even with our enemies now out of sight.

"Why is he here?" The question—one spoken quietly as Liam's strength dwindled—still packed so much fire, so much distrust as he stared at Nick.

My gaze shifted there too, toward Nick as he stared in the direction of where the others had just fled. He would have easily heard Liam with his heightened sense of hearing, but he barely seemed to notice us at all. His attention was likely focused on whether or not to go after our attackers.

I turned to Liam to answer his question. "He helped me," I admitted. "Without him, without the others, I never would've gotten to you."

His brow quirked at the word 'others'.

"His brothers are here, Chris, Lucas, Beth, Dallas," I shared, feeling my heart swell as I acknowledged again how brave they'd been to follow me.

There was still so much distrust in Liam's eyes when they shifted back to Nick, but the look soon faded as his consciousness slipped away.

My knees buckled beneath his weight, struggling to keep my grip as his blood-soaked t-shirt made holding on to him nearly impossible.

"Nick!"

I glanced up, thinking he'd come to my rescue, but he wasn't even aware that I needed him, didn't seem to notice I'd even called out.

There was so much tension in his arms—so much they seemed to grow as I looked on.

"I should finish this," he huffed, his broad chest moving with each rapid breath.

My brow tensed, wondering if he was slipping away, wondering if the darkness he fought to control within him had been sparked by his rage.

"What? No! Nick … I *need* you. Blaise isn't dead. In fact, he's probably halfway healed already. We have to get out of here, have to get to the others, and I can't do it without you," I pleaded, feeling the sting of tears in my eyes.

I was desperate. More than I'd ever been as I turned to Liam again as his lifeless body slumped against me.

Defeat spread quickly within when Nick didn't face me, seeming as though revenge, the need to settle the score, was the most important thing.

But then … his head swiveled in my direction and I saw something I wasn't expecting. Him.

No darkness.

Just … him.

He blinked, suddenly aware of how my grip on Liam was failing. He rushed to my aid and relieved me of half Liam's weight, tossing the other arm over his shoulder as we left that awful place. The Sovereign was somewhere in the darkness we emerged from, seething with the fires of revenge, no doubt. But we couldn't worry about that right now. We came here to do one thing, and one thing only — to rescue Liam.

And thanks to a handful of brave lycans and one fierce dragon with an iron clad will being at my side, we'd done the impossible.

Chapter Twenty

Evie

There was no scolding me when I walked through the door behind Dallas as he carried Liam's body inside. Elise took one look and shock froze her in place. The warning phone call when we made it off that mountain alive did nothing to prepare her for the sight of her loved one covered in a thick layer of his own dry blood.

We had to leave him this way—filthy and in pain. There was nothing any of us could do to fix either because our sole focus was to get him here where, hopefully, Hilda could do something.

The entire drive home, all eight hours, I was silent, sitting in the bed of the pickup while Dallas topped the speed limit the whole way. I cradled Liam's head in my lap, wiping away what I could from his face with my hands. I stared at him, counting his breaths, hoping each one wasn't his last.

Something was still wrong. He wasn't healing, wasn't getting any better, and my hopes were beginning to fizzle—the reason I was mostly numb when we stepped into the foyer. Hilda ordered Dallas to get him upstairs to the attic where she worked. I barely heard her because all sound was muffled inside my head, all time moved in slow motion. Dread filled me, the feeling that despite all our efforts, despite the brief show of strength when Liam came to my rescue, he still might not make it.

I sat near the door, still wearing clothes covered in my own dried blood, in Liam's. I couldn't move. There was an awareness of everyone rushing up both flights of stairs, but I couldn't follow them. Doing so would make things much too real. If I didn't go, if I didn't see him dying, it …

My fingers went to the band on my wrist, and at the feel of it, liquid heat streamed down my cheeks—tears, the ones I'd been warring with for hours now. He wouldn't have wanted me to cry, wouldn't have wanted me to worry. But I'd already done so many things to defy his wishes today, adding one more thing was somewhat of a moot point.

So, I let them fall. Not that I had much choice in the matter. I was a mess, painfully aware of all the years we missed out on already, and how I would now have to endure the same hell *he* had. Only ... there was no hope of him coming back. Not with his ring in the Sovereign's possession. If he died now, with the talisman so far away, it was of no use to anyone. As of today, it was just a useless piece of jewelry in the hands of a malevolent ruler.

My body shook with fear, with loss. A sound at the top of the stairs barely registered, even as Elise descended and joined me on the tile floor, letting her back rest against the front door. I couldn't even speak to her, couldn't open my mouth to explain how this happened, or why things turned out the way they did. Maybe because I didn't even fully understand myself. However, the warmth of her hand when it slipped into mine made it clear she didn't require any explanation.

"You did something amazing today," she said quietly, emotion clearly marking her tone when she wiped a tear from her eye.

I shook my head, hearing her, but the words only registered as a lie.

"No," I breathed. "I failed. We were too late."

My hand squeezed in hers and my stomach turned. I questioned whether I might have gotten to him in time if I'd gone on my own, if I'd had a bit more faith in myself and hadn't wasted time trying to round up others to help me fight.

"Evangeline, you did all you could, which was more than most of us could have accomplished," she assured me. "You brought him home."

Blinking water from my eyes, I scoffed. "And what good did that do? I brought him home to die?"

"You don't know that he won't make it," she reasoned.

Only, I kind of did. She couldn't feel what I felt. A small part of Liam lived inside me and it was almost nonexistent, which meant his soul was fading. So, if *anyone* knew he wouldn't survive … it'd be me.

I couldn't say those words to her, though. Couldn't force her to live with my reality. So, I remained silent.

My dragon was already beginning to mourn. Her presence, so strong, was heavy, weighing me down even more than I already was, consuming me. But she was quiet. It was during our journey home that I realized how Liam was able to wake up, how he was able to injure Blaise gravely enough that it created a means of escape. It was that show of defiance my dragon displayed when I should have cowered beneath Blaise's boot. While my human counterpart was full of fear, my dragon egged him on, practically *begging* him to do me bodily harm.

Because she knew the stakes had to be raised in order to jar Liam back to consciousness.

Our connection was weak, but still present. She knew what needed to be done to wake him and it worked. It provided me a chance to look into his eyes again, gave me the peace of mind knowing he'd at least know I came for him. At least he knew I tried.

Even if I didn't get to him in time.

Hours passed and the sun had set quite some time ago. There was silence upstairs where Hilda and Dallas had been with Liam since we first returned. I felt like such a coward for not moving from this spot, for not going to him, but fear of what I'd find when I got there kept me bound.

Elise sat beside me without a word. She hadn't moved all day, just sat beside me while I went insane with grief on the inside. That feeling only peaked when the tether—the last thing I had to hold on to—severed completely, leaving me with a sense of loneliness I hadn't even felt *before* I knew Liam existed. It was a jarring hollowness with no words in existence to describe it.

There was no doubt he was gone.

Slow steps trudged down the staircase and I didn't lift my eyes. The looks on Hilda's and Dallas' faces would have been too much. Elise stood, but I didn't.

Couldn't.

So many regrets rested on my heart in that moment. Among them, the acknowledgement that, during that brief moment where he was aware that I was with him, while the Sovereign could have stricken us all dead, I should have just said the words I felt—I should have told Liam I loved him. I was so concerned with escaping, so concerned with staying focused on the task at hand that I *missed* the task at hand. Making sure he knew how I felt should have been the only thing that mattered.

And now here I sat ... wishing I could turn back the hands of time.

Wishing I had one more chance to tell him he was the only important thing.

Hilda stopped in front of me and a deep breath left her mouth as she began.

"They tried to take his wings, but the amateurs the Sovereign sent in to do the job didn't realize they only manifest when a dragon has shifted. So, from the looks of things, they dug around in his back for a bit, he resisted the shift, and they beat him within inches of his life for not cooperating. Of course, the witches must have played a part, otherwise, he would have cut the lycans down where they stood."

Bile crept up my throat as I envisioned the torture he must have endured, letting my eyes drift closed.

"And as I'm sure you noticed, his healing mechanism never kicked in," she sighed. "My first thought was that he'd been hexed, that some curse had been placed on him to keep his flesh from mending, but then ..."

Silence. Whatever she was going to say, the words got stuck in her throat.

My eyes opened then, glancing up toward her when she stalled. She must have seen the plea within my gaze, because she went on.

"Then ... I found traces of candrenium. A bit in his hair, a little beneath his nails, which led me to swab the inside of his nose and mouth." Her expression remained grave.

"I've ... I've never heard of it," Elise stammered, nearly just as desperate as I was.

"It's an ancient herb," Hilda explained. "Used on a concoction only a few of the oldest witches have the recipe to create. And it serves one purpose, and one purpose only."

"Hilda ... please," Elise begged as my aunt broke this all down gently, to avoid overwhelming us, I guessed.

A sympathetic stare came my way, and then words. Words I never expected to hear. "Candrenium is the main ingredient in potion of sorts, one most effective in powder form. It's the candrenium that gives it its brilliant, purple color."

When she said that ... my heart nearly stopped, recalling the final moments as I followed Liam's command and ran from the Sovereign and his men. I recalled the witch Blaise called forth blowing a purple substance in his face right before his body slumped to the snow.

I focused on Hilda again as she went on.

"I'm assuming the spell used was intended to take effect slowly. Based on Dallas' retelling of the details you've given him, Sebastian must have wanted to ... *harvest* ... Liam's parts first." She nearly choked on that disgusting term the Sovereign used. "And then the spell would have made it easier to dispose of him when they were done. Or perhaps the purpose was to take some of the fight out of him," she guessed.

"Wait ... first? First before what?" I asked, getting to my feet.

She hadn't even had time to answer this question when I asked another.

"Is he alive?" The words were barely a whisper and, for so many reasons, I couldn't believe I asked it, but I did. Maybe out of disbelief. Maybe out of desperation.

Of course he wasn't alive.

The tether was gone.

We were too late.

But then I saw that shimmer of sympathy in Hilda's eyes when she shook her head, and it made me wonder if I'd been wrong this whole time.

"Yes," she answered. "He's alive."

I nearly sank back to the floor as I stumbled back, resting against the door for only the fraction of a second as I tried to let that sink in. But then, the *next* second, my eyes flickered toward the stairs and my only thought was that I had to go to him.

However, when I took a step, a huge arm and half a body blocked me.

Dallas.

There was a look on his face that let me know Liam still wasn't out of the woods. A look that meant there was still something wrong.

It was then that I went back over all Hilda had shared. Something stood out and I turned to her.

"What did you mean?" I asked, shaking, doing all I could not to let it show how frantic I was on the inside, but there was no hiding it.

"You … you said the Sovereign wanted to harvest parts from him *'before'* … something, but … before what?" My voice was panicked, but I didn't care. When it came to Liam, I didn't care that it was always so abundantly obvious that he was the one thing in my life that could make me come undone.

That dimness returned to Hilda's eyes when our gazes locked, and my heart sunk at the sight of it. It wasn't until a moment later, when she opened her mouth to speak, that I understood the cause of the remorseful look.

"Before, the transition is complete," she replied, sympathy weighing down each drawn out syllable. "Evangeline, he's—"

She stopped, and when she did, her gaze slipped from mine. In those fleeting seconds, I felt my knees get weak, long before the veil of secrecy had been lifted.

And then, with the words that followed … Hilda drove a knife straight through my heart.

"…They've turned him human."

*

To be continued in book four of
THE LOST ROYALS SAGA,
"Season of the Wolf".

Thank you for your purchase! I would love to get your feedback since you've finished the book! Please leave a review and let others know what you thought of

"Heart of the Dragon"

For all feedback or inquiries:

author.racheljonas@gmail.com

84165022R00209

Made in the USA
Lexington, KY
20 March 2018